Hang on Sloopy

Randy Rohn

This book is scary, but not as nearly as scary as playing Cribbage with my brother-in-law!
Randy Rohn
2012

L & L Dreamspell
London, Texas

Cover and Interior Design by L & L Dreamspell

ISBN: 978-1-60318-300-0

Library of Congress Control Number: 2011931748

Visit us on the web at www.lldreamspell.com

Published by L & L Dreamspell
Printed in the United States of America

Thanks to Lisa Smith for her kindness, patience, writing tips and editing.

Also, to Cindy Davis for brilliant editing.

And to L & L Dreamspell for everything.

For Linda, Kristin and Kurt. And, of course, Ringo Superpuppy. With all my love.

To the best parents ever, Dan and Jackie Rohn.

Also, to all those great garage bands for their perfect teenage music full of spit, swagger and snotty attitudes.

Cut 1
Let it Out

Her prickometer wasn't working.

For the first time in a long, long time, it failed.

And that destroyed her.

Mimi Johnston knew men liked to watch her. She had shocking blonde hair and lots of it. A tiny waist. An outrageous chest. And she dressed accordingly. Even her business attire tended to be strategically tight.

She always gave them a bit of a show. She would arch her back slightly. Put a little more English in her hip movement. She did it without thinking, whenever she sensed a man nearby.

And somehow she could always sense when there was testosterone in the vicinity. It was instinct. Radar. Even if she couldn't see anyone, she just knew.

"It's my prickometer," she'd say when friends saw the subtle shift in her demeanor.

However, this night the prickometer wasn't working.

Mimi Johnston didn't see the man standing in the shadows of the underground parking garage.

She didn't notice the same man peeking around the stairway exit as she got off the elevator. She didn't smell him or feel his vibrations.

Mimi was ready for a night at home. Long hot bath. Glass of wine. Maybe a cigarette. She was the only person she knew who could have the occasional cigarette, thoroughly enjoy it, but not become the least bit addicted.

Maybe she'd watch some TV. No, better yet, crack open a romance novel. One of those new ones with a vampire as the bad boy. How long had it been since she had time to indulge in one of those? She could use some sweet romantic illusions, followed by solo bedtime, after all the sweaty pseudo-romances she had experienced lately.

"You don't get much sleep when you're sleeping your way to the top," she once told a friend.

She didn't hear the man enter the apartment as she drew her bath.

Undressing, she had no idea a man watched. She couldn't hear his quickened breath.

She did, however, sense the man's presence as he came up from behind in the bathroom. The air felt different. The sound of the water running into her oversized tub had less echo. Someone or something was soaking up sound. She thought she heard breathing. A man's breathing, hoarse and raspy. Did she feel his breath on her neck?

She turned, slowly. And. He. Wasn't. There.

She turned back to the tub and saw him standing in the water. She didn't see his face. She saw his legs, knee deep in bubbles and lavender oil. As she tilted her head up to catch a glimpse of his face, she felt the cold sting of steel make a quick slice from vagina to vocal chords. A moment of nothing, no pain, no sound, no feeling, then she was engulfed in hot, wet agony.

She looked down at her own body, the body that had meant so much to her, the body that had given her so much, and her first thought was that the scar would be ugly. An ugly scar, and no man would ever want her again.

Another slash, but she was beyond pain. She thought that she wanted to see the face of her killer. She forced her head up, even though the instant exhaustion that engulfed her pushed it down.

There was something about the man's face. What was it? She recognized him, yet she didn't. If only she could remember. She thought it was very important that she recognize who he was.

Then, she had no thoughts at all.

The man watched Mimi Johnston slowly fall to her knees and then face first into her own intestines.

An artful kill.

Beauty. Symmetry. Visual poetry.

But, exceedingly unsatisfying. He could tell by her eyes she didn't recognize him. Therefore, she didn't know why he killed her. That wasn't how he planned it.

It felt hollow.

It felt limp.

He felt unfulfilled.

The next time he wanted the victim to know. The next time he wanted the victim to understand why he or she were being killed. The next time it would be slow. Extremely slow.

He felt the tiniest electric shock of pleasure.

Oh yes, the next kill would be slow, sweet and slow. And, oh so deliciously painful.

The killer rubbed his hand over his head. The scalp still didn't feel like it belonged to him. It felt like he had on a hat. A stocking hat. Or a bathing cap.

With Mimi still cooling in the bathroom, he walked through the apartment.

First he went to her bedroom. He looked in her bedside table. There was a tiny fake jewel encrusted case with two joints inside. There was a tube of K-Y jelly. Flavored oils. And a box of condoms. Oh Mimi, you naughty, naughty girl.

In her lingerie drawer he found a stack of love notes from various men, tied in ribbon. He put these in his jacket pocket to read later. He checked out her bra size. Hmm. He had guessed right. Just before he gutted her, he noticed that she was well-endowed. Not that she hid it at all when she was dressed.

He considered for a moment going back to the bathroom and slicing through one of her breasts to see if he could find any silicone, but decided against it. He didn't want to ruin the tableaux, the symmetry of how she had fallen in her own viscera.

He rummaged around for a few more minutes and didn't find anything that interested him.

He moved on to the TV room. There was a secretary with a computer. It was on. Splendid. He noodled around her screen desktop and found a file with names and addresses. Perfect. He found just what he was looking for. He printed it out.

Then, he took out his pocketknife, undid some screws and took out the hard drive. He didn't want the cops knowing what he did on her computer. Also, her hard drive might contain something that could connect Mimi to him. And that just wouldn't do.

Time for a cup of tea.

He went to the kitchen and found some Green Jasmine. Put on the kettle to boil. As the water heated, he searched the pantry and cabinets. He found a bottle of chlorine bleach in one of the cabinets and put it next to the sink.

By the looks of the refrigerator, she didn't eat at home much.

In the freezer he found something that made him smile, some packages he had sent her earlier. A goat's eye. Calf's liver. Part of a cow's stomach. The teakettle started hissing. He poured the hot water into a cup with the teabag. As the tea steeped, he rummaged some more.

In a little mop closet, he found, flattened and folded up, two of the boxes he had used to send the animal parts. He stacked those on the kitchen table; he would take them with him. He put some more water in the pot and sat to drink his tea.

He really enjoyed the tea and drank it slowly. When he finished, he washed out the cup with boiling water from the teakettle. Rinsed it again with bleach.

He went to the bathroom, emptied the tub and wiped it down with bleach. He also wiped down any surface he might have touched. He stuffed the towel he had used to wipe everything in a black plastic garbage bag along with the deconstructed boxes from the kitchen table.

While cleaning up, he imagined what he would do to his next victim.

He smiled.

He had already started the next ceremony, but this time the big finish would be much juicier.

Cut 2

Mirror of Your Mind—Twenty Years Ago Today

Although only a freshman, the boy was in a senior level Spanish class. Known by everyone in school as The Brain, he would graduate high school in two and a half years. The jocks called him Lame Brain or just Lame because it wasn't cool to be too smart in a small-town, small-minded high school. The boy realized he wasn't popular. He understood the key to acceptance was proficiency on the basketball court. This was Indiana, after all.

He didn't even run track, let alone play football.

Spanish class was a total drag. The Brain could speak Spanish better than the teacher.

A Mexican family helped around the house in the summer. The Brain had picked up the language listening to them. He spoke fluently by the age of five. He watched the Spanish station on cable television and turned on the Spanish subtitles whenever he rented DVDs.

For his tenth birthday, he asked his parents for a subscription to the Spanish-language edition of Reader's Digest. When he was twelve he read Don Quixote in the original Spanish.

So, he had a hard time paying attention to the teacher in senior Spanish. The teacher, Mrs. Hillcrest, was a dowdy woman who was tired. She had a tired body. A tired-looking face. She was especially tired of trying to teach hormonal teenagers anything. She was just marking time until retirement. Marking time today meant reciting the conjugation of the Spanish pluperfect verb tense in a bored, tired sounding voice that lulled the boy into the kind of daydreaming extreme boredom triggered.

It was a mild spring day. The sun poured down through the windows of the classroom and seemed to flow straight to the golden hair of the girl sitting one row up and one row over. Her name, Amanda, a senior and captain of the cheerleading squad. Of course, she had to be a cliché and date the captain of the basketball team, named, Chip, of all things. The Brain found the whole scenario gag-inducing.

However, that didn't stop him from being entranced with the way the sunlight danced off Amanda's hair with a tincture of brass and bronze and just the tiniest hint of white-silver, set against spun gold. He was fascinated by the myriad colors in her hair. She pushed the long hair back from her shoulders and it gently cascaded down her back. He loved the way she did that. The movement revealed a neck that was long and slender the color of soft butter-cream.

Her studied her profile, her perfect posture, the flawless skin, the way she crossed her legs. Her wondered what it would feel like to touch her legs. Just gently trace his fingertips from her exquisite ankles up her calves to that soft area behind her knees. He felt a tiny flutter in the pit of his stomach.

"Hey, Brain, what are you looking at?" Lisa, Amanda's best friend, who sat directly behind Amanda, whispered loud enough for half the kids in class to hear.

It was as if someone splashed scalding water inside his cheeks and behind his eye sockets. He focused on the book in front of him as sweat popped out on his hairline. He felt a drop slide down his forehead and into his left eye. He blinked it out.

"Hey, Brain, I'm talking to you." Lisa was looking directly at him with a big, stupid grin on her face.

"Leave me alone, Lisa."

"You're looking at Amanda, aren't you?"

"Be quiet, Lisa." His cheeks buzzed with heat. Pins and needles pricked his scalp. Sweat trickled down his back.

"Do you think Amanda is pretty, Brain?"

"Shut the hell up."

"Is The Brain getting flustered? Does looking at Amanda get you all frustrated?"

The boy felt everyone in class looking at him. He kept his eyes on the book, splotching it with fat plops of sweat. He closed his eyes wishing the moment would end, wishing he could run out of class and keep on running until his chest exploded.

He opened his eyes. Now Amanda was looking directly at him. God, her eyes were beautiful, blue with a hint of frost. Long, elegant lashes. He couldn't stop staring at them. She seemed to be reading his soul. He wanted to look away, but he couldn't. There was a faint smile on her lips.

She turned to look at Lisa. "Leave him alone."

"But, Amanda, he was seriously checking you out. I mean beneath that nerd exterior is a bona-fide horn dog."

"I wasn't checking her, uh…I was just thinking about stuff."

"Stuff you'd like to do to Amanda." If a whisper could be a shout, Lisa had perfected it.

"Come on, Lisa. Let the poor boy alone." Amanda smiled at him again.

"What's going on back there?" Mrs. Hillcrest had stopped conjugating verbs.

Could the day get any worse?

"Nothing, Mrs. Hillcrest," Amanda said.

The bell rang.

"Thank you God," the boy said under his breath. He stood up, careful to not look in Amanda's direction. He slammed the Advanced Spanish book shut and shoved it into his backpack. He had to make it to the door without bumping into anyone. He banged his thigh against the side of the desk. Damn, that hurt. He mustn't limp.

"Watch where you're going, creep." It was Billy Nester, Chip's best friend.

"Sorry."

The Brain dodged and pivoted to avoid desks and other students, walking as fast as he could to the door. He made it without further mishap, ignoring the ache in his thigh and the ball of fire burning in his chest.

He sprinted down the hall to the men's restroom. He shoved the door open. Crap, it was full of guys he didn't want to see. He spun around and went to the drinking fountain and gulped down refrigerated water until his teeth ached. He cupped some water and splashed it on his face.

One more period to go. Another fifty minutes of agony. He walked down the hall past the principal's office. There was a door to the outside, right next to the office, but students weren't allowed to use it without permission. He hit the bar and walked outside anyway.

The air felt cool and sweet. In the teacher's parking lot he began to jog. Past the cars, past the practice soccer fields, past the outdoor track. He climbed the fence, which surrounded the school property, and jumped a drainage ditch. He followed railroad tracks for about half a mile then cut across the scarred and pitted parking lot of an abandoned lumberyard.

He was going to his favorite place.

A small creek ran behind the lumberyard. He crossed the stream on a fallen log and cut through some tall weeds to a little clearing with a willow tree.

This was his spot. No one ever came here. He took off his backpack and set it down. He sat down and leaned his back against the tree. He closed his eyes and thought about Amanda. One day he would write a poem about her.

The Brain must've slept, because when he opened his eyes again, the light was different. His head felt clear. The throbbing in his thigh was dull, barely there. The burning in his chest wasn't as intense.

He pulled a book out of his backpack. It was a leather-bound journal his uncle had given him. He never let anyone see it. Never. He rummaged through the pack and pulled out a pencil.

He began writing. He was composing an epic poem about John Lennon. He had read everything he could about Lennon and by Lennon. He studied the lyrics to Beatle songs. He even read the letters Lennon had written to Rolling Stone and Melody Maker, an English music magazine.

Lennon once said that as a boy he used to see things, hallucinations, and was surprised when others didn't. The Brain felt the same way. Lennon had worshipped Alice in Wonderland. Ditto for the Brain. Lennon had been blown away by the artwork of Yoko Ono. The Brain was the only Beatle fan, or Lennon fan who thought Yoko was a blue streak genius.

The boy became lost in his writing. He stopped at one point and pulled out a paperback copy of "Through the Looking Glass" and "Alice's Adventures in Wonderland." He used "The Walrus and the Carpenter" from "Through the Looking Glass" as the model for his poem. The same cadence. The same meter. He wanted to use as many words and metaphors from the book, knowing Lennon himself had come up with the Walrus from that poem in "Through the Looking Glass" and also Lennon considered "Lucy in the Sky with Diamonds" a rock 'n roll version of the classic children's books.

As The Brain wrote in his journal the words began to flow. His pencil was magic. He didn't even have to think. It was if the lines were coming from the air around him.

A shadow appeared on the pages.

"Hey you." It was Amanda. She was standing right in front of him. He blinked and shook his head. It had to be an illusion.

It wasn't. It was her. The girl of his dreams and fantasies in the flesh. Amanda. "Hey you. What are you doing?"

"Oh nothing." The Brain quickly closed his journal.

"You sure seem to be working hard at nothing." She smiled. Was she mocking him? No, the smile seemed genuine. Real. Warm. "Mind if I sit?"

"Uh, yes. I mean, no, I don't mind. But yes, you're welcome to sit." He picked up the Lewis Carroll paperback and shoved it into his backpack along with the journal.

She sat beside him, her left leg warm against his right. "What are you reading?"

"Just a book."

"I know it's a book, silly. What book?"

"You wouldn't be interested."

"Why sure I am, that's why I asked."

"Trust me, nothing you'd like."

"Try me. Come on. What are you reading?"

He dreaded this moment. He wanted to run away again, but instead tried to divert her with a question of his own. "How did you find me?"

"I saw you jogging this direction when I was in Mr. Singer's class. I used to come here when I was a little girl to read Nancy Drew books."

"Really?"

"Really. Cross my heart." She made an X with her right hand over her left breast. The motion thrilled him. There was something very sensual about it.

"I used to read the Hardy Boys."

Amanda nodded enthusiastically. "I used to love the Hardy Boys. I must confess, for the longest time I had the biggest crush on Frank."

"Frank Hardy. I would've never guessed."

"Don't tell anyone. It'll be our little secret."

"Our secret." There was something about sharing a secret with the most popular senior girl in school, the most beautiful girl he could ever imagine, that made him blush.

"So, what was it you put in your backpack?"

The Brain pulled out the book and handed it to her.

She looked at the cover for a minute and then giggled. "This isn't at all what I expected."

He tried to grab the book back. "Give it to me."

"I'm not laughing at you. This used to be my favorite book."

He looked at her. Well, he might as well get it over with. He explained to her what he was doing, writing an epic poem about John Lennon based on the "Walrus and the Caterpillar" poem in "Through the Looking Glass." "Now, you can go tell your friends and have a good laugh about it. But, could I please have my book back?"

She handed him the book. “I’m not going to make fun of you. I find what you’re doing very interesting. Mind if I read it? The poem you’re writing?”

“Well, it’s not finished. And I’ve never shown it to anyone.”

“Let me read it. Please? Pretty please?”

There was something about her eyes. They seemed to look into him, touch him in a special place. He couldn’t refuse. He handed her the journal and immediately wished he hadn’t.

Out in the small field, a rabbit hopped around. It must be a sign. He flashed into a quick daydream in which he followed the rabbit down a hole, just like Alice had. The Brain wanted to jump up and run after the rabbit. He wanted to disappear.

“This is very good.”

“You think so?”

“Really.”

After a minute, Amanda stopped reading. “Why are you looking at me that way?”

“I, um, well I just didn’t expect that reaction from you.”

“Do you think I’m too dumb to get it? Just ’cuz I’m a cheerleader or something.”

“No, I mean, yes, I guess so. I don’t know.”

“Do you write much?”

“Oh, some stuff, here and there. Nothing special.”

“Will you show me some more of your stuff?”

“It’s at home. It’s not very good.”

“I would love to see it.” She handed the journal back. “I like to write, too, sometimes. Although I’m not nearly as good as you.”

She told him about her writing, her life, what she liked to read and the dreams she had. There was so much more to her than the airhead cheerleader he had imagined. He opened up to her as he had never opened up to anyone. The sky turned a rich turquoise and then a deep purple. He started to feel a bit of a chill. But he didn’t want the encounter to end. He would get in trouble at home for missing supper.

Finally, she stood up and said she had to go. “Let’s meet again here. It will be our place. Our secret place.”

That was the second time she used the word "secret." Imagine having secrets with the most beautiful girl in high school. They agreed to meet the following Friday.

That night The Brain couldn't sleep.

The next day at school he had a hard time concentrating. The burning in his gut was hardly noticeable. There was a certain lightness to everything. Everything looked a little cleaner. Brighter. Colors popped. He had a little more energy.

Whenever he saw Amanda in the hall, he looked for a smile, a special look, anything at all to acknowledge the time under the willow tree. Nothing. Wednesday was the same thing. By Thursday, he had come to accept she wasn't going to pay any attention to him in school. For whatever reason. To protect her standing in the brutal high school social strata. Or, because she wanted to keep that part of her life, the part with him in it, to herself. Or, for some other reason he couldn't fathom. Their relationship was a "secret." This made it all the more special, all the more romantic.

On Friday, they met. Even though she was right on time, he had been fifteen minutes early and was nervous she might not show up. He brought a bookbag full of sketches, poems, and a few short stories he had written. Again, it was a perfect day. The temperature was in the low seventies, the sun was out and the air was crisp. Although he was bashful about showing his work at first, gradually he took out almost all the pieces.

She, however, didn't bring any of her writing. She said she forgot it that morning. It didn't matter. As he showed her more and more of his writing, they had plenty to talk about. That night, she gave him a ride home in her car and kissed him on the cheek when she dropped him off.

When he awoke the next morning he remembered having seven dreams about her. Seven. Each one he remembered in vivid detail.

He felt elated. He thought he would walk to the donut shop in town and score a couple of donuts, something he never did because even at his young age, he was conscious of what he put into his body.

When The Brain got to the donut shop, there was a line of people getting donuts to go and only two people working behind the counter. Families with young children bought donuts by the dozen, which the kids picked out one by one. It seemed to take forever, but the Brain didn't mind. He thought about Amanda and the kiss she had given him. He remembered how her voice sounded, how her laugh was almost musical. He could hear it in his head. No. Wait a minute. That wasn't just in his head. He was actually hearing her laugh.

He turned around slowly and saw Amanda in a booth talking to two friends. She had her back to the counter so she didn't see him and the two girlfriends were intent upon listening to her. He backed up a little from the line so he was closer to the booth but still had his back to it.

He loved hearing her voice.

He backed a little closer, so he could make out some of the words.

"And he's writing a poem about John Lennon, you know, the dead Beatle? It has to be the dorkiest thing I ever read."

The other girls were laughing.

"He's such a douche."

"So lame."

"How can you keep yourself from just cracking up?"

The burning began in The Brain's belly and chest and roared into an unquenchable fire. His eyes stung. He had trouble breathing. He walked quickly from the donut shop. He wanted to bend over and vomit, but somehow made it all the way home.

Cut 3
Sunshine Girl

Louie Lewis woke up to a Public Execution.

It started, as it always did, with those stinging musical notes.

"Some words are best not spoken, some things are best not said." Always the singsong voice. Always the Dylan-cloned, nasal intonation. Always the talk about a two-wheel pony ride. The Public Execution was about to begin.

Louie didn't know if he was quite ready for it. But it didn't stop.

He loved it.

It was the only real hit by a group called Mouse and the Traps. The song came pounding out in glorious monophonic sound from one of four jukeboxes in his loft apartment above the old five and dime, now a consignment shop.

Louie had just finished up a job, one that kept him up past three in the morning the night before. His Seeberg "C" jukebox had for years been programmed to play ten songs, set on an electric timer to begin every morning promptly at seven. He stayed in bed through the "Public Execution," one of his favorite garage rock singles, and stumbled to the coffee maker in his kitchenette during "Psychotic Reaction" by 13 O'Clock.

If Louie had a vice, it was garage rock, music from that wonderful period in the '60s when American bands blasted out blues and soul numbers from American artists they had discovered by listening to English bands like the Rolling Stones, the Yardbirds and Manfred Man. The music had traveled across the ocean and ricocheted back.

Most of the garage rockers were high schoolers or college kids who could barely play their instruments. What they lacked in musical chops were more than made up for in attitude and swagger. Since most of the bands had the same set list, many of them tried writing their own bluesy songs and ended up with a beautiful three-chord mess. Or, many messes. That was the music he loved.

Although the songs were recorded before he was born, and most of his friends had far more contemporary tastes, Louie loved the loud, raucous stuff.

He took his big ceramic coffee cup with the picture of Captain Beefheart on it, and stood by the front window. He saw Hoss Harlan, a former semi-pro guard, walking a little longhair dachshund. Louie waved but Hoss was looking straight ahead. Louie could've yelled, but Hoss wouldn't have heard. The windows were triple-paned with a one-inch space for air, and then another three-quarter inch slab of glass. In effect, his entire loft was soundproofed. Double the insulation with one-inch cork walls, a layer of rubber on the original floor with a raised floor above it, and sound baffles in the ceiling.

Louie had spent more than he paid for the entire apartment for the luxury of rocking out whenever he wanted.

As he stood drinking his coffee, he knew by name everybody that walked by. It was a picture-postcard day outside, all hard, primary colors. He decided to go to the Tic-Tock Bar. The juke blared "Dirty Water" by the Standells as he stepped into the shower.

Some days are best for hanging out in bars. This was one of them. At least for Louie. It met the two important criteria to be a good bar day. He had money. He had nothing else to do.

Besides, who wanted to fight the heat? The sun had been unusually pugnacious the past couple of days. It hit with a bodyshot the second you stepped outside. It followed with stinging whiteout jabs to the eyes. It pounded the life right out of you. It wouldn't let up.

It was so hot it was stupid.

Inside, the bar was inviting, friendly, dark and cool. The colors were muted.

As a refuge from that chemical smell of overheated asphalt and car exhaust caught in the spongy atmosphere, the bar had an almost-sweet, slightly-stale beery aroma.

It was a good bar.

It was Louie's bar.

It had everything Louie valued. A good selection of beer. A good selection of whiskey. A good selection of guys taking it easy. No talk of politics or current events.

No goldfish. No soggy popcorn.

Just bowls of peanuts in the shells. You could throw the shells on the floor.

And, it had a jukebox. Not as cool as any of the jukeboxes in his apartment, Louie thought. For one thing, this one played CDs. But, about half the music on it was decent. No Britney. No Lady Gaga. No Cee Lo Green. Plenty of Beatles, CCR, LedZep, Stones. Some Neal Young, Dylan and the Boss. And a few real treasures, the McCoy's 'Greatest Hits,' the Kingsmen, The Gants and the Complete 'Nuggets' Boxed Set. The last four Louie had provided. For the donation, Louie could play the jukebox in the bar free of charge.

So, today the music rocked, which made the perfect soundtrack for a perfect day spent in a cool bar.

He enjoyed the sports talk and sex talk and dirty jokes. He enjoyed sipping on a cold draft beer and the occasional handful of peanuts. He enjoyed the feeling of solvency that so often avoided him.

Contentment. He was in a good bar on a good day in a town that he had made peace with. It was his town, Tivoli, Indiana. He liked the people. He liked the pace. He liked his job.

There had been a time when he wasn't so content in Tivoli. But that was in the past. This good feeling had been with him now for a couple of years. He had no desire for the big city rat race. He could live without unbridled ambition. He didn't need the big paycheck or the big house in the suburbs that came with a big commute and big headaches. He had everything he wanted and few of the things he detested.

The cool, mellow day he had envisioned was about to come to an end.

He saw Mean Old Sun first. The light knifed into the blue-tinged darkness and spread into a pie wedge as the door opened further and a woman stepped inside. He saw her silhouette and then, as his eyes adjusted, he saw who she was.

Her name was Susan Louise Petrie. She was the first girl in Louie's class to develop curves. And man, did she develop. She was considered one of the most desirable girls in junior high and high school. She was extremely beautiful now.

Like every other man in the bar, Louie did the up and down with his eyes to make sure she still had the body. She did. Curiosity satisfied he went back to his beer.

She walked right up to him.

"Louie." He was the only Louie in the bar, so he turned on his stool to face her. The years had been kind. Even up close she was a knockout. She was *still* a knockout.

"Sloopy."

"Omigod! I haven't heard that in years."

"No, I guess you probably haven't."

She laughed. "You're the only one who called me that. It never really stuck with anyone else."

"I always liked the name."

"Since you were the one who made it up..."

"Well, actually it was the title of a song."

"I know that."

"Besides, there were lots of Susans, but only one Sloopy. I liked it. Sloopy was always easier to say. Besides, it kinda went along with Louie Louie, same chord structure, anyhow."

"Can we talk?"

"Looks like that's what we're doing."

"I mean, someplace private."

"Sure, would you like to grab a booth?"

"I was thinking maybe someplace quiet, maybe a little more private?"

"No prob. Where would you like to go?"

"How about my house?"

"Let me settle up and I'll meet you there."

"Why don't you ride with me?"

"Okay."

He threw a small percentage of his newfound wealth on the bar and slid off the stool.

"You in some sort of trouble or something?" he asked as they were walking out.

"Yes. No. Kinda. How did you know?"

"You haven't spoken to me in fifteen years. Being an experienced law enforcement professional, I am pretty good at detecting the motives of people."

He didn't tell her he was halfway kidding. Inside he was hoping maybe she tracked him down because she had a wild pornographic whipped cream fantasy about him and wanted to make it come true. Or, maybe she finally came to her senses and realized she made a mistake fifteen years ago and now wanted to get back together. Or, maybe she saw him walking in from the parking lot and wanted to compliment him on the nifty new white linen shirt that looked just as good as the designer labels but purchased at a fraction of the price found in fancy department stores.

But no, she was in trouble.

He later found out it wasn't an easy kind of trouble.

It was a hard-core, badass, death and destruction kind of trouble.

Cut 4

Sometimes the Good Guys Don't Wear White

Elliot Blake loved his job as the Chief of Police of Tivoli, Indiana. Sworn to uphold the law, he was, at this moment, upholding it to ridicule. How many crimes was he committing? He wasn't sure. But he was sure most people had no idea he was breaking the law.

The few people who would find out certainly wouldn't care, because the crimes he committed, he committed for them.

So a kid robbed a convenience store. Big stinkin' whoop. The kid got away with less than two-hundred dollars cash. And the Big Chain Convenience Store probably had insurance or some such shit to cover it. Even if Big Chain Convenience Store didn't, it was a big chain for Chrissakes, they could afford to lose a coupla bills now and then.

Elliott popped the kid about two hours after the call came in. The dumbass was parked by a fire hydrant in front of his girlfriend's house, waiting to take her to breakfast or something.

Anyway, when Elliott tapped on the driver's side window to wake dumbass up, he noticed a blunt in the ashtray. So he frisked the kid and found the stolen money, some weed, and a snub-nosed .38 revolver.

Okay, now he could go by the book and book the kid. Or, he could have a little weed for the weekend, a little hooker money and a throw-down if he ever needed it.

But that wasn't the real reason he didn't book the dumbass kid. The real reason was that the kid was the son of a real important man in town. A rich dentist who was friends with the mayor, three or four city councilmen, and everyone else who was important in Tivoli.

Oh yeah, Dumbass Dentist's Kid made his day. Ol' Elliott would take the dumbass to the station house, throw a little scare into him, and then take him home as a "favor" to Daddy Dentist. Keep the money, dope, and gun. Probably get free dentistry for the family, especially since the cheap-ass medical and dental plan of the City didn't cover braces, and his son's teeth had as many gaps in them as a senator's morality.

Dr. Brian, the dentist, would tell his friends what a great guy Chief Elliott Blake was, how he didn't let the law get in the way of common sense and all the other blah blah. Probably get free tickets to Colts or Pacers games; those rich shits were always buying season tickets they used about a quarter of the time.

The friends of Dr. Brian would throw a few other bones his way, an open invite to all the best parties and weddings and whatnot. With a C-note or two pocket change, if he could get a couple off-duties to help with the parking.

But, first things first. He had the ski mask the kid wore. Put it in a garbage bag. He would take the kid home, get the thanks and backslaps from Daddy Dentist. Maybe a nice tight hug from Silicone Mommy, who was the dentist's second wife and quite a looker.

He would go to the kid's car still parked illegally at the fire hydrant and search it for anything else that might be incriminating. Then, throw the garbage bag in the dumpster behind the grocery store. Get Joe Sizelove and Dave Singer to drive it to the kid's home.

Elliott would come back to the station and mess up the security camera tape that caught Dumbass Dentist's Kid robbing the Big Chain Convenience store. No one from the store would ever look at it again because he would assure them the cops had made a copy. They'd just pop it back in their machine and tape over it. Hell, while he was returning the tape he would promise the store manager that the mobile units would keep an extra close watch on the C-store. Drive by every hour past midnight. That should be good for some free jerky and donuts on top of the free coffee he already got.

It was great to be chief.

Elliott Blake delivered the kid to Dentist Daddy. Damn it, Silicone Mommy wasn't home. He drove through town whistling to himself, on his way to clean up the kid's car when he saw Louie getting our of Susan's car and walking to her house. What did Louie used to call her? Oh, yea, Sloopy.

What was chickenshit Louie doing there? What on earth could she ever see in him? What a goofball.

Louie and Susan were an item once upon a time, but now she was Elliott's personal trim. He was gonna carve off a piece of her ass one of these days.

Oh sure, she had turned him down, but it was just a matter of time. She still needed the police chief to protect her from the joker who was harassing her.

Probably some kid who had a crush on her. Or, her no-good, faggoty husband.

Anyway, Elliott didn't bother running tests on the stuff anymore. Waste of time. He just threw them in a dumpster and told her some story about what was in the package and where it came from.

God, she was a beautiful woman. Cute little bubble butt. Nice rack. Flat stomach. An inny, if he remembered correctly. Yeah, he could make her very happy.

What was she doing with a loser like Louie? Louie, who hadda buncha modern theories about law enforcement. Didn't wanna carry a gun. Whatta wuss.

Almost became chief.

Well, Elliott had done enough favors for enough important people to nip that in the bud. He had beaten Mr. No Guns. Had to do some fancy footwork and call in some favors. But it had been Elliott who came out the winner. And then, like the loser piece of shit he was, Louie had quit the police force. Whatta stinkin' loser.

What was Louie doing in Susan's car? How could she let that chimp even near her car? Should he stick around and do a little peeky-boo, see what was going on inside? Naw. Better get back to Dumbass Kid's hunk of junk.

Elliott had to think of a way of getting Louie out of the equation. It shouldn't be too hard. Louie was a bit of a Boy Scout. A goodie-goodie who could be easily manipulated.

Louie would never know what hit him.

Cut 5
Nobody But Me

The Man with the Lightbulb Head thought about blood.

He thought how best to keep it off him as he performed his weekly tasks. He thought about how to make sure there were no traces of it in his workshop. Blood was such a pain. It splashed and oozed, leaked and leached, dripped and dribbled. It might explode in an impossible-to-control spray if you cut in the wrong place. It could shoot straight out in a ribbon. It pumped out in gouts. It cascaded over surfaces. It trickled down a face in odd patterns. There was so much of it, yet the tiniest missed speck could tell the forensic squints enough information to pack you off to prison. Scrubbing with soap and water wasn't enough to get rid of it from a surface it touched.

It was a challenge. That's what made it fun. And the salty-coppery smell of blood was intoxicating.

The Man with the Lightbulb Head pushed his cart along the aisle of the grocery store. He saw, out of the corner of his eye, a child staring at him. She was with her mother and they were in the same aisle. He turned his head slowly and looked at the little girl. Her eyes opened wide.

"Mommy, I want to go."

"Just a minute honey."

"Mommy, I want to go, now. Please, mommy."

"I said, just a minute." The woman frowned in concentration, comparing the prices of aluminum foil.

"Pul-lease, mommy."

"Sarah, use your inside voice or I'll give you a timeout when we get home."

"Mommy. I. Want. To. Go."

"Now hush, or you'll be in big trouble, young lady."

The woman put the rolls of aluminum foil back on the shelf and bent to talk to the little girl. As she spoke to her in urgent hissy whispers, the woman caught sight of the man. She stopped speaking and stared for a beat.

"Okay, let's go." The mother pushed the cart rapidly and pulled the little girl's hand.

"Mommy, that hurts, you're squeezing too hard."

"I'm sorry, dear. Let's go."

The Man with the Lightbulb Head chuckled to himself. He had that effect on people. Especially children. It was better to be left alone. At first it made him feel bad having a face that scared people. Now, he was used to it. Now, he actually cherished being left in peace. There was something comforting about the solitude.

Let the little people with their little minds stay away. He needed to do what he did without anyone seeing, that was for sure. He could prepare for his tasks much better, without an audience. It was better for him. It was better for the mission. Let the little people with their little minds live their little lives. He had bigger fish to fry. He corrected himself. He had things much bigger *than* fish to fry. He chuckled. He was one of the funniest people he knew. Too bad others couldn't enjoy his wit.

He pushed his cart to where the woman and little girl had been. He put two seventy-count packages of extra-thick garbage bags, four rolls of Saran wrap, ten rolls of wax paper and several packages of sandwich bags in his cart. He rolled on further down the aisle and got eight gallons of generic chlorine bleach. He threw in several packages of kitchen gloves and some scouring powder.

Pushing his cart down another aisle, which quickly became deserted, The Man with the Lightbulb Head grabbed three packages of disposable plastic tablecloths. He pushed his cart down the personal hygiene aisle and put in several bottles of liquid hand sanitizer and several bottles of hydrogen peroxide.

Finally, he picked out three big bags of beef jerky.

He felt that nice warm feeling in his mouth. It was the feel of saliva forming. God, he loved jerky. He wanted to tear open the bag and stuff some in his mouth right there and then. But he was too smart to lose control. Not in a supermarket. Not with all the mommies and their little puppies looking. That wouldn't do at all.

Standing in line at the checkout, he felt the tenor of the conversation change. He heard the whispers. He saw the rug rats and their parents stealing glances at him. That was okay. He was the boogieman. He was the monster under the bed. The fear of others only made him feel more powerful.

The contents of his cart would seem strange to the checkout girl and the bag boy. They would probably talk about it.

But he was several towns away from where he lived. He never shopped in the same town twice.

His head might look like a light bulb to some, but he wasn't a dim watt. He laughed out loud at his own pun. People around him looked at the floor. No one wanted to make eye contact.

Cut 6
Why Pick on Me

Men stink.

That's what Susan thought. Not figuratively, literally. Well, maybe figuratively, too. She had seen the way the men had looked at her when she walked into the bar. She was used to it by now. She'd gotten used to it by the time she was seventeen. About the same time she had started using it to her advantage, sometimes, truth be told.

What was the deal? Most of the men in the bar had wives and most the others had girlfriends. And about a third of the wives and girlfriends were good-looking women. Some were younger than she. Some were skinnier. Some had more fashionable clothes. A few, in Susan's mind, were even prettier. So why was every single male checking her out? Because men were pigs. Stinkin' pigs.

Although...although, she liked it that she still had it. The day men ignored her, well that was the day she would...what? She didn't want to think about that day. She hoped she would be like Sophia Loren or Diane Lane, one of those older women with enough grace and beauty to still turn a man's head.

But she was getting off track here.

Men, at least the men she had been with, stank. Smelled bad. Someplace or another on their body. And it's not like she had been with skanks. No, what few men she had been with were rich men, successful men, well-groomed men. But when the clothes came off, the odor came out. Usually, not very strong, but a little something. They smelled a little like chicken soup. Or worse.

They couldn't help it. It was just they all sweat under their suits. And the pheromones or hormones or toxins that came out with the sweat just smelled. And the expensive cologne just made it worse somehow. Made it sting her nose.

She hadn't thought much about the odor of men, until she saw Louie again. The thing she remembered most about him was how he smelled. He always smelled good. A faint whiff of Ivory soap. A very subtle hint of cologne. Sandalwood. That's right. He mail ordered Sandalwood cologne from someplace. And he used a Sandalwood deodorant from the same place. How did she remember that?

He was meticulous about hygiene. She remembered that, too. No other man she knew was so particular. She knew he usually showered twice a day. After every shower, he always put on fresh clothes. Not expensive, necessarily, but clean and pressed.

Even when he was doing something that caused him to break a sweat, it was somehow clean smelling.

But that was years ago. She wondered if he still smelled so good.

What a weird thing to be thinking about. Here she was scared half out of her wits, worried for her life, and she was thinking about the smell, for cryin' out loud, of the man she was going to ask for help.

So why did she come to Louie in the first place? She hadn't spoken to him in a long time. She had hurt him bad. All his friends made sure she knew that.

It felt safe, coming to Louie. That was the only reason, wasn't it? That feeling of safety. Even in high school he always seemed so in control. He never got rattled. He never talked about woulda-shoulda-couldas. He just seemed to have an uncanny sense of the right thing to do, no matter what the situation.

Besides, he was from a long line of cops. His grandfather had been in the FBI, and then opened a private security firm in Chicago. His dad had also been a G-man—did they use that word anymore?—until he quit and came to Tivoli to be chief of police.

Louie had gone to Chicago to be a cop and for some reason come back to Tivoli. He was in line to be chief, too, until some unfortunate business with Elliott Blake, the bastard.

Then Louie's dad moved to Chicago to take over the grandfather's firm. Louie stayed in Tivoli. No one was quite sure why.

Now her former boyfriend had his own one-man PI shop.

So, Louie was certainly qualified. That's why she looked him up. He was qualified and he made her feel safe. Not that he smelled nice, or used to smell nice. Not that he was still pretty good-looking. His wardrobe could use some help most of the time. Although the cream linen shirt and jeans he wore today were kind of sexy.

But those blue eyes. And he still looked to be in pretty good shape. Many of her girlfriends in town still talked about him as if he were a hunk.

Medium-brown hair. Combed back. He reminded of her of some guy that fronted a rock band way back when rock bands were important. Back before she was born. Who was it? Bon Jovi? Nope. Not Springsteen. Creedence. That was it. He looked like that guy from Creedence Clearwater Revival. What was his name? John something. John Fogerty. That was it. Louie looked a little like John Fogerty.

"What?" she asked. He had said something, sitting by her in the front seat of her Beamer.

"I said, 'What's up, Sloopy?' How can I help you?"

She took a deep breath.

"You're not going to believe this, Louie."

"Try me."

What happened next she didn't want to happen at all. She wanted to be professional in every way. The last thing she wanted to play was the damsel in distress. But the tears came and she couldn't stop them. "My life for the past three months, m-my life has been a nightmare. A very weird nightmare. I think someone wants me to go insane. Either that, or someone's going to kill me. I'm getting these threatening things in the mail. I'm afraid,

Louie, something bad's going to happen."

"Nothing bad's going to happen to you. I promise."

Susan Louise Petrie, Sloopy, believed him. For the first time in many months, she felt safe.

"So what's going on?" he asked.

"I don't know where to start."

"Just start at the beginning."

"I've been receiving these packages."

"Packages."

"About one a week. They are awful."

"Where are they from?"

"What?"

"Where are they from? Who are they from? The packages."

"I don't know. I mean, they're from all over."

"By mail?"

"Sometimes. Sometimes from UPS. Sometimes from other services. DHL. FedEx. Sometimes they just show up."

"What do you mean?"

"They're just there. On my porch. When I wake up, sometimes one is just there. They arrive one at a time."

"When you say from all over, what do you mean?"

"Well, each time they're from a different place. Indianapolis. Chicago. Columbus, Ohio. Muncie. Peru. Valparaiso. Evansville. Terre Haute. Springfield, Illinois. Uh, let's see, Bloomington. And, and, Jesus, I don't know. I've got a list."

"College towns."

"Well, yeah, I guess. The ones I could trace."

"How did you trace them?"

"The ones that came by mail, I saw the postmarks. The others, I called up FedEx or whoever and asked."

"Well, if they came by FedEx of UPS or whatever, they would have to have a return address."

"Always fake."

"How do you know?"

"The police told me."

"The police?"

"Yeah, I've always turned them over to the police."

"Who?"

"Huh?"

"Who in the police department?"

"Elliott Blake."

"What did he say?"

"He said the addresses are fake."

"What else?"

"He said not to worry about it. It was just someone playing a joke. A sick, sick practical joke."

She started crying again. "What kind of monster would do this? I-I know it wasn't Tim."

Tim. Her first husband. The man she left Louie for fifteen years ago.

"Sloopy, why did you say Tim?"

"Because, that's who Elliott said it was, probably, a domestic dispute of some sort and Tim was doing that awful thing."

"Does he have any evidence that it is Tim?"

"No, I don't think so. I don't know. You don't think it's Tim, do you?"

"I don't know. Let's get back to that."

"Here's my place."

She turned into her driveway. She lived in a rather upscale housing development east of town. The house was a three story brick colonial. The garage was a two door, four-car with plenty of room on the sides.

Sloopy parked in front of the garage door closer to the house and turned off the car. The engine was ticking. She took both hands off the steering wheel, put them on her lap and turned to Louie. "I'm waiting for the next question."

Louie stared at her deep chocolate brown eyes. Flecks of gold. Rimmed in an even deeper brown, almost black. They seemed to absorb him. He remembered how he used to just look at her eyes for hours at a time. He loved her eyes. He had to concentrate to find his voice. "I figured you'd tell me when you're ready."

"What's in the packages?"

"I imagine that's the key to the whole thing."

"It's pretty gross, but come inside and look. A package arrived this morning."

Cut 7

I Had Too Much to Dream Last Night

Peter Brown liked to be alone. He had his iPod, comic books, his anime and DVDs. They were all part of his own little world. Brownworld. In Brownworld, no one teased about his unnaturally high voice or lack of muscle tone. No one commented on his smooth face or almost feminine features.

In Brownworld, Peter was a boxer, the heavyweight champion of the world. In Brownworld, Peter was the son of Elvis Presley, not some smarmy Account Executive at a third-rate advertising agency. In Brownworld, the next-door neighbor, a pretty divorced woman, came over to Peter's basement every night.

Peter got off the school bus last, so he wouldn't have to walk with the other kids. He loitered a minute at the corner to make sure all the kids were well ahead of him. He put on the ear buds connected to his iPod. He listened to the Jonas Brothers. They were so uncool among the jock crowd at school. But Peter liked them. He liked their energy. They made him feel a little sexy. Like he was one of them. When the music started, he quickly stepped into Brownworld. Tonight the neighbor woman was dressed in a pink Secret Embrace Invisible Lace Bra and Pout Pink Lace Thong just like in his mom's Victoria Secret Catalogue.

Because he was in Brownworld, he didn't notice the man with the oddly shaped head, totally bald like Lex Luthor, who sat in an idling SUV at the corner on the other side of the street.

As Peter walked home he could see the Pink Secret Embrace Invisible Lace Bra strap slowly fall off the neighbor woman's shoulder. Her darker pink tongue licked lush red lips.

The man followed Peter, barely touching the accelerator. The man had his own world, too. Although his world was one of fantasies and dreams much nastier than Peter's. It was a world awash in blood. It was a world of gleaming steel and screaming pain and the long dark night. The man who followed Peter, unlike Peter, lived in a world that wasn't all fantasy.

The man pressed down slightly on the gas pedal, quickening his pace. His world and Peter's were about to collide.

Peter Brown slowly unzipped his next door neighbor's skirt. She was, in fact, wearing a light pink thong. The sight of the lace caused his breath to quicken. Her curves were pure poetry. He stopped to look at her. She said, "don't stop" and leaned over to lightly kiss his ear. Her breath was warm and fragrant.

And then it was cold and wet. A rough, wet cloth covering his face. A sharp, metallic smell. He breathed in. An abrupt, reflexive intake of breath. The world tilted. His eyes watered. He quickly left the warm kisses and pink lace bras of Brownworld and slipped into a world of cold nothing.

The Man with the Lightbulb Head carried Peter over to the black Trailblazer parked at the side of the street. An SUV was not an unusual sight in this neighborhood. The backdoor was already open and he pushed the boy inside. Before the the odd-looking man got in on the driver's side, he looked around to see if anyone had seen the snatch. The kidnapper wore a baseball hat to hide his distinguishing features. The entire operation had taken less than fifteen seconds. It appeared no one had seen him. Even if they had, he was in a stolen car, which he would abandon within ten minutes.

He drove off slowly down the street. In a few minutes a new game was about to begin. He smiled.

At a small neighboring playground the man parked beside a white van and shut off the engine. He left the keys in the ignition. He opened the back door to the Trailblazer and the side door to the van.

He quickly moved Peter Brown from the SUV to the van and slammed both doors. Although the Man with the Lightbulb Head wore gloves, he vacuumed the back seat with a hand vac and quickly wiped down everything with an alcohol-soaked rag.

Within ten minutes he drove away from the playground.

When Peter awoke he was cold. It felt as if he were naked, but he couldn't be certain because his eyes were taped shut. He was in a sitting position. He tried to move but he seemed to be taped to a chair. He started to shiver.

Cold air surrounded his body. His feet grew numb from the cold.

"Good evening Mr. Brown."

"Mmmmf, mmmoof."

"Oh, don't try to speak. There's a handkerchief in your mouth and duct tape over it. Now, here are the rules of the game we are going to play. When I ask you a question, you are going to shake your head yes or no. Understand?"

Peter tried to scream through his muffled mouth. Suddenly a pain shot up through his groin and he almost passed out. Vomit lurched up from his stomach but he held it back with rapid swallows.

"That was just a little tap. Your genitalia, do you understand the word genitalia?"

Peter shook his head vigorously up and down.

"Good. Your genitalia, your gonads, your balls, if you will, are as naked as the rest of you and laid out on a two by four inch block of wood about ten inches long. Every time you don't answer me, I will hit one of them with the ball peen hammer I have in my hand. Do you understand?"

Another affirmative shake of the head.

"Okay now. We're doing very well. Are you hungry?"

Peter shook his head yes. He realized he was famished.

"Well, don't worry because I'm feeding you nutriments intravenously. Are you cold?"

Head shake. Yes.

"Thank you for being honest. I will throw a blanket on you in a minute. Okay, what's the coldest part of your body? Your penis?"

Head shake no.

"Your ears?"

Another no.

"Your lips."

No.

"I didn't think so. It's protected from the chill by the tape. Your nose?"

Pause. Head shake no.

"Are you sure?"

Head shake yes.

"How about your toes? Your toes must be cold from the freezing concrete. Is it your toes?"

Slow head shake yes.

"You're absolutely positive your toes are the coldest part of your body?"

Another head shake yes.

"Good job. Hold still now."

The man picked up a roll of duct tape and started wrapping it around Peter's head and the back of the chair.

"Okay let me go over to the workbench here and mix myself a Dubonnet and club soda, when I return I will cut one of your toes off to get the blood flowing."

Peter strained against the tape and tried to thrash about. He tried to turn his head to the side but the tape had it locked. He heard the man walk away and then, return.

Another tap on the nuts and then the sound of some sort of scissors or clippers snapping shut and the cracking of bone. For an instant, no pain. Then, an excruciating hot slash of pain shot up from his below his ankle.

"There, there Peter, I'll give you a few minutes to feel the total effect of the amputation, and then I'll give you a shot of something to put you to sleep. Oh, this is going to be a fun, fun night."

At that, Brownworld went black again.

Cut 8
I Just Don't Know

It was pretty damn gross. Whatever it was. Louie wasn't a doctor. Or a vet. But he guessed it wasn't plant material, because of all the blood. And, he didn't think it was fish, although it might have been from a really big fish or one of those mammals that live in the ocean like fish, swim like fish and look like fish. Dolphins. Whales. Porpoises.

He had cleaned fish and dressed a deer and seen dead bodies. But he had never seen anything like this.

Maybe it was a peeled eyeball. Or, a skinned grape that had been marinating in cow's blood. Or some other gland, he didn't want to think too much about. Or, maybe it was the frontal lobe of a brain. Or, the whole brain of a skunk or something. Hell, he didn't have a clue.

Here's what he did know. It was about the size of a single male testicle. Louie smiled. It could have been a married male, but it was single testicle size. It was bloody. It was wrapped in wax paper, placed inside a sandwich bag, wrapped inside butcher's paper, in a cardboard box that had been placed in a FedEx envelope and put on Sloopy's doorstep.

FedEx didn't deliver it, someone just used a FedEx envelope. Louie turned to Sloopy. "How many of these have you received?"

"Fifteen or so. About one a week. Sometimes two."

"Any particular day of the week?"

"No."

"Any pattern? Like every five days? On the first day of the month? Anything like that?"

"Not that I can tell. In fact, one time he skipped a whole week and sent three packages the next week. Three days in a row. Monday, Tuesday, and Wednesday."

"You said he."

"Huh?"

"You said 'one time he skipped a whole week.'"

"I guess I did."

"Why did you say he?"

"Well it seems like something a he would do. It doesn't feel like a she thing."

"But you don't know. It could have been a she."

"It could have, but I doubt it."

Louie let it drop.

"The first thing we ought to do is check out butchers. A butcher would have the knives and the skill to do this. And this one was wrapped in butcher paper."

"I think the others were too, but I couldn't swear all of them were. But, yes that makes sense. A butcher."

"Where are the rest of the packages?"

"I gave them to the police, to Elliott."

"What did he do?"

"I'm not sure. He tested them, I guess. He told me what animal parts they were. He traced the packages."

"Did he interview anybody? Did he offer any theories?"

"He thinks it's some elaborate prank. And there's something else."

"What?"

"It's no big deal."

"No, what?"

"It has nothing to do with this. Well it does in a way."

"What is it?"

"Well, he kept trying to hit on me."

"Are you sure?"

"Louie, a woman knows."

"But he's married."

She snickered.

"Never mind."

"When I made it clear I wasn't interested, he lost interest in the packages. Kept telling me they were pranks. He started treating me as if I were a nuisance, the sonovabitch. I don't think they—the police—are trying very hard anymore to solve this thing."

"Did you always receive something that looked like this?"

"Like this?"

"Do they always look like, uh, testicles?"

"Oh no. This is the smallest thing I've received so far. I've gotten a cow stomach, sheep's intestines, rabbit brains, chunks of muscle, I can't remember them all, I don't know if I've been told what they were all the time."

"But it was never part of a human."

"Oh no. No. Definitely not."

Louie closed his eyes. He opened them again and scratched the side of his head absently. "Did Elliott tell the FBI about this?"

"The FBI, no, why?"

"Well, didn't you tell me sometimes the stuff was sent by mail?"

"Yes."

"Well, I believe if you commit a crime using the U.S. Postal service, it is a federal offense and so the FBI would become involved."

"I don't believe he ever contacted the FBI. At least he never told me about it."

"Okay."

Louie wrapped the bloody organ back up and put it in the box.

"Where are you going?"

"I'm going to take this to a guy I know who might be able to give me some information. Then, I have an errand to run. I will be back about suppertime. Do you want me to bring something? How about Chinese?"

"Chinese will be fine."

"In the meantime, I want you to make two lists. On one list I want you to try and remember the days of the week you received packages and on the other I want you to write down where the packages originated. Let's see if we can find a pattern to these things."

"You won't be long, will you?"

"I won't be long, I promise."

Louie took the keys to Sloopy's car and drove to a neighboring town's toy store and made some purchases.

He then drove to the house of a pathologist, a buddy, who also did some work for the state police. Sheldon King, the pathologist, usually worked until three. When Louie rang the doorbell, the doctor answered with a rocks glass in hand.

"Louie, good to see you. Come on in. Care for a scotch?"

"No, I don't have much time. I need a favor."

"What can I do for you, buddy?"

Louie handed the pathologist the package.

"What's this?"

"You tell me. I'm not sure what it is, or what it came from."

"So, is it plant, animal, mineral?"

"Animal."

"It's not human, is it?"

"I'm not sure, I don't think so. I wondered if you could tell me what it is, what animal it came from, how fresh it is and anything else you can find out."

"Well, well, well. A mystery. Any background you can give me on it?"

"All I know is that it arrived this morning and that's it."

Sheldon stepped out on the porch and closed the front door.

"I don't want to upset Dana with this. So, I tell you what. I'll open the garage door and you put it in the back seat of my car and I'll take it to the lab tonight after supper."

"Sounds good. I owe you a bottle of single malt."

"You know what I like."

"*Caol Ila*. You got it, bro."

After depositing the package in his car and hitting the automatic garage door button, Louie got in Sloopy's car and drove back to Tivoli. He stopped at the town's one butcher shop and talked to Randy the Butcher.

Randy was one of those guys who always seemed to be happy and always had a joke or two for his customers. He was a big man, six feet five with a belly that was softening up. He had permanent crinkles around his eyes from laughing and smiling. "Louie, how about I fix you up with a T-Bone that's so good and tender it would convince Paul McCartney to open a steak house? Just got 'em in; I'll cut one extra thick for you. Slap that bad boy on the grill and you'll thank me until the day you die and save a place in heaven for me even after."

"Not today, I'll take a rain check."

"I've got some beautiful pork chops just in."

"No, I've got a few questions for you."

"Well shoot. See I don't mind saying that to you 'cuz I know you never carry. Hell, if I said it to Chief Elliott, he'd have two in the heart and one in my head before I could even begin to say 'figure of speech.'"

Louie asked if anyone had been around asking for funny cuts of meat or animal parts.

"By funny, do you mean a chuckling chuck roast? Slapstick salami? Wisecracking cracklins?"

"No, I mean funny as in strange."

"Well, I always thought gizzards were pretty strange. Funny, too, now that you think about it. Just say the word out loud, gizzard, it just sounds funny. Headcheese sounds kinda funny too, if you ask me."

Louie explained what he was looking for.

"Other than some of the old-timers who still get cow's tongue, or Mrs. MacReady who orders tripe, never could understand how anyone could eat that crap, no one has ordered or asked for anything unusual."

Louie next stopped off at another friend's house, Carson Catlin, who was a genius computer nerd. Louie was glad to have him as a friend. Louie always said he didn't know doodley squat about computers and didn't want to learn. He hated computers.

He thought they did more harm to society than good. But, in his profession, they were excellent tools. So, even though he fought having them in his personal life, he didn't mind having a friend who was comfortable in the digital world.

He explained to Carson what he wanted. Carson agreed to do some snooping around cyber space.

Louie drove to Church Street just three blocks off the main street. This was still a cobblestone street lined on either side by older single dwelling homes built in the thirties and forties. There were plenty of mature trees on the lots. Some of houses were rather tiny by today's standards, but a few were bigger and featured wraparound porches.

Louie stopped in front of a white Cape Cod with black shutters. There were a few little paint blisters and some light peeling. It was one or two years away from needing repainting. The front yard was immaculate but small. The asphalt driveway was cracked but had been repaired and sealed several times.

Louie got out of the car with a package and looked around to make sure there were no neighbors snooping out their windows.

A breezeway connected the one-car garage to the main part of the house. A kitchen door led to the breezeway. It was locked, but he used a credit card to open the screen door and a pick to open the kitchen door. He stepped inside and re-locked the door.

In the small dining room off of the kitchen, he placed the package on the dining room table and laid an envelope on top of it.

"I could have you arrested for trespassing. Or maybe I just ought to shoot you," said a voice from behind.

Louie turned around.

"Hi, Diane."

She was holding a shotgun.

"I knew it was you all along. Why do you keep doing it?"

"Doin' what?"

"Don't play me for stupid."

He shrugged.

"You don't have to, you know. You don't owe me anything."

"I know."

"So what did you bring this time?"

"Guitar Hero III or IV, whatever the latest one is."

"What's in the envelope?"

"A couple hundred bucks."

"I'm not a charity."

"It's from your husband."

"It's not from my husband, the jerk. He hasn't given me a dime since he ran off." She put the shotgun down.

"Well, it was some money I owed him."

"You don't owe him anything, and you know it. For some reason you think it's your duty to help me out."

"Just take the money, Diane. Buy yourself something nice."

"You know, I figured it was you all this time. I won't say I don't appreciate the help. I can't say I don't need it. But you don't have to do this."

"I want to. He was my friend. He is my friend. You are my friend. Just keep the money and the toys. Do it for your son."

She opened her mouth and then shut it. She turned her back on Louie for a moment and then turned around again.

"Oh Louie. I love you."

She came over and hugged him. He stroked her hair. She was very cute. Short red hair. Perky little body. Something stirred. He pushed her away, slightly.

"We could be friends. Friends with benefits. I would like that," she said.

"So would I. But I can't."

"Some sort of guy thing, isn't it?"

"I guess."

"Can't mess with your best friend's girl, can you?"

He didn't say anything.

"Well then, you better leave now."

"Okay."

"And take your money."

He left, but didn't take the money.

Cut 9
Lies

Elliott Blake drove back to the station from the kid's car. He liked driving. It gave him time to think. Right now he was thinking about a lot of things. His mind seemed to be ping-ponging all over the place. He thought about the high school girl he saw walking down the street about two blocks back. She was one hot little number.

She had interrupted his thoughts as he was reliving that one time in junior high when, as an end, he caught a twenty yard pass and ran another forty-three for a touchdown. It was junior high wasn't it? Most the time when he told the story, he was in high school. Lies were funny things, you tell them enough and they began to seem like truth.

Who was that girl he saw walking down the street? Was that Jim Mitchell's daughter? Man, she had grown up. Filled out. Elliott was wondering if he could come up with an excuse to pat her down.

His stomach growled and he thought about steak. A big, juicy New York strip at St. Elmo's in Indianapolis. A shrimp cocktail with sauce that would blast the back of your skull off. A vodka martini or three. Go to a strip club. PTs. Yeah. What was the name of that blonde with the big boobs that gave you a lap dance that would turn you inside out? Heidi? She was a dental hygienist. No, she was going to nursing school. No, she was going to dental hygiene school. That's it. Elliott liked the way she nibbled on his ear. Most lap dancers wouldn't do that.

Okay, had he promised the wife he would be home for supper? Anything going on with the kids? No school plays or soccer games? Soccer, now there was some pussy sport. Sure, his kid played it. That's what young kids do these days. He went to the games 'cuz he loved his kid. But, now, really, who gave a rat's ass about some faggy European sport that bored the bejeezus out of him?

What the hell, he was going to Elmo's tonight.

First he was gonna circle the block and see if he could catch another look at the high school trim with the belly ring and cutoffs. And…

What the hell?

It was Susan Louise's car again. What was it doing parked in this part of town? Whose house was it in front of? Yea, that was Diane Baker's house. Boy would he like to make a sandwich out of Suzie and Diane. While listening to Deep Purple's "Smoke on the Water" at full volume. Doin' a little weed.

Wait. Who was that leaving Diane's house? Son of a bean pickin' mongrel whore. It was that asswipe Louie Louie again. Damn it all to hell.

Diane, too? What the… When did Louie start becoming the town's pussy hound? Damn. Her husband, Louie's old buddy, had taken a powder six months ago, give or take, and Elliott was taking his time, working her slowly. Being the good friend. Giving her a shoulder to cry on. Listening to her boring-ass chick whining and acting like he cared.

Oh. That fried his oysters. Louie was getting all of the grade-A trim in town. This had to stop.

Elliott had killed nine people in his life. Two were righteous shoots. Six were questionable, but they were scumbags and Elliott had used a throw-down piece. One person had simply disappeared.

The steak, the teenage girl, the lap dance were all forgotten. Elliott used every available brain cell figuring out how he was going to make that stupid ass Louie vanish from the face of this earth.

Elliott followed Louie into town.

Louie stopped off at the Jade Garden and ordered enough Chinese takeout for four. Waiting for the food, he looked out the window and saw the police cruiser drive by, the second time so far.

Why the hell? Louie thought.

He stepped out the front door. The police car was stopped at a light. Louie's hands tightened into fists.

Should he turn this into something? Elliott was one of the few things in town Louie didn't like.

He took a deep breath.

Leave it be.

He turned back and waited for the food.

The cruiser followed him as he drove to Sloopy's. It kept going after he stopped.

When Louie came in the backdoor, she told him there was a bottle of white wine chilling in the refrigerator. They had a couple glasses of wine and gorged on Chinese food.

The whole time they didn't talk about the packages or the present. They just reminded each other of silly stories that had happened in their lives. The kinds of stories that are only funny if you lived them and knew the people involved. "Remember the time" stories that involved milk squirting out someone's nose, or slaw dripping on black pants, or when the class clown cut loose a five minute fart during a convocation.

Louie realized he hadn't laughed so much in years. It felt good.

"Louie?"

"Yea."

"What are you doing here?"

"You asked me here."

"No, you big dope. Here in Tivoli. What are you doing here?"

"I like it here. I like my home. I like the people. I'm happy."

"But why do you like it here? You could make more money in Chicago with your Dad."

"Yes, I could."

"So."

"So. Well, I guess I don't like things to change too much."

"But even here, things change."

"I know they do. But I don't like change. I liked things as they were in the sixties. The Beatles. Cell animation. Mom and pop stores that would stay open as long as there was one customer left. Companies that had personalities rather than conglomerates that have quarterly sales goals."

"The sixties were all about change."

"But, it seems to me, they were about informed change. Change that had a certain rhythm to it. Change that had to prove what came next was an improvement over what came before. Now it's just rapid and out of control. It's change for change's sake. I don't know."

"But you weren't even born in the sixties."

"I know. It all might be romantic hoo-hah from a silly fool."

"You do have some quirky ideas about things."

"Perhaps I do. That's why I don't talk about them much."

"And what does this have to do with Tivoli?"

"It's where I grew up so I don't have to change my friends and the places I know. And it's a small town, slow to change."

"But, Louie, it has changed."

"Not for the better. And the change has come more slowly than in other places. Look I'll fight change as much as I can. But there are some changes I've made peace with. I use cell phones, even though they are just tracking devices for the government. I have a buddy that looks stuff up for me on the computer. Uh…I carry an iPod with me, just because I can't fit any of my jukeboxes in my pocket."

"But you still prefer the sixties to now."

"You've got it, babe."

"You're a strange one, Mr. Louie. A cop—"

"Former cop."

"Who doesn't like guns. A man who wants to return to a way of life he never even experienced."

"I watched a lot of Dick Van Dyke."

"And a man who lives in a broken down old town when he could be making some decent coin in the Big City."

"You live here too."

"So?"

"So, why do you live here?"

"Because it's home," she said in a matter-of-fact tone of voice.

"Well, that's the reason I live here, too."

"You shoulda just said so."

"Mighta saved a lot of gum flapping by me, huh."

"No kiddin'."

"No kiddin'."

"So, is that it?"

"I guess."

"Okay." She said it with that tone of voice that meant it was less than okay.

"What's that supposed to mean?"

"Nothing."

"Are you sure?"

"I just thought there might be other reasons."

"None that I can think of."

"None?"

"Nope."

"Okay."

They moved on to other subjects. Catching up on their lives.

After a while the conversation wound down. They had been eating the food in her living room on the couch. Louie sat back and looked out the front picture window at the street. There wasn't any traffic. He felt sort of zoned out. Just thinking about how right everything was. How good everything felt. How good it would feel to hold her.

He wanted to say something, to ask her about Tim, but it would ruin the moment. So, he kept quiet. Still, he thought, it was a sore spot that needed to be lanced sooner or later before it infected their whole relationship, whatever that was and whatever it was turning out to be.

"Louie?"

"Yea."

"Are you staying the night?"

It didn't sound like an invitation. But, he wasn't sure.

"I better not."

"Well, I'm getting really sleepy."

"Let me help you clean up. In fact, you stay there and I'll clean up."

There wasn't much to do, just throw away the take-out boxes and chopsticks and wash two plates and two wine glasses.

"Hey, Sloopy, do you have those lists I asked you for?"

But she was sound asleep. He debated whether he should carry her up to the bedroom and tuck her into bed. He looked at her a few minutes and then took off her shoes and threw a comforter on her.

It was a pleasant night. Slowly walking back to the bar, Louie rolled his shoulders and shook his hands out. There was a looseness to his body he hadn't experienced in a long time. He thought about Sloopy. He thought about the packages. He thought about Tim Ferman, her former husband. Tim had to be involved somehow. But where was the proof?

Tim was one of those guys who was all designer clothes and ambition. Louie didn't like the type. Could that be swaying his thoughts? He imagined scenarios that didn't involve Tim.

The first Louie became aware of the van was when it screeched to a stop beside him. Two men with ski masks pulled down over their faces jumped out. One of them had a baseball bat. The other had something in his hand, Louie couldn't tell what. Baseball bat went for a rib shot but Louie dropped to the ground and kicked the attacker's legs out from under him. The other man circled around behind and jumped on Louie's back, yanking a wool hood of some sort over his head.

Louie couldn't see. He reached up to pull the hood off and the guy on his back twisted Louie's arms behind his back. Nylon handcuffs ratcheted his wrists together. Louie's face was pushed into the dirt and the man with the baseball bat squirmed out from under.

Louie knew he had to get away. So he rolled to the street. He'd started to get up when the van accelerated. It hit him with a glancing blow and, as he struggled to his feet again, something crashed into the side of his head.

The world went dark.

Cut 10
Knock Knock

Sloopy awoke to the sound of a door clicking shut. She thought about calling out to Louie, but decided against. The poor lug was probably walking home. His car was at the Tick-Toc Bar. Maybe he'd drop in and have another beer.

It was amazing how comfortable she felt with him. It was like all the years hadn't happened. They laughed just like they did when they were together. There were no awkward silences. None of that slight self-censorship, the white lies, or the filters you put on when you're with anyone except the very closest of people. She hadn't felt so uninhibited in conversation for years. She certainly was never so totally open with Tim.

How did the whole Tim thing happen? She did love him once. But was it ever as much as she loved Louie? Did she ever feel as comfortable with Tim as she felt this night with Louie? Something to think about.

She wasn't one for self-recrimination. But Tim had been a mistake. She didn't feel the same kind of love for Tim she felt for Louie. She admired Tim. He was good-looking and a good dresser. He treated her very well. Took her to nice restaurants. Took her to plays and movies and concerts. Tim was always fun. He had a surface confidence that was appealing.

But beneath the surface, he was a bit unsure. He primped a little too much for her taste. He dropped names all the time. He never let a conversation go by without talking about the latest fabulous vacation they had been on. He bordered on being boorish.

He never did anything spontaneous. Everything seemed calculated to impress.

He watched sports so he could talk sports with his buddies. She could tell he didn't really like them. That he tried so hard to impress people in this little town wasn't very impressive at all.

She shook her head. Why was she doing this? Why was she bashing Tim in her mind? Four years into her marriage, she could see it was over. He began going to bed after her so he wouldn't have to have sex with her.

And that was okay. The sex was never that great. There was never the wild abandon, the lust that made romance such an adventure. In fact, there was more lust in the eyes of the half-drunk old men at the bar today than she ever saw in Tim's.

She felt the electricity between herself and Louie. Even though he hadn't tried anything, she could see how much he wanted her.

Was that why she asked for his help? To see if he still wanted her? To see if he still cared about her?

She hoped things would go on after the whole bloody package mess was over. She wanted to see whether she and Louie had a future.

The doorbell rang. Sloopy smiled to herself, Louie had returned. Would he make up some sort of excuse like he left his wallet or something? Or would he just say he wanted to be with her?

She opened the door.

It wasn't Louie.

She tried to slam the door, but the man stuck his foot in and then shoved.

As he pushed his way in she didn't wonder if the man was going to hurt her, but how much.

Louie awoke blind.

Slowly more feelings emerged. Pain in the leg. A head that hurt when he didn't move it and hurt much more when he did.

Something blocked his vision, a hood or pillowcase of bag of some sort pulled down over his head. Fragments of memory started to fit together in his mind like a jigsaw puzzle he couldn't finish. The picture still incomplete. He remembered a guy with a baseball bat. He remembered a van and two guys getting out. He remembered…what? Not much more.

As his senses slowly reasserted themselves, he became aware of traffic noises, talking, the cold feel of metal beneath his hands, the vibration of a moving vehicle. He must be in the back of the van that had let the two goons out and then later on clipped him on the leg. That was a new memory. The van hitting him on the leg.

Without causing too much body movement, he twisted and pulled his arms to work out of the wrist cuffs. No luck.

He slid sideways on his butt seeking a sharp corner to cut the nylon restraints. Again, no luck.

Okay. This was probably an execution. The hood. The fact that they were going somewhere out of town, probably an abandoned corn or soybean field.

He didn't think he had much of a chance, but he had to do something.

He scooted to the side of the van. With his back against one wall, he pushed with his legs. He slid up the side until his head bumped on the top.

He stopped and listened. The voices came from his left. That meant he was against the right side of the van, the passenger's side. The driver was at an angle.

He tried to calculate the correct angle, ducked his head and bulldozed to the front. He screamed with a throat-shredding growl and pounded his feet as loud as possible.

"What the…" someone up front said.

He hit the left side and shot straight forward. He banged against one of the seats. The seatback snapped. The driver smashed against the steering wheel. The horn honked and the van swerved crazily.

He didn't want the driver regaining any sort of control so he jerked and thrashed as much as he could and kicked with his feet to keep the pressure on the back of the driver's seat.

The hood caught on something so he yanked his head back and forth to get it off. It finally came off and he could see for an instant that the van was in a skid, heading for the side of the road, the driver fighting the steering wheel. Louie head butted the driver's head against the side window. The window spidered but didn't shatter. Louie brought one of his feet up and kicked the passenger in the back of the head.

A loud thump and the world turned on its side. Metal shrieked, Glass shattered. Then, scraping, scraping, scraping. And…silence. No, not quite total silence, a ringing in Louie's ears. He crawled out through the shattered front window.

The van had tipped over on its side and skidded to a stop in a little weedy strip between the road and a cornfield.

Two guys in the van both were unconscious. One of them, the passenger, had his eyes open but they were going opaque with the unblinking stare at eternity. The other was bleeding and moaning, his face against the mosaiced side window. The third guy was unaccounted for.

Louie rummaged around and found the baseball bat and a .38 snub-nosed revolver.

He threw the .38 in the field and took the bat to use as a cane or as a weapon, if needed.

Louie thought he recognized the location, but wasn't sure. There were many cornfields surrounding Tivoli, Indiana and he was having a hard time remembering which side of town this particular one was on.

Louie made sure the driver wasn't moving.

There was no traffic on the road. Not unusual for a country road late at night. Ahead, there was a house in the about a half mile away with an outside barn light on. From the other direction, he heard traffic sounds in the distance.

Louie walked toward the traffic.

Cut 11

Twistin' the Night Away

Peter Brown found it hard to stay alive. In fact, even though he was only fourteen years old, he didn't know if he wanted to live.

He wanted the pain to end. He wanted The Man with the Lightbulb Head to quit cutting him up.

First his toe had been snipped off. Now, all his toes had been removed, his fingers were gone, as were his ears and long ribbons of skin.

And, his testicles. Gone. At least those had been removed with a surgeon's knife. But it hurt more than anything he could imagine. Not that he ever spent any time imagining pain. In his young life, a few scrapes and bruises were all he ever experienced. He never even thought about pain. In Brownworld, everything was based on pleasure. He tried to take his mind to Brownworld. But he couldn't. His mind was fixated on the universe of hurt coming from the center of his body.

His eyes were next. The Man with the Lightbulb Head already told him. That would be awful. That would be unbearable. He couldn't imagine a world without vision.

He decided he wanted to die, for sure.

He jerked and squirmed to remove the IV. He tensed his muscles to pop the crude stitches. He willed himself to die. Nothing worked.

He prayed. So far, no answer.

He must've passed out because The Man with the Lightbulb Head now stood right in front of him.

"The end is in sight," the man said and giggled. "Of course, for you, there'll be a considerable length of time when nothing is in sight." He giggled again.

"What I'm going to do, is put this knife in the corner of your eye and slice through the muscles that hold it in place and pop it out. I've done it on animals. It should work on humans. Then I'll pack the socket with cotton balls and antibiotic ointment. I'll do one eye now and the other in four or five hours. How does that sound?"

The man took a sip of from a tiny stemmed glass.

"This, my dear boy, is Manzanilla, a dry sherry like a Fino, but with a nuttier taste. I love sipping sherry while I work , it just makes everything a little more civilized. Don't you agree?" When Peter didn't respond, he said, "Oh Peter Peter Pumpkin eater, I asked you a question."

Of course Peter Brown didn't answer. He didn't struggle much anymore. He *couldn't* struggle much anymore. But, what he lacked in struggle, he more than made up for in smell.

The Man with the Lightbulb Head pinched his nose. "My goodness, you're rank. I suppose I can't expect rotting flesh, excrement and urine to smell like Chanel number five, but still... The next time I'm going to rig some sort of catheter system to drain off the urine and cut a hole in the chair with a slop bucket underneath for the crap. Yes, that's exactly what I'll do. In the meantime, we must do something about your appalling lack of hygiene."

The Man with the Lightbulb Head held a can of Lysol Disinfecting Spray, which he used all over Peter. Waiting for the mist to dissipate, he turned his back on Peter to get the baggie-lined box ready.

Peter pushed his head forward with all the strength he could muster as he also pushed down with his feet. This was his one chance. He worked through the pain and fatigue. The duct tape on his forehead had loosened and stretched a little over the past few days. The moisture of the Lysol helped loosen the adhesive a little more. Even though the chair was bolted to the floor, the constant pushing with his feet had stripped some of the threads and he was able to tilt the chair back almost two inches.

The Man with the Lightbulb Head turned around and walked over to Peter Brown in his chair. "Well, it smells a little better. Let's get to work, shall we?"

He took a last sip of sherry and licked his lips.

The Man with the Lightbulb Head carefully pushed the knife into the corner of Peter's right eye. Peter pushed backward as far as he could with his head and the chair. When the knife was in as far as the man with the Lightbulb Head was going to push it, Peter Brown quit pushing with his legs, dropping the chair forward while simultaneously thrusting his face forward as far as it would go. The surgeon's blade drove through the socket into Peter's brain, killing him instantly.

"Oh my, my. Now that wasn't supposed to happen. Shame on you, Mr. Brown. You've certainly ruined my entertainment with your untimely and very selfish death. Just what am I going to do with you now? I know. I'll just cut you up while you're dead. Won't be quite as much fun. But I can still use your parts for other fun time activities. After all, parts is parts. I guess I should get to it. Chop-chop."

As the freakishly-headed man went to work cutting, slicing and dicing, twisting and cracking and sawing, he whistled.

Pretty soon, he'd get someone else in the white van. Drive the white van to his special place. His chop shop. The fun was just beginning.

Cut 12
Last Time Around

Lee Brian, Dumbass Dentist's Kid, was about to do another dumbass thing. He was going to rob the convenience store that he robbed two nights earlier.

"Hey, if at first you don't succeed," he thought.

Even though he hated when that cop called him Dumbass Dentist's Kid, he knew he was a dumbass dentist's kid. He was always doing dumbass things. In fact his dad, the dentist who very rarely swore, had once called him a dumbass.

So, yes, he was a dumbass. He was the mayor of dumbass city, a town without pity. Like the time he shot out the streetlights in town. One or two might've been fun. One or two might not have gotten him caught. But the beer and the pot and his posse egging him on, made it seem like it would be really cool to shoot out all the streetlights on Harrison Street, the main street of town. Now, that was a 100-proof, high octane, pedal-to-the-metal, no-doubt-about-it dumbass with a capital D kind of move.

Then there was the time he stole two crates of candy the band was using for a fundraiser. He should not have hidden the candy in his school locker. Or, given a couple of bars to a girl in study hall. Grade A, government-inspected prime dumbass move.

Oh, he could go on and on. Unfortunately, it was only after he got caught that the sheer dumbassiness of the move occurred to him.

So, he decided to keep the dumbass stuff to a minimum. He had another one of his dad's pistols. If he dropped it, that would be a dumbass move on two counts. The cops would trace it back to him. Even if they didn't, his dad would miss it and get pissed. So, hold on to the pistol, no matter what. What else? Keep the ski mask down and, oh yes, take out the video camera first thing.

Disguise his voice somehow. It didn't do any good to wear a ski mask if they recognized your voice. And, since everyone knew one of the two patrol cars always made a circuit at fifteen minutes past the hour, every hour, it would be a dumbass move of the highest magnitude to try and rob the store then. Do it on the half hour.

And, finally, don't go into the place if other people were inside. They could be potential witnesses.

Well, it was 3:30 a.m., no cars in the lot, no one in the store. Adrenaline thrummed through his body and he was ready to boogie.

He pulled down the ski mask.

Showtime.

He walked across the highway and the parking lot. Just as he was opening the door, another car pulled into the lot.

Crap. Lee felt like the dumbass express was pulling out of the station and he had just jumped on board.

Lee Brian quickly pulled off the ski mask and shoved it into his pocket. As he entered the store, head turned away from where he knew the camera to be, he walked to the corner the furthest away from the camera with his back to it the entire time.

He examined the energy drinks in the coolers to keep his face hidden from the camera, as up front, the tinkling bell announced someone else entering the store.

Two girls giggled and walked toward him. He recognized the voices.

"Lee? Is that you?"

"Sandy. Denise. How are you?"

Both of the girls were what he considered "hotties" but Denise had a body that turned boys into men just looking at it.

"So, what are you doing here?" Denise asked.

"I uh, gee I was just, I mean, you know," Lee stammered.

"Yeah, we are too," Sandy giggled.

"We're just getting some Red Bull," Denise said.

"Yeah, lots and lots of Red Bull," Sandy added.

"Sandy's parents aren't home and we're having a par-tay," Denise said.

"Yea, the old man has a case of vodka in the garage. He won't miss a bottle or two," Sandy said.

"Hey, that's great." Lee grinned at them.

"You don't happen to have any weed do you?" Sandy asked.

"Well, as a matter of fact." Lee patted his pocket.

"That's cool, why don't you join us?" Denise said.

Oh man, oh man, this couldn't be happening. Partying with Denise and Sandy. This friggin' rawked!

"Yea, sure."

"Why are you walking backwards? Come on, let's do this thing," Sandy said.

Lee stopped. He had promised he would rob the convenience store tonight. That was the deal.

"Listen, I'll catch up to you two in about a half an hour. I got to get something here and take it to my old man."

"Well hurry, 'cuz we're still in the part-tay mood. Won't last forever. We're not near as much fun when we're not in the part-tay mood. Are we Denise?"

"We're not near as frisky."

"Oh don't worry, I'll show up."

"Are you sure you're okay? You're acting kinda strange," Denise said.

"Yeah, yeah, I'm fine. See you soon." Lee stepped back toward the corner of the store.

"Bring some beer if you got any," Sandy said over her shoulder.

"Sure, okay."

He opened the cooler, took out a Red Bull and pretended to be reading the label. The girls were at the front of the store talking with the guy behind the counter.

He heard giggling and more chatter but he couldn't make out the words. Would they ever leave?

Finally there was silence. Had they left yet? He didn't hear the tinkling of the bell. What was going on? He couldn't turn around because the camera would pick up his face.

He put the Red Bull back.

Wait, what was that? Over the whoosh of the refrigerator door opening he thought he heard something. Was it the front door? Were the girls leaving or did someone come in the store?

More silence. Lee could hear the sound of his heart beating in his ears. He'd give it another minute or so.

"May I help you?" the guy up front said.

"No, no. I'm fine."

"What are you doing back there?" the man called out.

"Nothing. Uh…just looking." Shit! He was using his normal voice.

"Can I help you find anything?"

"No. I got it." He did it again! Well, there was no use trying to disguise it now.

He couldn't hang around the energy drinks forever. He took the ski mask out of his pocket and slipped it over his head. He pulled the gun out from the back of his pants and dropped it.

It skidded across the floor.

He bent down to pick it up and almost tripped. His hands were so sweaty he couldn't grab the gun. Finally, he wrapped his fingers around it, started to stand up while running forward and fell over a display of nuts.

"Hey, what's going on?" the man yelled as Lee scrambled to his feet.

"Put your hands up!" Lee screamed, although he couldn't see the man.

Lee made it to the front of the store holding the gun. Where was the son of a bitch?

"Come here, goddammit, or I'll blow your head off."

Lee remembered the camera and pointed the gun at it. Pulled the trigger. Shit, the safety was on. He flicked off the safety and fired three shots, all of them missing the camera. One shot blew out the fluorescent lights in the front of the store. The next hit a carton of cigarettes behind the counter. It exploded in a cloud of paper, smoke, and powdered tobacco. The third shot killed the Mr. Slushee machine, sending icy blue raspberry everywhere.

When he turned back, the man behind the counter had just put the second shell in a double-barreled shotgun and was snapping it shut.

Dumbass didn't begin to describe how Lee felt just then. He twisted his torso and fired just as the man pulled the trigger on the shotgun.

There was a blue flash and then the world exploded. Lee was knocked off his feet and the gun was again knocked out of his hand when he hit the floor.

The shotgun blast, besides hitting Lee, shattered the front window, which knocked over the magazine stand and a huge salty snack display.

Lee's bullet went through a two-liter bottle of soda, which took off like a rocket and hit the clerk in the face. As the man toppled backwards, his finger twitched setting off another shotgun blast, which turned a display of donuts into white dust and exploded the glass door of a refrigerator case. Dozens of soft drinks squirted carbonated fountains of colored, fizzy sugar water.

Lee pushed himself off the floor. Holy crap, the store looked like one of those things on the news when a terrorist bomb went off in central London or something. There was a rainbow of colored liquids and glass and shredded snacks everywhere. Not to mention plaster dust roiling around the air.

His nose was bleeding from when he hit the ground, but there wasn't any blood on the front of his body. He could stand. But walking hurt. Was he hit? He patted down his legs. No blood, but some gooey blue raspberry Mr. Slushee syrup on his crotch.

His hips really hurt. No, it was his butt. The right cheek was sticky with blood. The back of his pants was pocked with tiny holes.

The counterman moaned and stirred around behind the

counter. Well Lee may be a dumbass with a bloody ass, but he wasn't about to get his ass shot up anymore.

Where was that gun? His dad would be pissed. Never mind. He wasn't getting shot looking for his old man's piece.

Time to cut and run.

Lee Brian had parked his car pretty far away from the C-store. With buckshot in his ass, it hurt every time he took a step. There were two mighty fine chicks waiting for him, so he could work through the pain. What would they say when they saw his bloody butt? He would stop someplace with a restroom and clean it up a bit first. He thought maybe he had a pair of sweatpants in his car.

He increased his pace. He could definitely use some weed tonight.

Two blocks from his own car, he saw the blue and red disco lights of a cop car. Well, he must've done some dumbass thing or another, 'cuz the cops were already onto him.

He was in trouble. He just didn't know how much.

Cut 13

A Question of Temperature

Louie made it home just as the sun was bruising the sky a painful shade of purple and magenta with a slight tinge of pink in the east. He thought that when the sun gathered its strength, it would batter everyone again in all its white hot fury.

He was not a hot-weather guy.

He was, however, a hot bath guy. He ran a scalding bath and spiked it with Epsom salts. He went to one of his jukeboxes and pressed the buttons to play about twenty singles. He went to the tub and gingerly submerged inch by inch and soaked until the water got cool.

Louie got out of the tub, sat on the bed dripping wet and started toweling off. A black flash of time and he awoke at four in the afternoon with the telephone ringing.

He sat up and caught his reflection in the dresser mirror. Terminal bed-head. Crap.

It was Sloopy.

"Louie, another package arrived."

"Today?"

"Within the last hour. Could you come over?"

"Was there a postmark?"

"No, someone left it on my front porch. Could you come over now?"

"How do you know—"

"Louie, please. I'm frightened."

"Yeah, yeah. Sorry. I'll be right there."

He hung up the phone. Should he put on a hat like some middle-aged baldy trying to hide his chrome dome? He decided against it and threw on his best jeans, that is, the only pair that were clean at the moment, a favorite black Paul Revere and the Raiders T-shirt and a pair of running shoes. He splashed water on his head and finger combed it into some semblance of something.

He went to the garage. No car. Where was it? Then he remembered, it was still at the Tic-Tock Bar, about a ten-minute walk away.

At the bar, he cursed. Someone had flattened all four tires. He wondered if it had anything to do with his kidnapping last night.

Now what?

Maybe he could go inside and get one of the regulars to give a ride. No, he decided, that wouldn't be a good idea. He didn't want any rumors starting about Sloopy. Not yet. As the song went, let's give them something to talk about, first.

No other choice but to hoof it. As predicted, it was one hot mother of a day.

The first thing Sloopy said when she opened the door was, "What took you so long?" The second thing she said between laughter so hard it gave her the hiccups was, "What the hell happened to your hair?"

"Long story."

"Well, come in. Would you like something to drink? Water? Something stronger?"

"I could sure use some coffee. Black. As strong as you can make it."

"Are you sure? You look all sweaty," she said and broke out in laughter again.

"Please."

They went to the kitchen and she pulled out a bag of Starbucks French Roast beans from the freezer. She ground two big batches and dumped them into a French coffee press.

As she put on the water to boil, Louie asked to see the package.

"Why don't we have some coffee first? I'm not sure I'm up to looking at it right now."

The coffee press made a mug full apiece and they sat on the couch in her family room and drank it.

"So what's the long story about why your hair's such a mess?"

"Oh, I had a late night and fell asleep with it wet." He didn't want to scare her with the van story just yet.

"My Lord, Louie, you're usually so put together."

"Well you asked me to come right over."

"It took you long enough."

"Oh yeah."

"What happened? You could've showered twice in the time it took you to get here."

"I walked."

"Why?"

"Car trouble."

"I see." She knew he was holding out on her.

"This is good coffee."

"Uh-huh." She was pissed.

"Nice and strong. Like I like it."

"Yea."

"Very good coffee."

"Thanks."

"You're allowed to utter two or more syllables, you know."

"You're keeping something from me, Louie, and I don't know why."

"Look, it's really a whole lotta nothing. I don't want to bother you with it."

"Okay."

"Okay."

There was a pause so pregnant, Louie wondered if the water had broken.

"Okay, I'm here."

"Thanks for coming."

"Why don't you show me that package?"

"Okay. It's on the dining room table.

She set her mug down, left the room and came back. "Louie, I'm so scared. I think this is human."

"Let me see. I'm sure it isn't."

But it was. It was very human.

Wrapped inside wax paper, inside a baggie, inside a box that was probably used for jewelry, was a human toe.

Louie looked up at Susan and squinted. "Sloopy, what happened?"

"I just found this package on my porch when I got home from work."

"That's not what I'm talking about,"

"What are you talking about?"

"Your arm."

"Oh, that's nothing."

"You're bruised."

"I must've bumped into something."

"What did you bump into?"

"Why all the questions?"

"Those look like finger marks."

"Maybe they are."

"Well?"

"I don't know. Maybe somebody squeezed my arm too hard. I don't remember. It's not important."

"Which?"

"Huh?"

"Which is it? You don't remember or it's not important."

"It's not important."

"Well someone would've had to squeeze pretty hard to leave marks like that."

"Why don't we just drop it."

"I don't want to drop it."

"Well, I do."

"Sloopy, if someone's hurting you, I want to know. I've got to know."

"What gives you the right to pry into my life?"

"You invited me in."

"Into what?"

"Your life. You invited me into your life."

"I did not. I invited you to help me with a problem."

"Well maybe they're related."

"What?"

"Whoever's hurting you and whoever's sending you packages with animal and people's parts in them."

"They aren't."

"Are you sure?"

"Positive."

"Well why don't you tell me?"

"Because it's a one-time deal. Nothing to worry about. A mistake."

"So, tell me."

"No."

"Why not?"

"Listen, you've got your secrets, I've got mine."

Louie opened his mouth to say something and then shut it.

Cut 14
Louie Louie, the Banned Version

Louie slept on Sloopy's couch. No, he didn't, not really. He sat on Sloopy's couch. He stretched out on Sloopy's couch. He stared at the ceiling. She wanted him to stay the night because she was "afraid." He didn't think it was only the packages.

He had heard from his State Police buddy. There was no evidence that a van had wrecked out south of town where he knew it had. The area had been sanitized pretty well. No dead bodies had turned up anywhere. Bill, the statie, had checked around with the local hospitals, morgues, the police, sheriff, and local towing services. Nothing to indicate there had ever been a wreck out on the county line road.

Then he checked in with Sheldon King and found out the package to Sloopy before the toe, was a dog testicle.

He was all knotted up. He rolled over on his stomach. He was worried about the missing van and the missing kidnappers, someone had to have some serious juice to make it, and them, disappear so fast and so completely.

He tried to make a connection between the animal parts Sloopy was getting and the kidnapping. He couldn't. Carson Catlin had come up with some information Louie might find interesting. He said he'd drop by Carson's house tomorrow. So Louie willed himself to put all this in the back of his mind to let it ferment and foment in the subconscious until an idea bubbled up.

So, that left Sloopy. Was something happening? She walked back into Louie's life when he was neither expecting it nor wanting it. Since then, things had been moving at such a pace, he hadn't had time to think about the possibility of another hook-up.

Sloopy and Louie Louie seemed to be such a natural fit.

When Louie was in fifth grade, he had moved to Tivoli, met Sloopy and developed an immediate crush on her. Louie's dad, like his grandfather, was a good cop and former FBI agent. His dad came to Tivoli and became chief of police, a post everyone assumed Louie would inherit someday. He almost did, except for Elliott Blake and Elliott's shenanigans. That was why Louie quit the force and went private.

Sloopy and Louie Louie. Two of the great garage rock songs of the sixties. The same chords. The songs every rock band learned first.

Sloopy was the nickname Louie gave her.

Louie Louie wasn't a nickname; it was his real name. Actually, Louie Louis Lewis. He was named Louie after the song. And not just any of the more than nine hundred versions of the song, but the most famous one.

Not the beautiful original recording by Richard Berry. Nor, what Louie considered the way cool version done by Paul Revere and the Raiders. Or, the even cooler version done by the Pretty Things. Or, the gritty soulful rendition by Wilbert Harrison. Or even his absolute favorite version done by Ike and Tina Turner. Not any of the versions done by everyone from Joan Jett to the Washington Square Marching Band.

But Louie was named after the oh-so-sloppy version by the Kingsmen. The version done in one take with one microphone suspended from the ceiling in a studio primarily used for recording radio commercials. The one in which Jack Ely, the lead singer, comes in at the wrong time, stops and the drummer has to flail away to fill the space. The garage-rock staple. The frat party anthem. Yeah, that Louie Louie.

In 1964, Louie's grandfather was in charge of investigating Louie Louie.

All because of one of those teenage pop culture blips.

According to his dad, it was a craze one summer. Every spirited teen from junior high on up had to have a copy to the "real" lyrics to Louie Louie. It was in three-ring binders, spiral notebooks, bookbags, taped to the inside of lockers, scribbled on restroom walls, hidden in diaries, folded up and nestled beside the never-used rubbers in high school boys' wallets.

They weren't what was on the record, just what hormonal teenagers thought they heard. Every once in a while a too-nosy parent got hold of these lyrics and listened to the record, Wand #143-A, and wrote a letter to someone in the government. What was going on? Something had to be done. Louie Louie was corrosive and corrupting. Why, the song was *filthy.*

Actually the song wasn't. It was badly-recorded. No one could really make out the words. There'd been a variety of reasons given for this. Jack Ely, the lead singer, was wearing braces at the time, so his enunciation left much to be desired. The lone boom microphone was placed too high, so Jack had to stand on his tippy toes and scream out the lyrics, hence the distortion. The Kingsmen had done a Louie Louie marathon at a local club the day before and Jack's voice was shot. The primitive recording techniques turned the words into mush. Or, all of these things together conspired to make the vocals an aural mess.

Whatever.

There were rumors that if you played the 45 rpm single at 33 1/3, you could make out what Jack was singing and what Jack was singing was naughty. Why, it would make Rusty Warren blush. This song might cause horny teenagers to think about, uh, sex. It was some kind of conspiracy.

And J. Edgar Hoover chose Louie's grandfather to investigate, using the ITOM, the interstate transportation of obscene materials, as the reason.

Louie's grandfather was a lieutenant navigator in the Army Air Corps. His grandfather went to Harvard Law and then through all the rigors of Quantico because his grandfather had always wanted to be a great cop. And the FBI was the toppermost of copperdom. It was the most elite police force in the world. Louie's grandfather had dreams of being Elliot Ness, wanted to do something legendary, wanted to crush commies and catch bad guys.

Instead, the aspiring FBI man spent two years of his mid-career buying singles of Louie Louie and sending them to the FBI lab, sitting hour after hour with headphones on listening to that opening dadada-dada organ riff and playing with volume controls and speeds. Louie's grandfather cranked up the treble. He cranked up the bass. He slowed it up and sped it up. He couldn't understand any of the words.

The FBI agent interviewed the Kingsmen individually, grilling the lead singer especially hard. He did two lengthy interviews, only to find out that, Lynn Easton, the current lead singer wasn't the singer on the record. The singer on the record, Jack Ely, had quit the band right after the song was recorded. But you could tell Louie's grandfather was losing interest because he didn't even track Jack Ely down.

Everyone who knew anything about it told the FBI the same thing: Louie Louie was a sea shanty. Nothing dirty about it. The lyrics weren't even written by any of the Kingsmen, but by a guy named Richard Berry.

So, Gramps and another agent flew to Los Angeles and talked to Richard Berry. They went to Portland, Oregon and interviewed the head of Wand Records. They interviewed the secretary. The record producer. Some of the kids who had seen the Kingsmen live doing the Louie Louie marathon.

Louie's grandfather and his team filled out forms in triplicate. They sent in lab reports. They even got copies of the "real" lyrics, actually many copies of the "real" lyrics, all of them different and all of them, to one degree or another, sexual. None of the "real" lyrics, however, had anything to do with the actual lyrics sung on record.

Finally, Louie's grandfather sent in the report, page after page of testimony, analysis, lab findings, etc. The conclusion? Nothing dirty about Louie Louie, except the muddy sound.

Nope, not good enough, said the FBI brass. Attorney General Robert Kennedy was just sure that Louie Louie was a potty paean to pubescent lust. Matthew Welsh, then governor of Indiana, banned the song, for cryin' out loud. Investigate some more.

So, Louie's grandfather sent the single to another FBI lab. The lab boys still couldn't make out the lyrics. The FBI agent and another agent followed the Kingsmen on tour. They went to every concert, frat party and dance for a year and dutifully transcribed what Lynn Easton, the new lead singer, sang when he sang Louie Louie. He interviewed Mark Lindsay of Paul Revere and the Raiders, another Portland group that was friends with the Kingsmen and who, incidentally, recorded another version of Louie Louie two days after the Kingsmen, in the same exact studio, using the same lyric sheet the Kingsmen had left behind.

You could understand the lyrics in their version. Kinda goofy but kinda sweet. A tad poetic. A sea shanty, to be sure, sung in pidgin English.

That was the period at the end of the sentence. Louie's grandfather was sure he was chasing his tail. Okay, the lyrics weren't dirty. And, even if they were, what did it matter? You couldn't hear the damn things.

So, what do you do if you're a dedicated G-Man? You follow procedure. You send in another report with all the same stuff as the first report. Throw in the new lab reports. Come to the conclusion that your investigation is inconclusive, because like everybody who's ever listened to the song, you can't understand the lyrics no matter what speed you play them and no matter what filters you use.

The song was like clouds. You could see what you wanted to see. Ice cream castles or scary wolves or women's breasts.

When this report—conclusion? no conclusion—was accepted, Louie's grandfather quit the FBI and opened a private consulting firm. The man had a young family to support. Enough of this Louie Louie nonsense. To agent Samuel Lewis, his career at the FBI was now a joke. Little did Lewis know how long the joke would last.

Louie's Dad, in an act of rebelliousness or humor, or who knows what, named his firstborn son three Louies. Louie was the first name, Louis, the middle name and Lewis was the family name. Louie's dad put the Louis in the middle, just to make sure everyone got the joke.

So it was Louie Louie and Sloopy. She was the tomboy who lived in the same neighborhood. They were buddies, then sweethearts, then lovers and then nothing. They drifted apart when Louie went to college. He wanted to be able to concentrate on his studies. He didn't want to date any other girls, but didn't want to feel he had to come home every weekend for Sloopy.

So it seemed to both of them, maybe a two or three year cooling off period wouldn't hurt.

Louie always thought they'd end up back together.

He was wrong.

Someone once told Louie that most suicides happen between three and four a.m. He wasn't sure if that was true. He also heard they mostly happened during the day. But three a.m. does have a certain depressing quality to it. The feeling of loneliness is most acute. Even if you're not a lonely person, three a.m. is a lonely, lonely time.

Louie laid awake on Sloopy's sofa. The blinds were drawn but enough light leaked in from the yard lamp that was on all night. Mad shadows that his imagination slowly moved around, danced on the ceiling. He heard traffic sounds way in the distance. He heard Sloopy's house fidgeting through the night. A slight creak here, a muffled pop there. The sound of moving air.

"Louie?"

A soft sound like sheets rustling. Louie wasn't sure if she called his name or if it was his too-tired mind playing tricks, as it had with the night shadows.

"Louie?"

That time he heard it. He heard his name called.

"Yeah."

No reply. Perhaps it was the wind. Perhaps, tricks of the mind.

"Louie, do you want to come upstairs?"

Upstairs is where the bedrooms were. Upstairs is where Sloopy was.

"Yes, I think I do."

Louie threw off the afghan. He had on boxer shorts. Was he taking too much for granted? Should he put on pants?

He walked across the room and up the stairs.

At the landing, he didn't know which way to turn. A soft pink light came from beneath the second door on the right. He padded barefoot to the door, hesitated, then slowly and quietly knocked.

"Come in."

She was under the bedcovers. The room had that womanly smell, a slight whiff of a fragrance he always associated with Sloopy.

"Would you sleep beside me tonight?"

He would and did.

He was back where he belonged, beside Sloopy.

Cut 15
Man with Money

Tim Ferman hadn't really talked to his former wife, Susan Louise, since their divorce nine years ago. They spoke the first year or two after the split, but only to wrap up matters in their marriage.

Everything had been oh-so-civilized. They had been very businesslike with the divorce. They were professional, courteous, very adult.

There was a certain detachment to the whole thing. He never yelled. She never yelled. Or cursed. Or cried. As far as he knew, she had never badmouthed him. Of course, this lack of passion had been symptomatic about what was wrong with their whole marriage. It just wasn't there. No ups. No downs. Just a cool, comfortable relationship.

Sure, he gave her a good chunk of money when they split. But that was okay, he had inherited a much better chunk, so he could afford it. It didn't sting a bit when he signed over the check.

She was a bright, attractive woman. She was kind. She had been the perfect wife. He just didn't love her. So, she deserved every penny she got. He still had her in his will, so she would get more when he died. He was fine with that.

Tim Ferman owned a successful marketing/advertising agency in Indianapolis, Indiana. He had been the boy wonder of the advertising world. He helped create an advertising campaign that had propelled a local hamburger joint into a nationwide chain. It not only helped the business of his client and, by extension, his business, but it had won all sorts of industry creative awards. Clios, Tellys, Silver Microphones, Webbys, and even a Cannes Lion.

He was featured in ADWEEK and Advertising Age. They called him the "Boy Wonder."

Then his agency helped elect the Governor of the state. More awards followed. Tim was asked to speak at Advertising Clubs around the nation. He had even been on Donny Deutsch's television program. He was on the juries of all the big ad competitions now.

They called it the Hoosier School of advertising. Some of the trades even compared him to the late, great Leo Burnett. Like Burnett, he was credited with bringing back bedrock values and tonality to the world of advertising.

He was asked to all the best parties. He was friends with all the movers and shakers in the state. He was seen with some of the state's prettiest women. Models and actresses. Daughters of shopping mall magnates.

He was living the dream.

Unfortunately, he was also living the nightmare. His own personal nightmare. There was a curse on his bloodline. An insanity he could trace back to his grandfather, who had started a successful coal-mining operation in Evansville, Indiana. It was the source of the family fortune. His grandfather had gotten pneumonia after a night of hard drinking which ended with his falling into a snowdrift outside the family mansion at a little past midnight. He was found the next morning, almost dead from cold. He died two days later. That was his grandfather's way of dealing with the curse.

Tim's dad had chosen a rope.

Now, Tim's life was spinning out of control. He knew it, but didn't know what to do.

He should call Susan, come clean. The animal parts, the packages, it was all going wrong. It had to stop. He picked up the phone on his desk. He started to dial and then stopped. He put the phone back in its cradle. He picked it up again placed it against his cheek. Tears were streaming down his face. He wiped his face with the sleeve of his silk robe.

He couldn't call. He would rather die. He threw the phone across his study and it stuck in the wall in a puff of plaster dust. It hung on the wall for a second, then fell to the floor.

Tim Ferman opened the lower left hand drawer to his desk and pulled out a bottle of Macallan 25 year old scotch and a cut glass tumbler. He filled the tumbler to within a finger's width of the top. He drank it all in one swallow. The honey-toned liquid went down with a fiery smoothness that caused him to shudder. He poured another and downed it.

He opened the middle drawer to his desk and brought out an oxblood leather box. He opened the box and looked at the Colt .45 nestled in black velvet.

He took the gun out of the box and placed it on his desk. He stroked the barrel a few times and debated having another scotch.

He picked up the pistol and put the barrel under his chin. He held it that way for almost a minute. He slowly lowered the barrel and sat the gun back on the blotter of his desk.

He picked up the gun again and put the barrel in his mouth. He could taste the gun oil as he wrapped his lips around the sight.

Tim had found his snowdrift. He had found his rope.

Cut 16
Leave Me Alone

Lee Brian wanted to run away.

"We're getting to be regular pals, aren't we?" Elliott slapped Lee on the back.

"Yeah. I guess so. No. I don't know. What do you mean?"

"I mean we might as well become poker playing-buddies as much time as we're spending together."

"I don't play poker."

"Naw, I guess you wouldn't. That takes a little common sense. You're too busy turning your brain to mush smoking weed and huffing whatever you kids huff these days."

"Hey, there's nothing wrong with weed."

"Relax, I've been known to have a hit or two myself. Don't worry, I'm not judging."

"Sorry about everything."

"Well, what you have done could result in a shit storm, but I think with a little work and a little planning we can turn this all around to our advantage." Elliott slapped Lee on the back again, this time a little harder.

They were in one of the patrol cars. All the colored lights of the radios and GPSs and the other gear turned Elliott's face a ghastly shade of green. He looked like one of those dead people in a cheap zombie movie. Lee shuddered.

"Say, let's get some coffee and then start cleaning up the mess you've made of everything. Whadya say?"

They turned into a donut place.

"You stay in the car."

"No prob. Uh, could you get me some donuts?"

"Got the munchies, huh?"

"Well yeah. I mean no. Not those kinda munchies."

"Relax, kid, I got your back."

When Elliott returned with the donuts and coffee, he asked Lee, "Say, who's that chick that walks around town in the cutoffs?"

"I don't know."

"Sure you do. The one you were talking to at the ZipMart before everything went to shit."

"I was talking to two of my friends there."

"I'm talking about the one with the rack."

Lee thought for a moment. "Rack of what?"

"The rack. You know. The nice hooters. Melons. Tits."

Lee broke into a smile. "Oh yeah, Denise."

"Denise who?"

"Denise Mitchell."

"Jim Mitchell's little girl."

"I guess."

"Wow she's all grown up."

"Yeah."

"Have you ever..."

"No, but I prob'ly coulda, if that dude at the store hadn'ta shot me in the ass."

"Whadya mean?" Elliott wore a big grin on his green face.

"All the buckshot went in my ass. Didn't you know?"

"No. I mean, are you saying you could've gotten some trim off of Denise?"

"Trim?"

"Snatch. Pussy. The good stuff."

"Oh well, they invited me over to their house to do some Red Bull and vodka right before everything happened."

"No shit?" Elliott burst out in laughter. He had to set his coffee on the dash to keep from spilling it.

"No shit." Lee couldn't help but laugh because Elliott was laughing so hard.

It appeared to Lee that Elliott was going to reach across and tousle his hair like his dad always did. Or maybe slap him on the back again.

"Do you realize what you just did there?" Elliott asked as he smashed Lee's head against the dashboard.

"Hey, what the… That hurt."

"It was supposed to hurt. You. Stupid. Shit." Elliott banged Lee's head against the dash to punctuate the last three words.

"Stop it." Lee sprayed half-eaten chunks of donut all over the front of the dash, getting some on Elliott's shirt front. Tears and snot ran down the youngster's face.

"Stop it," Elliott mimicked in a baby's whine.

"Please." Lee started to wipe the donut debris off of the dash. That made his hands sticky so he wiped them on the front of his shirt.

"Stop it or you'll do what? Huh? You'll do what? You little spoiled, pansy dumbass."

Elliott started the car and pulled out of the parking lot. "Here, take a napkin. The first thing you're gonna do when we get to where we're going is clean up the inside of the car. The next thing you're gonna do is dig a hole."

They were silent for a while.

Finally, Elliott turned toward Lee. His eyes were black smudges.

"Do you know why I banged that noggin' of yours off my dash?"

"No."

"Because I told you to never talk about the robbery. To no one. See how I tricked you? Well, what if an FBI guy or somebody got hold of you? Could they trick you so easy?"

"I don't know. I suppose. No, I mean no."

"You better learn to keep your mouth shut. Just don't talk about what happened to no one. Got it?"

"Got it. But it was you."

"I don't care if it's Angelina Jolie and she's promising you a night you'll never forget. Don't tell no one nothing."

"Okay."

"That's good. Say, you wanna listen to the radio?"

Lee didn't answer.

"Yoo hoo. I'm talkin' to you. Do you wanna listen to the radio?"

"Who's the hole for? It's a grave isn't it? You want me to dig a grave."

"Whatsamatter? Are you scared, pansy-boy?"

"Well, duh. You've got the gun."

"Naw, what did I tell you? We're gonna make this all right for you and for me."

"Okay."

"Speaking of guns, I got the one you dropped in the ZipMart."

"Wow that's great, Mr. Blake."

"I told you I got your back."

"Well, as long as my old man don't find out."

"Don't worry."

They turned off a country road down another that had a dead end sign posted. From that they turned onto a lane that went back about three miles.

"Where are we?"

"This is an old stripper pit. Not sure who owns it now, but I've never see anyone back here."

"What are we doing here?"

"Like I said, digging a hole and like you guessed, in what was probably one of the smarter moments of your life, it's a grave."

"But who? Why? I mean, I didn't kill anybody."

"No, this is another piece of business related to our business. Let's get out. Get the shovel in the back and start digging."

Elliott shoved the scared teenager.

As the kid dug, Elliott said, "You know, I thought we were up shit's creek when Sizelove brought you in last night."

"Didn't you just tell me not to talk about this?"

"Don't volunteer any information. But you can listen."

"Okay."

"As I was saying, what was supposed to be a nice clean robbery turned into a mess. I had to get the surveillance tapes again. Convince the night manager to not remember a few details and put a little bit of the squeeze on Sizelove to forget the whole thing. Man it was one screwed up situation."

"I appreciate the help."

"I know you do. We just got to do a little fancy footwork, throw the scent off here and there. Keep the state boys outta this and things are gonna be just fine."

"Thanks again."

"Well, your dad's been really good to me and will continue to be, I'm sure. You know, what are friends for?"

Lee continued to dig. The earth was soft, but he so was he. It wasn't fast going. Elliott nursed his coffee and didn't comment for a while.

After about an hour of digging, the hole was about three feet deep, more egg-shaped than rectangular. This kid was worthless, Elliott thought. "Here, hand me the shovel, take a break."

Elliott, who was in much better shape, dug down another two feet and shaped the hole up a bit. He was sweating through his uniform by the time he finished. Good thing he had another couple shirts fresh from the dry cleaners hanging from the hook in the back seat.

"So, what are you gonna put in there?"

Elliott threw Lee the keys. "It's in the trunk."

Lee walked over and opened the trunk and promptly threw up. "Ohmigod, oh shit, ohmigod."

"Never seen a body before, have you, kid?"

"No. And the smell." Even though the body was wrapped in plastic, some of the odor leaked out.

"You never get used to it," Elliott said. "Why don't you let me drag the body over to the hole and you fill in the dirt."

"Works for me."

Elliott tugged the body out of the trunk and threw it into the hole face first.

"Who is—who was that?"

"A dead person."

"No, really."

"A guy that got into a car wreck."

"So why are you burying him out here?"

"He fucked up."

"How?"

"By getting into a wreck. He was kidnapping someone at the time."

"I don't understand."

"He was a beaner. Don't worry about it."

"Okay."

"I'm gonna Lysol the hell out of that trunk when we get back. Nothing worse than refried beans." Elliott laughed.

Lee didn't get the joke, if there was one. So he began filling in the hole. As Lee worked, Elliott walked back to the car. Lee wondered what he was doing.

Elliott came back and finished buttoning up a fresh shirt. He threw his soiled shirt into the hole.

"Make sure you give me Dad's gun," Lee said.

"Okay," Elliott shot the teenager in the back of the head. Lee dropped in face first on top of the other body.

"I told you I got your back."

Cut 17

You Dove Deep in my Soul

Louie awoke before Sloopy and went downstairs to make coffee and toast. He filled the old-fashioned cast-iron teakettle with cold water, set it on the stove and ground some Starbucks French Roast beans. Rather than watch the pot, he called up Carson. The hour didn't matter. Time in the traditional sense was irrelevant to Carson. The computer whiz might stay up for thirty-six hours straight on a Ding Dong and caffeine high and then crash for twenty hours. Or, maybe be awake four hours and sleep one hour, keeping the pattern for weeks at a time.

If Carson were awake and wanted to answer the phone, he would. If he wasn't and didn't, he wouldn't. As simple as that.

Carson was and did. "Jetson, here."

"Hey Carson."

"Uh Louie Lou-eye," Carson sang.

"What's goin' on, big guy?"

"Got some four one one, dude."

"Same place?"

"Minus-two."

Carson sometimes didn't trust phones, especially cell phones. Sometimes, it didn't seem to matter. So, if Carson didn't begin the conversation with some obscure pop reference, he and Louie spoke in a semi code. Four one one meant he had some information, not hard to figure out. They usually met at a truck stop outside of town, same place. Their second meeting location was a coffee shop in town—minus-one. And the third place was a bakery in another town—minus-two. They had never used the minus-two place before, so Carson must've come up with something he thought was dangerous.

"How about noon?"

"Ten o'clock."

They always subtracted an hour from the last hour said. So, Louie was to meet Carson at nine. It was a code, not terribly sophisticated.

"Ten o'clock," Louie repeated and clicked off.

The bakery in town was about 45 minutes from where Sheldon King lived and worked, So, Louie would have time to drop off what looked like a human toe to find out if it was, in fact, human and a toe. Louie still didn't trust the cops in town.

The kettle started squealing just as Louie's cell phone started chirping. He flipped open the phone and said "wait a minute" and then walked over to the stove to take the kettle off the burner.

Louie put the phone up to his ear. "Hello."

"Stay away or your dead," a voice at the other end of the line said.

"Stay away from what? From who?" But the connection had been broken. Louie looked at the menu on the cell phone. The last call was unlisted. He tried the call back button twice, but got one of those recordings that say the number is not in service.

"Who are you calling?" Sloopy stood in the doorway to the kitchen. Louie thought she was more beautiful than he had ever seen her. But, to him, her beauty intensified by the minute.

"No one. No answer. I've made you some coffee."

She went over to the counter and poured two mugs. "That was really nice, last night, I mean."

"I agree."

"I feel really comfortable with you."

"You don't regret it, then?"

"I would've regretted if I hadn't asked you to hold me."

Louie took a drink of coffee. Damn it was hot. Somehow doing a spit take seemed like it might spoil the moment. So he swallowed as fast as he could and let the coffee scald his throat and esophagus.

"Why are you giving me that funny look?"

"I, uh, was just thinking. Sorry. It's nothing."

"For a second there, you looked like you had heartburn or something."

"No. No, I'm all right."

"Will you stay tonight?"

"Sure."

"I'll get a couple of steaks. Fix some creamed peas and onions."

"That'd be great."

Louie nonchalantly walked over to the sink and poured a glass of tap water. He took a mouthful and let it trickle down his throat. Sweet Jesus, did that feel good.

"There's bottled water in the fridge."

"No, I'm fine. But I could use an ice cube." He went to get one.

"So, what's on the agenda today?"

"Well, first, let's see if there're any surprises on your porch or in your mailbox. And then, could you give me a ride to Sayer's to pick up my car? He should have the new tires on by now."

"Sure."

The new tires were on the car. Unfortunately, now Louie's wallet was flat.

He drove through town and dropped off the toe with Sheldon. There had been no new packages this morning, so that was all he had to give the pathologist. Sheldon looked at Louie in a strange way and asked if he were doing anything illegal. The doctor didn't say much as Louie left the house.

Next Louie went to see Carson. Carson held onto a laptop and was bouncing in his seat when Louie got to the bakery. Carson was a big lug of a guy, six-five, probably close to 300 pounds. He had a shaved head and a goatee. He looked like the movie cliché of a biker, or a heavyweight wrestler. He looked like he could kill. He looked like he wanted to kill. But Louie knew Carson was one of the gentlest people anyone had ever met.

The computer nerd liked to talk about two things: what a genius he was and every little ailment he had.

Carson always wore a T-shirt with some saying or some drawing on it. Most of the time Louie didn't understand the context. Most of the time very few people understood Carson's shirts. Once in awhile Louie did, like the one Carson had on today that said "Easy as 3.1415926535897932..."

"So you've got something for me?" Louie sat in the booth across from the gentle giant.

"Dude, once you see what I got and how I was able to get it, you're going to bow down and worship at the alter of the genius Carson."

So Carson went through his spiel and tapped away at his computer. "Looky here," he said.

Louie lookied there and saw on the screen a newspaper article about a woman who was murdered in Cincinnati, Ohio. "That's too bad Carson, but what does that have to do with..."

"Patience young Skywalker, and learn from the master."

"Baiter?"

"Shut up. Now looky here."

"Hmm. That is interesting."

Carson had opened some police files. Apparently Mimi Johnston, the murdered woman had lived in Kettering, Ohio before moving to Cincinnati and reported receiving packages containing bits and pieces of dead animals. She filed several reports, but the police in Kettering, like the police in Tivoli, couldn't find out who was doing it and concluded it was probably a prank.

The FBI was called in because some of the packages were sent by mail, but they didn't give it top priority. They also thought it was some sort of prank and in these days of terrorism alerts, didn't spend much time on it. They did seem to take an unusual interest in Mimi's vigorous sex life and concluded it was probably a jilted lover harassing her.

"Did she report anything when she moved to Cincinnati?"

"No, she didn't. So the Cincy cops don't know about it. Besides, they have other suspects they're looking into."

"How do you know this?"

"I am the almighty Carson. Knower of everything." Carson tapped some more keys. "What I'm doing here is busting through some..."

"That's okay, Carson. You don't have to tell me what files you hacked into and how you did it, just give me the Reader's Digest version."

"Okay, okay. Basically, not many people liked her. Apparently she stepped on a lot of toes while on her back."

"What do you mean?"

"She slept her way to glory. She was a starfucker. Every place she worked, she tended to sleep with the big boys. It made her co-workers mad. It made the spouses mad. It made the men she ditched as she moved up the ladder mad. There are many men with motives. There are several with means and opportunity. A few of them don't have alibis."

"I see. So what's the connection to Sloopy? Did Sloopy even know her?"

"I'll get to that, but first you should know something else."

"What's that?"

"Her killer took the hard drive from her computer."

"So?"

"So there was probably something on it he didn't want the cops to know."

"Okay."

"But the great and powerful Oz was able to get some information even the cops don't have."

"What?"

"I was able to get her email."

"But how?"

Carson explained to Louie about tapping directly into the server but Louie understood about a third of it, if that. "So what did you find out?" he asked.

"Well, for one thing, when she moved to Cincinnati, she was still getting packages."

"How do you know that?"

"She kept in touch with a girlfriend from her college years. She mentioned the packages to this girlfriend in several emails."

"Why didn't she tell the police?"

"Mimi realized the cops weren't doing anything about it. And she herself began to think it was just some harmless prank from an old lover or something."

"Did the cops find any evidence of this when they studied the murder site? Wasn't it her apartment?"

"Yes and no."

"Carson, yes and no to what? It wasn't her apartment where she got killed?"

"No. I mean, yes, she was killed in her apartment, but the police didn't find any evidence of the packages with animal parts. Not that they were looking because, of course, they knew nothing about it."

"Carson, think back on all the emails and the police reports. Was there a pattern?"

"Pattern?"

"Yea. A pattern of any sort. Like when she received them. Where they came from. Anything like that?"

"Give me a day or two and I'll see if I can figure something out."

"Okay. Also, see if you can find out if there was a pattern to what she received."

"What do you mean?

"Like did it go from pig parts to cow parts? Toes to head. That sort of thing. What was the last thing she received before she was murdered?"

"I'll check into it. Unfortunately, it will take a while. I've still got some digging to do. Some hacking."

"Why? I thought you got into her emails. What more can you find out?"

"Well, I haven't been able to tap into her work email yet. See, she and her friend exchanged emails at least once a week. Sometimes more. Well, that stopped about a month ago. My guess is that she started using her work email account for that."

"I see. Do you think you can get into that? Her work email account? Do you think you can get those emails?"

Carson looked at Louie like the man had brain damage. "Of course, Jimmy. Superman can get anything if it's ever been on a computer."

"Well, let me know."

"I will. Should take about a day or so."

"Where did she work?"

"I've been waiting for you to ask me that. This is where the power of Carson really shines."

"What do you mean?"

"Well, digging around a bit, I found the connection between Mimi and your Susan."

"What is the connection between Mimi and Susan?" Louie asked Carson.

"Mimi worked at a marketing firm in Cincinnati called Flicker Advertising. Flicker Advertising broke off from a bigger firm called Sabat/Brown Branded Entertainment. This firm specializes primarily in getting product placement in movies and television shows."

"Okay, but I don't see the connection."

"Sabat/Brown Branded Entertainment is the…well, the branded entertainment division of one of the Midwest's largest advertising agencies."

"Which is?"

"Wild Imagination Advertising in Indianapolis," Carson said with a note of triumph.

"I still don't see…"

"You've never heard of Wild Imagination Advertising?"

"Sorry."

"It's owned by Tim Ferman."

"Well, well, well. Now that's interesting."

"Well, well, well, indeed. Am I just the greatest, or what?"

"You are the Muhammad Ali of cyberspace."

"Nobody calls it that anymore."

Louie sat back in his seat to think. "Carson, I can't thank you enough."

"It's nothing."

"So how's that rash been treating you?"

"It's gone thanks to Gold Bond. That stuff works miracles. Thanks for turning me on to it. However, I am feeling a funny tingle in a couple of my toes."

"Probably your shoes are too tight."

"You think so?"

"Hey, listen, be sure to call me the minute you find out anything more about Mimi's packages, okay? I gotta run now."

"Sure. Okay. Where are you going?"

"I've got a couple of things to do but eventually I'm going to Indianapolis—to pay Mr. Ferman a visit. I think he holds the key to this whole thing."

"So, when are you going to Indianapolis?"

"As I say, I've got a couple things I want to check out. So, probably in a day or two. But, I'm going for sure. Besides, I kind of want to see what Timmy looks like these days. I'm not gay or anything, but from the photos I've seen, he's one good-looking dude."

Louie was standing beside the table and sat back down. "You wouldn't be able to pull a picture up of him on that thing could you?"

"No prob."

Carson tapped a few keys and turned the computer screen.

"Damn," Louie said.

"What's wrong?"

"He *is* good looking."

Cut 18

I Like It Like That

Joe Sizelove was pissed off. Not just pissed off, royally pissed off. Hot, fuming and ready to kick some ass pissed off. And, as he sat in one of two uncomfortable wooden chairs in front of the Elliott Blake's desk, there was more bile adding to the ureic poisoning of his anger. Elliott looked out the window, the back of his cushy leather desk chair mocking all those who were not chief of police. Joe wanted to push the chair, with Elliott on it, out the window.

Elliott slowly turned back toward the desk and placed his hands on mahogany desktop as he nodded for Sizelove to speak.

"So where is the punk?" Sizelove got right to the point.

"I let him go."

"What do you mean you let him go?"

"I mean, I undid the cuffs, opened the front door and said 'See ya later.'"

"For cryin' out loud, Elliott, that kid tried to rob a convenience store, shot it all to hell and threatened a man with a gun."

"Says who?"

"Says me."

"Says you."

"Says the store manager, too."

"Okay, where's the evidence?"

"The store manager is an eye witness."

"The store manager said he saw somebody with a ski mask

run to the front of the store and say 'put your hands up.'"

"Sounds like attempted robbery to me."

"But even the store manager, what's his name?"

"John Dumont."

"Even John Dumont says our boy didn't ask for any money."

"He's not our boy. I don't want anything to do with the little son of a bitch."

"Okay, then don't worry about him any more."

"Dammit, Elliott."

"You're skating on thin ice, Sizelove. I'd zip it while the zippin's good."

"But..."

"No buts, I don't want to hear anything more about it." Elliott signed heavily. "Look, most of the damage was done by Dumont and his shotgun."

"We pulled out some slugs."

"We did, but we haven't found a gun. The Brian boy didn't have a ski mask on him. The tapes show nothing."

"They don't?"

"Nope, I looked at 'em myself."

"About the gun. Dumont says it was on the floor when you came to investigate."

"I didn't see no gun."

"And it's gone now."

Elliott slapped the desk. "What are you trying to say? Choose your words very carefully now. I'd choose 'em real careful."

Sizelove looked at the Chief for a half minute and then bowed his head. "I ain't sayin' nothing."

"Okay then."

"But what about his car?"

"So his car was parked near the ZipMart. That ain't no crime."

"And what about his bloody butt. Huh? His butt full of buckshot."

"Enough already."

"Well what about it?"

"He fell on his ass 'cuz he'd been drinking and skidded down some steps on his ass."

"So, there was no buckshot."

"Nope."

"Yeah sure."

"I examined his butt myself, not that I'm bragging about it. But he just scraped it up a little. It was a coincidence. It looks to me like Dumont didn't hit jack shit when he started blasting away. Killed a few fluorescent tubes. Gut shot a picture window. Just forget about it, okay? We come up with some evidence, we'll arrest somebody. In the meantime, let the insurance company buy the store a new window and some potato chips and call it a day. Are we in agreement?"

"I guess so."

"What?"

"Yes."

"Well, okay. Now speaking of butt, why don't you get yours out there and catch some speeders or something."

The chief turned to look out the window and turned back.

"Why are you looking at me like that? Go already."

Carson Catlin was Twinkin' out. AC/DC cranked up to ear-bleed, can after can of Monster KHAOS Energy Drink, and boxes of Hostess Twinkies were giving him the mother of all buzzes. He was on a new plane, a new orbit, hell, he was a supernova in a different universe, a gadzillion gigawatts of pure energy. He had been on his computer all day and all night and all day again checking out stuff for Louie Louie. Sleep? That was for trolls. He owned the night. That was when the computers were half asleep, and he could sneak in the backdoor, past the firewalls, through the safety nets, crack some codes, get some dope.

He was the king of cyber space, trippin' the light fantastic, becoming the emperor of the digital realm.

Oh this was friggin' sweet.

He had found out stuff nobody could find. He had been zippin' and zappin' all over the world, pinging around like a pinball, hackin' into police computers, reading private email, unearthing government secrets.

He wasn't just good; he was awesome. Beyond awesome. Awesome times infinity squared.

Just one piece of the puzzle still eluded him. Then, he would have the complete picture.

He shoved another Twinkie in his mouth. Taptaptaptaptaptappity tap. His fingers were just dancin' over the keys. Fred Astaire and Michael Jackson and Dancin' with the Stars, all channeling themselves into his ten fingers of pure magic, hot wired directly to a brain that was jacked up, pumped up, hittin' on all twelve cylinders.

Dr. Sheldon King, the pathologist, finished examining the sample Louie brought him earlier. This was a whole new ball game. A new level of crazy. Whatever Louie had gotten himself into, it was flat-out weird.

The Man with the Lightbulb Head took two packages out of the freezer. One was the right hand of Peter Brown. This, he would send to Peter Brown's father, Stuart. The other package he would send to Susan Louise Ferman.

It was Peter's brain.

He thought of sending a note in the first package. He wrote several different lines:

Need a HAND?

I've Got to HAND it to You.

Give Yourself a HAND.

HANDle with Care.

This will come in HANDy.

Get a GRIP.

Reach out and TOUCH someone.

This is your last HANDout.

A threat and a pun. Perfect. He had to make sure to write it on something that was non-traceable. Maybe he would go to a Kinkos in a nearby town. Or, maybe he would do it at a library. Better yet, a library at one of the nearby colleges. That would work. He had to be sure to wear a hat so he wouldn't be remembered.

Now, should he deliver the package himself or send it by courier service? This one he would send by some sort of courier. FedEx? UPS? DHL? Or, maybe A1.

The brain he would deliver himself. What should it say?

Get aHEAD.

Don't Lose Your HEAD.

I want to give you some HEAD.

Oooh, that was delicious. A tease. A threat. A pun. Pretty damn good. What else?

HEADing Someplace?

You're Soon to be HEADline News.

HEADS, You Lose.

Hmm. He liked the last one. He liked the "give you some HEAD" one too. Decisions. Decisions. He took a sip of his Dubonnet and soda.

There was almost too much on his plate right now. There was just so much to coordinate. He had been masterful with Mimi Johnston. No one suspected a thing.

The police were clueless then. They were still clueless.

The last package to her had summed everything up, so nicely. But she was such a moron, she didn't get it. But who cared? She got something else. He giggled to himself. A little poke, but not the kind she usually got.

Anyway, no need to get sloppy now.

He would have to put the brain back in the freezer and concentrate on Stuart Brown for today. He got busy wrapping Peter's right hand in wax paper, putting that inside a plastic bag that would go inside a box and another box.

He wondered if Stuart Brown would understand the significance of the hand. Probably not. He would know his kidnapped son was probably dead. After a couple weeks of worry, it would just add to the misery. Too bad Stuart's wife died a year ago. It would have been nice to take her apart. The Stumeister might have really gone bonkers over that.

But Stuart was probably scared and worried, in extreme mental distress. Soon, the pain would be more than mental. Soon, the payback would be complete. And he would move on to Susan. He meant to do them both simultaneously, but there was only so much one man could do.

Susan, dear, you may have postponed the inevitable.

But not for long.

Cut 19
I Go to Pieces

Stuart Brown was dead, but didn't know it yet.

He thought he was dreaming. He tried to sit up and felt straps tighten against his chest. What the hell? He tried to raise his arms. They were strapped down too. And his legs. But these weren't really straps. It was duct tape. He was duct taped to his own bed.

His head, however was free. Something was wrong with his mouth. He wanted to scream, but he couldn't. The inside of his mouth and throat were in agony.

"Wakey wakey," a voice said.

Beside his bed was a plastic trashcan lined with a black poly bag. Knives, saws, a propane torch, and a hammer rested on a clean white towel beside him. Except for a light shining in his face, the rest of the room was in darkness. A man stood at the foot of his bed.

"Aren't we Mr. Sleepyhead tonight?"

The voice was familiar but Stuart was too groggy to place it.

"Of course, maybe it was the two Ambien the doctor gave you to help you sleep after the bad day you've had. Or, maybe, it was the sedative I shot into you after you fell asleep. But it doesn't matter. What matters is that you're awake now." The man in the shadows giggled.

"What's the matter—cat got your tongue? Oops, sorry, I guess I do."

The man in the shadows held up a pair of pliers. There was

something in them. The man flicked the pliers and a bloody red tongue landed on the pillow close to Stuart's head.

Stuart tried to scream, but his mouth was filled with a face-cloth and taped over.

"I took the liberty of removing it when you were out. I hope you don't mind. From now on I promise to make sure you're aware of everything I take from you. Oh, and don't worry, I cauterized the inside of your mouth where your tongue was, so you didn't have to swallow any of your nasty old blood."

The man moved to the side of the bed and picked up a ball-peen hammer.

Stuart caught just a glimpse of the face before the man moved back into the shadows.

"Have you ever read the book, *Misery* by Stephen King? Great book. They made a really good movie of it, too. One of the best movies they ever made from one of Stephen King's books. Did you see it?

"Don't bother to answer. I'm sure it left you speechless. Oops, that was me again."

The man giggled.

"I also liked *The Shining*. Wasn't that a great movie? Did you know Stephen King hated that one? Can you imagine, hating a Stanley Kubrick movie? Anyway, I digress. In the book and the movie, *Misery*, a woman named Annie Wilkes decides to hobble Paul Sheldon by hitting his foot with a sledgehammer. I thought, now isn't that fun! Do you think I ought to try it? Yes? No? Hmmm. This isn't exactly a sledge hammer, but let's see."

The man swung the hammer. There was a sound like a pencil breaking. Stuart felt a hot burst of pain in his left foot. He tried to thrash around, but was restrained by the tape.

He looked down at his foot and saw that his big toe was bent inward at a ninety-degree angle.

"Tut tut. This little hammer could only get the piggy that went to the market. Oh well. Time for a little nursery rhyme. Okay the piggy already went to market. Now this little piggy went home."

The Man with the Lightbulb Head swung the hammer and smashed the second toe.

"This little piggy got roast beef."

He smashed the next toe.

"And this little piggy got none."

The man swung the hammer again.

"Made you flinch. I am such a tease."

This time the man swung the hammer and hit the fourth toe.

"And this little piggy said 'Wee. Wee. Wee. Wee. I. Want. Some.'"

With each word the man swung the hammer down, tearing flesh and cracking bone, finally turning the top of Stuart's foot to pulp.

Stuart tried to contain the pain. Kept telling himself it was just his foot. But he couldn't keep the pain down. It flowed up through his legs. It seemed to saturate every cell in his body. It was terrible. And every time he thought it couldn't get any worse, it did.

"Well, your days dancing ballet are over. What next?"

The Man with the Lightbulb Head walked over to the side of the bed and placed the bloody hammer on the towel. As he bent to pick up a knife, Stuart caught a good look at his face. That was when Stuart realized the tormenter's identity.

"You know, you may not realize it, but tonight you're just coming apart. Get it? Do I have a way with words or what? Of course, you already know that, don't you? I am such a cut up. Do you hear me?"

The man sliced off Stuart's right ear. He held the bloody ear an inch from his lips.

"I said, I am such a cut up. And tonight I am going to practice my trade. Oh, and by the way, you'll never see your son again. Unless, of course, there is an afterlife. In a day or two, you'll find out. I always say, if you can't bring the son to the father, send the father to the son."

Two days later, The Man with the Lightbulb Head walked

out to his car carrying a garbage bag with bloody tools in it. He put the bag in the trunk. He opened the front door and sat in the driver's seat and waited. A half an hour later, the house exploded in a ball of blue and yellow flame.

"Oh, my my, an unfortunate gas explosion. I wonder if it was suicide or an accident? We might never know. The poor unfortunate man has had such a terrible time lately."

The Man with the Lightbulb Head started the engine and drove away.

Junkyard Slim and the Belladonna Boys were in a pole barn, behind a house, on a plot of land in the middle of nowhere.

On the door of the barn was a hand-lettered sign, "The Highest Order of the Belladonna Brotherhood and Bourbon Society."

The inside of the barn was about twenty by fifty feet. There was a workbench on one end with greasy tools piled up on it. The other end had a bar made of two bourbon barrels with a sheet of plywood on top. A huge flat screen TV sat atop cinderblocks. Seven recliners, three covered in brown vinyl and four in black, were scattered about the floor. There was a card table made of a telephone cable spool with a green felt patch of cloth on top.

"Louie Louie, what brings you to this neck of the woods?" Slim asked from his spot on the bench of a bench press machine covered in red cracked vinyl and silver duct tape. Behind him, a calendar advertised a hunting magazine. On the cover, a busty woman posed holding deer antlers that barely hid her chest. The caption underneath read: "Nice Rack."

"Just thought I'd drop by and say hi."

"Hi," three or four of the Belladonna Boys said in unison from their recliners. The air was thick with sweet brownish smoke.

"Care to do a little smokin' or did you come here to drink?" one of the Belladonna Boys asked Louie. Louie wasn't sure but thought the questioner was named Skeets.

"I might have a short bourbon."

"Well, we got bourbon," one of the other Boys, Jimbo, said.

"We got expensive bourbon, we got cheap bourbon. We've got good bourbon and we got more good bourbon, 'cuz there ain't no such thing as bad bourbon," the man who might have been Skeets said.

"Only bad bourbon drinkers," Jimbo continued. They all laughed, but Louie had the feeling this line had been used before.

Louie walked over to the bar. There were bottle after bottle of bourbons in all shapes and sizes, one bottle of Canadian whiskey and one Tennessee sour mash. No vodka, gin or tequila. Nothing that wasn't brown. Nothing from Scotland. Louie poured two fingers of Evan Williams in a paper cup and sat in one of the recliners.

Two of the Belladonna Boys, Samson and Manny were passing back and forth a hand rolled cigarette.

The Belladonna Boys were all farmers in their late forties and early fifties who had come under the spell of belladonna back in the eighties. One of them, Steven James aka Junkyard Slim had originally smoked his grandmother's Asthmador as a kid. He got his buddies to try it. Soon, they started buying it for themselves. Louie didn't know if anyone made Asthmador anymore or if the boys grew their own belladonna plants.

Sometime after high school graduation, the group of rural guys who had developed the odd habit of smoking belladonna, started calling themselves the Belladonna Boys. Everyone in town did too. Sometimes the Boys said they were a club, sometimes a fraternity, sometimes a religion. No one quite knew what they were.

But every Tuesday and Thursday, they met in Junkyard Slim's pole barn/clubhouse and smoked the stuff while drinking bourbon. The only thing Louie could tell it did to them, was make their pupils huge.

Louis sipped bourbon as they talked sports awhile and carped a bit about the government. Louie was dying to get to the point of the visit, but he knew he would get better cooperation if he didn't rush things.

"So, how's the dick business?" Jimbo asked.

Again, they all chuckled. Louie had heard variations of that one more than a million times.

"Oh, I'm paying the rent."

"You dicking around now?"

"As a matter of fact, yeah. I have a question or two I wanted to ask you guys. Saturday night there was a wreck about a mile up the road."

"I didn't hear anything about that," Possibly-Skeets said.

"Me either," Ray replied.

"I didn't ask if you heard about it." Louie smiled and took another sip. "I wondered what you knew about it."

"Now that's a whole different question," the man who, now that Louie thought about it, was *most probably* named Skeets said.

"Yes it is," Ray said.

"A massively different question," Probably-Skeets said.

"So, do you know anything about it?"

"Yeah, we know about it," Slim said.

"What do you know?"

"That there was a wreck up the road," Slim said.

"And we don't think it would be wise for us to get involved," Probably-Skeets said.

"Although we saw the wrecked van," Slim said.

"But we still choose not to get involved," Probably-Skeets said.

Louie thought a moment. He had gotten all the information he would get from them. It was enough.

"Well, okay, thanks for the drink, boys. I owe you all one."

"Do you know Arnie Summers?" Slim asked as Louie was walking out the door.

"Lives about five miles north on county line road, right?"

"Yeah, that's the one. Well, you know, he's always fixing up cars. And he has himself an old tow truck." Slim was giving Louie another piece of information.

"Maybe he likes to get cars that have been totaled and strip 'em for parts," Louie said.

"Yeah, maybe."

"Well, thanks again."

"You know, something else peculiar, that doesn't have anything to do with you, but peculiar nonetheless...someone's been planting something at the old Baxter farm. Wonder what it is. You don't think it's Mary Jane or anything, do you?" Slim was still trying to tell Louie something.

"I might check it out. I'll let you know."

"Hell, pick me some if you run across it."

Cut 20

It's A-Happening

Louie called Sloopy and said he'd be late and probably miss supper.

"Don't worry. I won't start the steaks until you get home."

"You really don't have to wait for me."

"I know I don't. But, I will. Just be careful."

He promised he would and hung up.

Louie drove to the old Baxter farm. A lane covered in weeds led up to a barn that had lost all its color and was too old and tired to stand up straight. The barn was about three hundred yards from the road and the lane looked as if someone had driven on it recently. That didn't mean much, because for years, kids had been driving back there to make out or smoke weed or drink beer, or all three. About ten yards north of the barn was the foundation where a house had once been.

Louie drove back to the barn and got a flashlight out of the glove compartment. Beer cans and cigarette butts and an old condom or two littered the ground. He walked around the barn, went inside and looked around. He didn't see where the ground had been disturbed.

Louie went back to the car and sat on the hood. He could hear crickets and the wind blowing through the trees, and the night sounds of wild animals.

Behind the barn was an old bottled propane tank. Louie walked to it and looked around. Nothing. He walked back to the car, opened the door to get into the car and stopped. He thought a moment, then went over to the foundation of the house. In the northwest corner was a big chunk of concrete. In the flashlight beam, it looked like some of the weeds around it had been flattened. He tried to move it with his foot but couldn't budge it. He set the flashlight on the ground and tried to pick up the concrete chunk by one of the sharper pieces jutting out. He got it about belt buckle high and couldn't hold on so he let it drop. He flapped his hands around to cool them.

Louie didn't have a chain or rope in the car. He didn't have gloves. Neither did he have a shovel to dig with once he moved the chunk out of the way. He decided to get some equipment and come back later tonight or tomorrow night and do a little digging around.

Louie got in his car and drove to Arnie Summers' farm. As he passed, he noticed several cars and a truck in the driveway. There were no lights on in the house. About a half mile north of the farm was a patch of grass big enough to park a car. He grabbed the flashlight from the glove box and walked back across a bean field to the back of the Summers' farm.

Arnie had a good half-acre of wrecks that he stripped for parts in back of his house. Louie wanted to see if there was a white van among them.

A half moon lit the sky, so Louie didn't need to click on the flashlight.

He had to climb a fence to get on the property. A chained dog in the backyard started barking furiously. Louie stood like a statue gazing at a mishmash of cars and half cars scattered all over what could optimistically be called backyard, but Louie didn't see a van from where he stood.

The light above the back door turned on. Louie was far enough away to still be in the shadows. The door opened and a man stepped out on the tiny concrete pad behind the door. "What is it boy, are you all right?"

The dog calmed down a bit. The man walked over and petted it. Even though it was only a silhouette, it looked to Louie like a Lab of some sort. It certainly was big. The man stood up and scanned the yard. Apparently he didn't see Louie, because he walked back into the house.

Louie moved slowly around the perimeter of the property, hugging the fence.

The dog started barking again. Louie climbed over the fence at the far end of the property and crouched.

The man came out again, and walked over to the dog. "You hush now, you hear?"

Louie stayed still for another five minutes.

Enough of the dog. This wasn't working. Louie decided to go back to the car. He thought of a better way to check out the farm. There was a small grass airstrip west of town. The owner took Louie up every once in awhile just to fly around and keep his skills honed.

Louie decided to see if he wouldn't fly over the farm tomorrow at first light. Louie could check out if there were a white van among the field of wrecks. It seemed like a good plan. Hell, it was a great plan.

When Louie stood up, a voice said, "Gimme one good reason why I shouldn't blow your head off."

Louie was trespassing and had a shotgun pointed at his head. Not good.

"Hey Arnie, how are you doing?"

"Who is this?"

"Mind if I turn around? It's me. Louie. You know, Louie Louie, and all that. I was two years behind you in high school."

"Louie, how's it hanging?"

"Good, good. You mind lowering that thing?"

Arnie lowered the shotgun so it wasn't pointing at Louie's head anymore. However, it was still pointing a little south of his stomach. Louie had a quick flash of something not pretty happening.

"So, what are you doing sneaking around on my property?"

Louie didn't have a good answer.

"You know, I have every right to shoot you where you stand just for being here without asking."

That wasn't exactly true, but Louie didn't think it was the

time to argue. “You sure can Arnie. I hope you don’t. I didn’t mean any harm.”

“So, what are you doing?”

“I just wanted to see something and I didn’t want to wake you up.”

Arnie lowered the shotgun so it was pointing at Louie’s feet. “What were you trying to see out here in the dark?”

Louie decided to go with the truth. “Well, you see, some guys beat me up and put me in the back of a van which wrecked about six miles from here. I was wondering if you had the van.”

“Why should I tell you?”

“Because I’m looking for it.”

“I didn’t do anything wrong.”

“I know. It’s just that the van has disappeared and I wondered where it got to.”

“Why?”

“I was just curious.”

“What are you gonna do if’n it is here?”

“Nothing.”

“Then why do you want to know?”

“I…uh…well, as I said, I’m curious. There were three fellas in the van and I wondered what happened to them.”

“There weren’t nobody in the van.”

“Then you have it?”

“I didn’t say that.”

“Arnie, I’m not here to cause any trouble. If you tell me you have the van, I’ll take off and leave you alone.”

“Elliott said I could have it.”

“You can. I promise.”

“But if’n I do have it, you can’t tell anyone. I don’t want no trouble. I had nothing to do with no kidnapping.”

“Shoot, Arnie, I know that. You’re not the kind of guy that would do that.”

“Okay. I’ve got the van. There, you satisfied?”

“Thanks, Arnie. I appreciate you telling me.”

"Now git."

Louie decided to push it a bit. "You mind if I look at it?"

"Why?"

"Just to see if I can figure out who did kidnap me."

The farmer thought a minute. "Okay, I reckon' you can. But it's my van."

"Sure, sure. It's your van. No problem."

He led Louie to the van. The driver's side was crumpled. The windshield was cracked and spidered. There were no license plates.

"Hey Arnie, do you have the plates that were on it?"

"There weren't no plates."

"Okay."

Louie ran the flashlight light over the van. He opened the back doors and looked around inside. There were no clues that were obvious.

"Well, okay, thanks Arnie. I'll be leaving now. Sorry to bother you."

"Where's your car?"

"About a mile up the road."

"Need a ride?"

"Naw, I'll walk." Louie started walking up the driveway.

"Hey Louie."

"Yeah?"

"Next time you want something, just come to the front door."

"You got it, pardner. Thanks for your help. Sorry again to bother you."

God, I'm having bad luck, Louie thought.

Cut 21
Last Time Around

Tim Ferman woke in a bed he didn't recognize. He was totally naked. His head hurt. He didn't want to move. So, he stared at the ceiling for several minutes. The ceiling was white. Not much could he deduce from that.

Some familiar objects nearby. A telephone with a card attached to it. A "Do Not Disturb" hanger on the door handle.

Okay, he was in a hotel room, someplace. Good. He wasn't in some stranger's bedroom. He rolled out of bed with as little motion as possible, since every movement detonated a tiny bomb inside his head and unleashed a tsunami of burning acid in his stomach.

He spotted his clothes all wadded up in a corner. What a way to treat a $5,000 suit. Oh well. He rummaged around the pile, searching for his underwear. Oh no. Oh shit. Not again. He pulled out his shirt. It had splotches of blood on it. A boiling cauldron of vomit almost erupted from his stomach. He had to close his eyes and breathe in slowly through his nose to keep from spewing whatever was sloshing around down there.

He opened his eyes again, threw the shirt to the side, rummaged some more and finally found his underwear. He put on the Sea Island cotton boxers imported from England and walked to the bathroom. It was a big one. He figured he was in an expensive place. He bent over the sink and splashed water on his face. Glass tumblers wrapped in wax paper surrounded a liter glass bottle of Evian water on a tray. Beside the Evian was a bottle opener. He snicked off the old-fashioned cap, poured half a glass and drank it down slowly. It stayed down. So he poured another and drank it a little faster.

He walked back into the main room of the suite. It was furnished elegantly in antique furniture. He sat at the writing desk, opened the middle drawer, and pulled out a leather folder with stationery and a listing of the hotel amenities. He recognized the hotel name. It was what he considered the finest hotel in Cincinnati.

Cincinnati. Oh no. How did he get here? And, more importantly, what did he do? Oh please, he hadn't seen Mimi had he? No wait. He would never see Mimi again. Poor thing.

Well, then who?

Where did the blood come from? He shuddered. His stomach flipped on him and he almost blew chunks again. Okay. He had to pull himself together. First take a shower and get dressed. He could wear his suit with a T-shirt. That would work. Shades of Don Johnson without the pastels.

After showering, he walked back into the main room, feeling almost human. He noticed an envelope pushed under his door. Maybe the hotel bill could give a clue. It looked like he had checked in a little after 11 p.m. He signed for drinks at the hotel bar. HPNOTINIs and Johnny Walker Blue on the rocks. He had quite a few JW Blues. Interesting. He usually drank single malt. Did one of the girls at the office drink HPNOTINIs? It seemed like the kind of drink an ad woman would have. Something trendy. Cosmopolitans were out. Appletinis were just a short phase. Pama was cooler that HPNOTIQ. But HPNOTINIs with the glow sticks were still pretty hip.

Okay, if he had been with one of the girls from the office last night, who? Where was she now?

Damn, thinking sure as hell hurt. He wanted to lie down again. What time was it? A few minutes after noon.

The last thing he remembered was being in his study in his home in Zionsville, Indiana. He was drinking Macallan's Scotch. The bottle of 25 year old. Now, that was what a scotch should be. And he also had the revolver out. What had he done with that?

He went through the pile of clothes once again. Not there. He checked around the bedroom and the sitting room. No suitcase. No gun. No sign of any woman.

What now? Maybe he should call the Cincy office to see if he had been with one of them. Maybe he should call to see if everyone was okay. He went back to the pile of clothes and looked through his pants pockets and jacket pockets. He couldn't find his cell phone. It was a workday, wasn't it? Now, what was the telephone number? He called information from the hotel phone and they said they could connect him for a minimum charge. What the hell?

When the receptionist answered, he learned that Stuart Brown hadn't shown up for work yet, would he like to leave a message? Sure. He got voice mail.

The beep shot through his head like a rocket, causing him to grind his teeth in pain.

"This is Tim. Call me at this number." He gave the hotel number and room number and hung up.

He paced walked around the room and then into the bathroom for another drink of water. The phone rang. That hurt. There was a phone right beside the toilet. So he sat and picked it up.

"Stuart," he said.

"No this is the front desk, sir. You have a Do Not Disturb sign on your door. Are you planning to stay another day?"

"Yes. Yes. I will be staying another day."

He dropped the phone with the woman still talking and threw up into the bathtub.

Already this was turning out to be a lousy day.

Cut 22

Twenty Years Ago Today, Reprise

The boy couldn't bear the thought of seeing his parents. He couldn't bear the thought of seeing anyone. Shame burned inside his gut. Anger boiled in his veins. He went to the willow tree behind the abandoned lumberyard. He sat against the trunk, pulled his knees up and hung his head.

He was such an idiot. Such a fool. How could he ever imagine a girl like Amanda would have anything to do with a loser like him? He looked up and saw a rabbit. Probably the same rabbit as the day Amanda read his poetry. His stupid epic poem about John Lennon.

He watched the rabbit for several minutes. A dark gray rabbit. Nose twitching. Sitting fifteen yards away eating clover. Soon the rabbit was joined be three tinier rabbits. Barely bigger than rats. Two were dark gray and one a lighter gray.

The boy everyone called the Brain, slowly stood up with his back against the trunk of the tree. The rabbit jumped at the movement and then stopped. The Brain took one step forward and then stopped. The rabbit didn't move. Another step, longer this time. No movement. The boy slid his feet to the right and bent over to pick up a three-foot long tree branch from the ground. As he straightened up the rabbit was still there.

The branch felt good in the boy's fist. Wood rot and insects hadn't softened it up yet. It was solid, a little bit thicker than a baseball bat.

The boy stood stone still watching the rabbit. Slowly took

another long step in the direction of the rabbit. The rabbit turned and faced away from the boy, still eating clover and grass. The baby rabbits jumped around the bigger rabbit, no more than two or three feet from the parent.

The boy took another step. And then another. He was close enough now. He took one more step just to be sure. Brought the branch up over his head and the rabbit jumped. But the Brain was expecting this, he dove for the rabbit at the same time bringing the branch down like a club. He aimed a little to the right, knowing rabbits never ran in a straight line. He had a fifty percent chance of being right.

He hit the ground on his stomach and chin. Knocked the wind out of him. Heard a loud popping sound from his jaw. A white jolt of pain shot through his head. He turned on his back, mouth working like a guppy. Needed air. Couldn't get air. Tilted his head back and arched his neck. His diaphragm loosened and his lungs filled with air. Sweet, sweet air.

Rolled over again on his stomach. Heard a baby crying. A loud, awful sound. No, it was the rabbit screaming. A terrible high-pitched scream. The rabbit lay on its side screaming, one leg twitching. The Brain smiled. Got up on hands and knees crawled over to the animal. Picked the rabbit up by one leg, and tore it apart. Literally tearing it limb from limb. The rabbit was jerking, alive while this was happening. The screaming stopped when the boy twisted off its head.

The boy remembered when he was four or five years old. A deep, burning anger at his dad. His nutso dad. The boy ran out the back door after being slapped. Ran to the small wooded area behind his house, to a maple tree he liked to climb. The boy would climb the tree to be alone. Sometimes to read.

The boy climbed the tree and straddled a branch. Tears and snot running down his face. He wiped his face with the sleeve of his hoodie. Then he noticed something he hadn't seen before. A robin's nest. With little baby robins inside. The mother had flown away when the boy climbed the tree. The mother robin landed on the branch about four feet from the nest.

The boy could see four baby robins, their mouths open. Just the four, tiny open mouths above the rim of the nest.

The boy scooted toward the nest and saw the squirmy little robins inside. Eyes closed, mouths open. He raised his fist like a club and smashed it down on the nest. Once. Twice. Three times. Until there was nothing but bloody, furry pulp.

His fist was covered with goo, blood, tiny feathers and fur. He smiled. The hot ball of anger in his belly, gone. He felt powerful. Alive.

He wiped his hand on the front of his hoodie.

Now, he had rabbit blood on his hands, the sleeves of his shirt and splattered on his face. Again the feeling. Elation. Power. The burning in his gut was no more. No more anger. No more pain. Just like those many years ago when he smashed the robin's nest.

And he realized only through the pain of others could his pain be relieved. Quenched. Mastered.

He laughed. He never laughed. But now he laughed out loud. Laughed until his bruised diaphragm ached.

He really enjoyed the killing. It was gratifying.

From that moment on, there were fewer stray cats in town. Dogs disappeared. Turtles near the river were crushed with heavy rocks. Traps were set for squirrels and rabbits. The animals were caught and brutalized.

Yet, no one knew his secret.

The boy seemed so much happier.

His life was so much easier.

He prospered in school. He had friends. He was the guy everyone seemed to like. Nothing bothered him. Nothing could break his cool. He had a surface charm that was unflappable.

No one could imagine the monster within. No one could fathom what he would become.

The boy would grow up to be The Man with the Lightbulb Head.

Cut 23
Last Night

Louie woke beside Sloopy for the second day in a row. This time he was under the covers with her. He washed his face, went downstairs and stuck his wet face in the refrigerator. He pulled out milk, eggs, butter, an onion, olives and three kinds of cheese, only one of which he recognized. He found a garlic clove in the pantry and a bottle of pepper infused olive oil.

Louie got out a big cast iron pan and a mixing bowl. He didn't need no stinkin' omelet pan to make an omelet. Nosirree. He put a big splash of olive oil in the pan and turned the gas on high. He chopped up the onion and decided to add another onion and chopped it up too. Chopped up about a dozen black olives and smashed the garlic clove. He threw all that in a pan until it sizzled and then added a pat of butter and turned the heat off.

Louie broke four eggs into the mixing bowl, added a dollop of milk and whipped them to a froth. Poured it all into the pan with heat still off and set out the plates. He wanted to make her a breakfast in bed she wouldn't forget.

Louie found some French bread, which he sliced into two-inch pieces, brushed a little olive oil on both sides, put on a cookie sheet and popped it into the oven at very low heat.

"I've never heard you whistle before." Sloopy appeared at the kitchen door dressed in a pink silk robe.

"I guess I'm just happy."

"Because of last night?"

"No, because I'm about to have a big ass omelet. Next to steaks, that's my favorite meal."

"Last night had nothing to do with it?"

"Oh, maybe a little."

She came over and kissed Louie on the cheek.

Louie flipped the omelet. "Now sit down at the kitchen table and I'll serve you a kick ass breakfast."

"Kick ass breakfast, big ass omelet, you seem to have ass on your mind."

"Hmmm. Wonder why?"

Louie got back to work, turning the French bread pieces to brown the other side and grating enough of the different cheeses to cause a heart attack.

Sloopy made some coffee and Louie folded the omelet, cut it in half and slid each half onto a plate. He pulled out the toasted French bread pieces and tossed a couple on each plate.

As they were eating, she said. "This is nice."

"Yes it is."

"I could get used to it."

"I could too. I have to tell you, Sloopy, I don't think there has been a day gone by that I haven't thought of you."

"Do you think we could pretend those fifteen years never happened and start all over again?"

"I would like that very much."

They ate in silence for a while, a comfortable silence—the silence of people who enjoy each other's company.

"This sure is cheesy," she said as she rotated the fork to wind up a long string of cheese.

"It's cheese-licious."

"Oh gawd," she groaned. "Please don't ever go into advertising."

"Speaking of which," Louie said.

"Tim."

"Yea, I think I'm going to see him today."

"But why?"

"I have a hunch he knows something about the animal, and now human stuff you've been getting."

"No way."

"It's the only thing that makes sense."

"Why, because he used to be my husband?"

"No, I have other reasons to believe he might be involved."

"I don't believe you."

"Look, there's nothing I'd like better than to find out he doesn't have anything to do with it. But I have to talk to him to make sure."

She looked out the kitchen window and bit her lower lip. Louie finished the omelet and took both plates to rinse them off.

Finally, she said, "Okay, you can see him."

"Thanks. Sloopy, I have one thing I have to ask."

"Why I left you for him?"

"Nope. I don't care. We were young. Things happen. No, what I want to know is why you got divorced."

"Does it matter?"

Louie shrugged. "Maybe. Maybe not. I wouldn't ask, but it might be something that has to do with the case."

She started crying softly.

"I'm sorry Sloopy. You don't have to tell me, if you don't want to."

"No, no, it's alright. I just, I don't know, I mean, I don't know what I did."

"What do you mean?"

"I don't know what I did to make him stop loving me."

"Oh."

"You see, before we were married, he never touched me. I thought he was being a gentleman and wanted to wait until we were married. But after..."

"After?" Louie prompted.

"After, well we had a honeymoon and all. But he couldn't

really. I mean, we made love and all, but it was, difficult. He tried to be a husband but by the end of our first year he was sleeping on the couch in his study most nights."

"I'm sorry."

"Me too." She looked out the window as if she were watching her marriage fall apart. "He just didn't love me, I guess. Or, didn't find me attractive in that way. Oh, he was always kind and considerate. I mean, most of the time."

"When wasn't he?"

"Huh?"

"When wasn't he considerate? What did he do? Did he hurt you?"

"No, nothing like that. He never laid a finger on me. He always bought me nice presents and took me to nice places. He let me buy whatever I wanted."

"But?"

"Really, it's nothing."

"Yes it is. What is it?"

"Well, he liked to drink."

"Was he a mean drunk?"

"No. Not to me. He would just go on these benders and leave for long periods of time. Days sometimes."

"I see.

"I'm not sure you do. When he came home, he claimed he didn't know where he had gone or what he had done. At first I didn't believe him. But as time wore on I began to believe he didn't know what he was doing. I think he had blackouts like he claimed."

"Did you try to help him."

"I did. But he couldn't seem to help himself. I even suggested he seek professional help. He claimed he was, but I don't know. It was terrible. I just didn't know what to do."

"So, you left him."

"No, that wasn't it. Well it was, and it wasn't."

"What do you mean?"

"One time he came home and I could smell another woman on him. It's such a cliché, but there was lipstick on his shirt. And maybe some bloodstains."

"Big ones?"

"No, just a few drops."

"So what happened?"

"I confronted him. He said he had no idea what happened. I told him I couldn't take it anymore. I was hoping he would really make a commitment to get help. But he just looked at me and didn't look at me, if you know what I mean."

"I do, I think."

"He just looked at me and said, 'You shouldn't have to take it, Susan.'

"That was it. He promised to take care of me after the divorce. And he has. He's always given me plenty of money and he's been a perfect gentleman since we split."

"I'm sorry."

"I will never forget the way he looked at me. There was such sadness in his eyes. I will never forget that look. Never."

Cut 24
Shake a Tail Feather

Louie went to his house to change clothes, get a shovel from the garage, and the LockAid in case he needed to break into anything.

He thought about stopping at the Baxter Farm to dig around, but decided to leave the shovel in the trunk for the time being and went straight to Indianapolis. He was beginning to form a theory about who was sending Sloopy the animal parts.

In a nutshell, Louie figured it was Tim Ferman. He just didn't know the hows and whys. On the way to the circle city, Louie's cell phone rang. It was Carson.

"Now my head tingles."

"Huh?"

"My head. It tingles. Like my feet did. You don't think it's anything serious, do you?"

"Does is hurt-tingle?"

"No."

"Are you dizzy or anything?"

"Not that I know of."

"Carson, you'd know if you were dizzy."

"But you said 'or anything.' I don't know what that means."

"Figure of speech. I think you're okay unless start having serious headaches."

"Really?"

"Really. Now what's up?"

"Hacked into Mimi's work computer."

"And?"

"My God, I don't know how that woman finds time to work. The world wide web might crash just because she overloaded it with emails."

"What did you find out?" I asked.

"Well, I haven't been able to read everything yet, but I found out a couple of nuggets that may interest you."

"Let me have it."

"Well, she was having an affair with Sloopy's former husband that ended badly."

"That's interesting."

"In fact, I gathered from the emails that was why she was in Cincinnati. Also, in one email to him, she threatens to expose him and all his and I quote 'dirty little secrets.'"

"Even more interesting."

"Oh and get this, in another email she even tells him with what she knows, she could bring him down."

"Did he ever respond to her?"

"Only once that I can find. He just told her to be careful."

"That's it?"

"That's it. Nothing more. Two words: Be careful."

"Did you find out if she received animal parts when she moved to Cincy?"

"Big time. She didn't contact the cops because she thought it was some sort of prank, but she was receiving all sorts of animal pieces and parts."

"Anything human."

"Not that I've been able to find. But I've only gone through a third of the emails. Gimme a gallon of Red Bull and I might make it through them all. She wrote more words than the Encyclopedia Britannica and *War and Peace* combined."

"Well, keep on it."

"You got it. You owe me some Ding Dongs."

"As many as you want."

Louie ended the call and dialed Sheldon's number. Sheldon

wasn't home, so Louie checked with the pathologist's office and was told the doctor was in 'consult.' Everything Carson said bolstered what Louie was already thinking—Tim Ferman was the key.

Louie drove into Indianapolis at a little past eight. He had Mapquested both Ferman's home and company address. Louie wanted to ask Ferman some questions without giving the ad man time to formulate a response. So, Louie didn't call ahead.

First, Louie decided to see if he could catch Ferman at home. Ferman lived in Zionsville, a charming little village that grew a little less charming every time Louie saw it. Much of the land surrounding the village that used to be fields and woodland was becoming scarred with strip malls and McMansions built too close together.

Ferman lived in a bona-fide historical home on what looked like three acres of well-manicured land with mature trees. The land was surrounded by a black iron fence with an elaborate gate opening to a cobblestone driveway curving right then left up to the house. The gate was open, so Louie drove up to the house.

He walked up to the columnated front porch and rang the doorbell. And waited. Nobody answered. He walked around the house. All the windows had closed curtains and drawn blinds. He rang the doorbell again. Again, no answer. Louie could've used the LockAid to break in, but was sure there was an alarm system, which he didn't want to take the time to disable.

Louie got back in the car and drove to downtown Indianapolis. He remembered when Indianapolis was called India-No-Place. But a local shopping mall developer had spearheaded the drive to revive the downtown. Now, it had a new lease on life. It was full of new businesses and shops, all anchored by the Circle City Mall.

But Louie wasn't going all the way to the center of town; Wild Imagination Advertising was on South Meridian. The city's renaissance was just beginning to reach out this far. He parked in the parking lot behind the building. It was about half past nine, so the agency should be open.

There was a directory in the lobby of the building. Ferman's agency took up two floors, the third and fourth and his office was on the upper one.

Louie took the elevator to the fourth floor.

"May I help you, sir?"

Her name was Lisa. That's what the acrylic nameplate on her glass desk said. Her desk was in a modern glass and brushed steel reception area that greeted you the minute you stepped off the mirrored and brushed steel elevator.

She was in a twelve rounder against plump and still ahead on points. Jet black glossy hair, cut short, very pale skin and an impressive bosom.

Louie grinned and put his hands in his pockets. "Hi, Lisa, is Timmy around?"

"Oh, you mean Mr. Ferman. No he isn't. Do you have an appointment? Mr…"

"Is he expected any time this morning?"

"No, I think he's at our sister company in Cincinnati. Is he expecting you?"

"Well, he said if I was ever in the city to drop by and see him. Dang and double dang."

"Well, I'm sure he'll be sorry he missed you. Can any of our Account Executives help you?"

"No, I don't know any of them. I thought ol' Timmy and I might go out and have a few Bloody Marys and gab about old times."

"Would you like to leave a card or anything?"

"Nope."

"Can I tell him who called?"

"I didn't call. I came to see the crazy bastard, pardon my French."

She frowned. Louie frowned back. "So, when do you expect him back?"

"I can't really say."

"Can't or won't?"

"Huh?"

"Never mind. Well, see you later." Louie turned and pushed the elevator button.

"But sir, can I have your name?"

"No. Your name suits you better," Louie said.

The elevator doors opened and Louie stepped inside. She was still frowning when the doors closed.

Now what?

Louie walked to the parking lot and got in his car. He sat in the driver's seat. Tugged at his lower lip. He hit the steering wheel with the palm of his hand. Tugged at the lower lip again. Scratched his head. He started the car. Turned it off. Closed his eyes. Opened them again while tugging at his lower lip. Breathed out heavily.

Two minutes had passed. This was turning out to be a very productive day.

Louie got out of the car and walked around the parking lot. There were no spaces marked with Tim Ferman's name. Across the alley was an enclosed parking garage. It was connected to the building by a skywalk on the second floor.

He trotted to the garage and took the elevator to the second level. Right next to the skywalk entrance was the empty parking space for Tim Ferman.

Louie went back to his car and pulled into the parking lot. He backed into a space on the other side of the second level but with a good sight line to Ferman's parking space.

He rummaged around the glove compartment. Yes. The iPod was inside. He pulled it out and thumbed the little dial to the garage rock mix featuring almost all of the first Rhino 'Nuggets' Boxed Set, 'Teenage Head' by the Flamin' Groovies, and a smattering of songs from two or three Chesterfield Kings albums.

The music played but nothing else happened.

That's what a stake out is: a whole lotta nothin'. He sat and watched and waited and listened to some more great music.

It was a little past noon. Louie got out of the car and walked around to the front of the building. People were just filing out for lunch. There was a group of men in suits. Not especially stylish. Could be members of the accounting department. Maybe advertising Account Executives. Doubtful. They could've worked for any of the other five companies in the building.

Three women came out and two of them stuck cigarettes in their mouths. Dressed in pants and tops. Not denim. Again, not necessarily advertising types.

Another man came out. He had on an expensive suit. He stopped and checked his reflection in the plate glass window and spent a little time adjusting his hair. Probably an Account Executive. Louie was about to follow the preening Account Executive type when a car pulled up. It was a big black H2 driven by a blonde with silicone breasts. Preening man hopped into the car. Definitely an Account Executive. Louie thought about running around to the back and getting the car to follow the plastic people. But just as he was about to make a move, a group of twenty- and thirty-somethings of both sexes came out.

Denim and leather. Flip-flops and Converse Chuck Taylors in a variety of colors and patterns. One woman with purple hair. They were loud and laughing. The Creative Department. Louie followed them at a discrete distance. About a half a block north, they all piled into a beer and burgers joint. No doubt about it, Creatives.

Louie waited five minutes and walked into the bar.

Five minutes later he was seated at a table with three art directors and two copywriters from Wild Imagination Advertising.

One art director was an Asian, named Dennis. Another art director was from Kentucky. His name was Greg and he wore lots of jewelry for a man, a bracelet, three rings on one hand, two on the other, both ears were pierced with small gold loops and a couple of chains around his neck. He had a tattoo that said Vegas '08 on his forearm. He had on a sport coat, very wrinkled shirt, jeans and shower clogs. The third art director was a woman named Amanda with purple hair, black lipstick, black turtleneck, short black skirt, black fishnet stockings and black high top Converse tennis shoes.

One copywriter everyone called Squared. He had on a black Ramones T-shirt, white jeans, red Converse low tops and white socks. He was a native Hoosier, born and raised in a town not too far from Indianapolis.

The other copywriter was a woman named Nancy who had grown up all around the country because her father was in the military. She was over six feet tall, very pretty, with long butterscotch hair and a nice smile. She was dressed rather conservatively in a wine-colored sweater and black slacks.

Louie had told them he had come to Indianapolis to interview for an Executive Creative Director's job with Tim Ferman, who wasn't in today. Louie figured it would stir the pot a little if any of them happened to be the current Executive Creative Director.

"The Furryman loves to pull the old disappearing act every once in a while," Squared said.

"Do you know when he'll be back?" Louie asked.

"When the old man turns ghost on us, there's no tellin' when he'll reappear," Greg said.

"Why does he leave?"

"No one knows, man. He just does. One day he's here, the next day he's gone. It drives his secretary nuts, canceling appointments and making excuses," Squared said. "Thank goodness he only does it once or twice a year."

The conversation turned into speculation as to whether on not Tim was having an affair with Lisa.

"There's no way he isn't. Timmy likes his boobies," said Dennis.

"Remember Mimi?" Nancy asked. They all either nodded or laughed. Louie tried not to appear too interested.

"Who's Mimi?"

"She was Tim's secretary, receptionist, whatever you want to call her," Greg said.

"I know what I'd call her," Squared said.

"She was suddenly promoted to Account Supervisor," Greg said. "She had all the mental qualifications you need to get ahead here," he added with an obvious sarcasm.

"Did you say get ahead or give head?" Squared said.

They laughed.

"Be careful, guys," Amanda said.

"Hey, don't worry, I'm cool."

The burgers and beers came. The conversation shifted quickly to movies, music and TV shows. Louie found the Creatives funny, knowledgeable and interesting. He liked them.

As we were finishing up Louie brought up Mimi again. "So what's the story?"

"Look, the poor thing got murdered a few weeks back, we really shouldn't be bad mouthing her," Nancy said.

"Yeah, but the dude should know what he's getting into if he takes the job here," Squared said.

"Yeah, your predecessor became a victim of the Imagination Fornication Club," Greg said.

"Yeah, he got screwed, screwed over, and screwed up just because he didn't have the sweet stuff," Squared said.

"Ain't it the truth," Dennis said.

"I wouldn't go there," Amanda said.

"I take it you're talking about the last ECD."

"Yeah, good guy, but no longer here," Nancy said.

So that's why they weren't surprised when Louie told them he was interviewing for the ECD job.

"What does that have to do with Mimi?" Louie asked.

"Well, our last ECD came from Leo Burnett. Real nice guy named Paul Dabrowski. Great creative. Loved comic books. Anyway, his dream was to take a small Midwestern shop and turn it into a creative powerhouse. And, frankly he did it," Nancy said.

"You guys have quite a reputation."

"Thanks to all of us and Paul's leadership," Nancy said.

"So what was the problem?"

"You know the Burgerhut campaign?" Nancy asked.

Louie didn't but said he did.

"It put us on the map. That was Paul's idea," Greg said.

"Sounds like he did what he came here for."

"But he got it stolen from him," Squared said.

"By Mimi and Tim," Greg said.

"C'mon guys," Amanda said.

"Okay. Okay," Squared said.

"What do you mean?"

"Let me tell you a little how it works around here. Tim Ferman hires pretty people to be Account Executives. They don't know jack about advertising. Which is okay. Our clients don't either. It's not like we have P & G or McDonald's or any sophisticated marketers in our portfolio," Greg said.

"I understand." Louie didn't, really.

"Creatives are treated like second class citizens," Greg continued.

Louie nodded sympathetically.

"We aren't even allowed to go to client presentations. Tim says it saves the company money and besides the suits are better salesmen," Greg said.

"Bummer."

Greg stopped speaking and looked at Louie with a surprised expression. In fact, the whole table looked at Louie and snickered. "I haven't heard that expression since, oh I don't know, before I was born."

"Okay, maybe I should say it sucks the way Tim treats you," Louie said.

"It sucks, no doubt about it. But what really sucks big time is that the suits take credit for our work. Tim and his squeeze at the time, little Mimi hotpants, took all the credit for the Burgerhut campaign. Acted like they created it," Greg said.

"And then when they stole the Governor's campaign, and started showing up in magazines as the Hoosier Wonderkids, poor old Paul got royally pissed and confronted Tim. No more Paul," Squared said.

"What happened to him?"

Greg shrugged. "I think he went back to Chicago, probably working at Burnett or DDB now."

"And then Tim got tired of Mimi and she ended up in our Cincinnati branch," Squared said.

There was some talk about the Cincy office and names Louie didn't recognize. Then the talk turned to something they all saw on YouTube. Louie tried to think of a way of steering the conversation back to Mimi, but there didn't seem to be a way to do it, without it seeming forced.

"Well we better get back," Nancy said.

"Let me get the check," Louie said.

"No, I'll get yours," Squared said.

They divvied up the check.

"Sucking up, in case he becomes boss?" Greg asked.

They got up to leave. Except Amanda.

"You coming?" Nancy asked.

"I'll catch up," Amanda said.

"Talk about a suck-up," Dennis said.

When they were alone Amanda looked at Louie for a few minutes.

"So, what's up, Amanda?"

"You're a liar."

Cut 25
Liar Liar

"I'm sorry," Louie said.

"You're a liar," she repeated.

"Yes I am."

She started to say something and then stopped. Louie took another sip of beer. It was warm and starting to go flat.

"I knew you weren't really applying for a job here."

"No, I'm not."

"You're not really an ECD either," she said.

"You are correct, sir," Louie said imitating Phil Hartman imitating Ed McMahon.

"Huh?"

"Nothing. I am not an ECD."

"In fact, you're not really in advertising at all, are you?"

"Nope."

"I knew it."

"You're very perceptive."

"Then who are you?"

"My name is Louie."

"That's the name you gave us when you sat down and began lying to us."

"It's the same name when I'm not lying."

"I'm leaving." She stood up.

"Okay."

"I'm telling all my friends what a fucking liar you are."

"Well, right now I'm doing neither."

"What do you…oh, I get it." She sat back down.

"Why did you lie?"

"I wanted you guys to talk to me and I thought if you thought I might be your next boss, it would help."

"Why did you want us to talk to you?"

"I wanted to find out stuff."

"Did you find out what you wanted to know?"

"I think."

"You a cop?"

"Not anymore. Well, sorta."

"How can you be a sorta cop? There's no such thing. Do you ever tell the truth?"

"I used to be a cop. Now I'm a private investigator."

"That's a good one. What's your name, Jim Rockford?" Amanda started to get up again.

"It's true." Louie showed her his license.

"What are you investigating?"

"Tim Ferman."

"Why?"

"I'm protecting someone he may be trying to hurt."

"Who?"

"I can't say."

"Does this have anything to do with Mimi's death?"

"I think it does. Did you like Mimi?"

"Oh God no. She was a slut."

"I see."

"She gives all women a bad name."

"Why do you think she was killed?"

"Don't know. Don't care."

"Well, I do."

"Say, you don't think Tim had anything to do with it."

"I'm not sure. But, right now, I'm leaning toward that theory."

"But why would he, I mean, what does he have to gain?"

"That's what I'm trying to find out."

She leaned back in her seat.

"Buy me a beer."

"Sure." Louie caught the waitress's eye and ordered two more beers. They sat in silence.

"Do me a favor," Amanda said as the waitress set down her beer.

"I'll try."

"If Tim killed Mimi, and quite frankly I wouldn't put it past the bastard..."

"Why?"

"Because he seems to be a man of no morals."

"Okay."

"Anyway, if he offed the bitch, it probably has something to do with the whole Burgerhut campaign."

"Why do you say that?"

"It's just a feeling I have. The whole agency is built on lies and maybe Mimi was killed to protect the agency or Tim or both."

"Maybe. I don't know."

"Also, I haven't heard from Paul in a while and I'm worried about him. We were buds. He used to email me even after he left the agency. I'm worried about him. Paul knows the truth. If Mimi were killed to shut her up, Paul would be next. Will you check it out and make sure he's alright."

"My first priority is my client. But, I promise, once I've assured her safety, I'll do what I can for Paul."

"How do I know you're not lying again?"

"I guess you don't. But I wouldn't lie about something like this."

"Okay."

"Could you give me Paul's address?"

"I can give the last address I have. But, as I say, I haven't heard from him in a while."

She wrote down an address on a napkin. Louie put it in his coat pocket.

"Paul got a pretty good severance package from Tim. So he was living at an old farmhouse near Anderson and doing freelance work on websites," she said.

"Amanda, thanks for everything." Louie got up to leave.

"Where are you going?"

"To try and find Tim."

"I don't know if I believe you or not. But, whatever," she said.

"I just have one more question," Louie said.

"No, I won't meet you later for coffee."

"That wasn't the question."

"I won't meet you for a drink."

"I'm not hitting on you, Amanda."

"Okay what's the question?"

"Why is Squared called Squared?"

Amanda laughed. "Because his name is Robert Rawlson."

Louie shrugged.

"You don't get it?"

"No."

"Some detective you are."

"Amanda, I'm lost on this one."

"Robert Rawlson. Initials RR. Get it now?"

"No."

Amanda sighed theatrically. "RR as in R times R. R to the second power. R squared. Squared."

"Oh, I get it now."

"As Charlie Sheen would say, well, duh." Amanda made an exaggerated slack-jawed face. "You see, that's how I knew you weren't a creative."

"How?"

"You're too damn dumb."

Cut 26

What Kind of Fool Do You Think I Am

Sloopy was restless. The house seemed empty without Louie. She felt a little vulnerable. Exposed. Just sitting around waiting for something to happen. She didn't want to call him on her cell. That felt so needy somehow.

She tried to read a magazine. But found herself staring at the page and the words weren't registering. She put the magazine down and used the remote to turn on the TV. She wasn't in the mood for Oprah or Martha or Ellen. She zapped through the channels. Nothing seemed interesting.

She turned off the TV. And closed her eyes. She must've dozed because the quality of the light was different when her eyes opened.

Something wasn't right. She scanned the room. What was it? She scanned the room again, more slowly. There. She saw it. Shadow movement at the window. Was it just the wind blowing some tree branches or something else?

Her heart did a tom-tom in her chest. She took a deep breath and stood. There it was again. A shadow moving. She walked over to the window and looked out. Nothing. She looked as far right as she could and then left. Still nothing.

A sound on the front porch. She walked down the hall toward the door. By the hall closet was an umbrella stand. Her father had given her a hand carved walking stick which had been passed down to him from his grandfather. It was fashioned from a single piece of black walnut. She pulled it out and gripped it like a baseball bat.

She stepped up to the front door and looked out the peep-hole. Didn't see anything. She turned the deadbolt and opened the door. There was no one on the porch or the sidewalk in front.

But there was a package. An unmarked package, sitting on her welcome mat. She stepped out onto the porch but didn't see anything. A car slowly passed on the street in front of the house. The windows were tinted, so it was impossible to see the driver. The car drove out of sight.

She didn't want to pick up the package. Didn't want to open it without Louie. She left it and walked back inside. Just before shutting the door, she thought the bushes at the side of the porch rustled.

She almost opened the door again, but decided against it.

Getting antsy. Had to get out of the house. She went to the kitchen to get her purse and keys. Went back to the front room. Opened the door and picked up the package. Put the package on the kitchen table. Keeping a firm grip on the walnut stick, she walked into the garage.

Before getting into the car, she stopped again and listened. Didn't hear anything, so she opened the driver's door, got inside and hit the button that locked all the doors.

Tapped the garage door opener, started the car and backed out.

In the street she put the car in drive and drove toward town. She didn't see the van parked three houses behind her.

She didn't see it pull out to follow. Not being a professional, she wasn't used to looking for tails. However, she caught a glimpse of it in her rear view mirror once she turned the corner. However, the van was too far back to see the driver.

It was driven by The Man with the Lightbulb Head.

He was in disguise. He had a baseball cap on his head, Ray Ban sunglasses and a fake mustache and goatee. He followed the woman he knew as Susan Ferman, now Susan Petrie, for more than two hours.

That woman!

First, she went to the grocery store. Fine. People need to eat. And then a second grocery store. And then! The butcher, the baker and, well not the candlestick maker, but a health food store and *then* a candle shop. She bought one thing here, two things there, one or two things every goddamn where. Hadn't the woman ever heard of one-stop shopping? Did the idea of efficiency ever occur to her? The price of gas was outrageous, not that she seemed to mind. Was her life really so much better getting everything just so puking perfect by going from store to store?

Madness! But wait! We can't forget the coffee shop can we now, little bitch? A place for people with no taste to think they're actually doing something gourmet. She ordered some so-called coffee concoction with caramel, cinnamon and for God's sake! whipped cream sprinkled with shaved chocolate, topped off by a little chit-chat with some overweight bimbettes.

The conversation! Could any three people possibly use more words to say absolutely nothing?

Susan then bought a half-pound of some roast or another. God forbid she'd buy enough for a week or two. Oh man, the man felt like his poor old weird-looking head were going to explode. He wanted to grab her on the street and filet her right there.

But no, he would keep it under control. The heat was making his mustache and goatee itch. And she was making it so hard to remain inconspicuous with her fluttering to and fro. A quarter pound of this, a half pound of that—he couldn't wait to get her alone. He would make her death so slow. He would repay her for this day.

But at least it was comfortable here in the coffee shop. The air conditioning eased the itchiness of his fake facial hair. And the iced tea was quite good.

He thought, he couldn't snatch the snatch—he had such a way with words!—until she opened the last package. The one with the little surprise in it. The one she took inside and set on her kitchen table. So, he would follow her, until she went back home, just to make sure she saw what was in the package. But it had to be today. And if she didn't go home he would grab her anyway.

Just as he was about to get comfortable in the coffee shop, just as he was getting used to all the verbal pollution from the three women, Susan was up again. So, now he would have to throw away the tea he had just bought and follow her. Again.

Well, maybe another sip or two of tea. He couldn't walk out at the same time she did. One minute, two minutes, then it was time to get up and follow her. He sauntered to the door. As he hit the sidewalk, he looked right and then left. There she was. And then, horror of horrors! She was walking into a greeting card shop. No way. Wasn't gonna do it. He was not loitering inside or in front of the damn card shop for hours on end.

He got in the car and started the engine. The stupid bitch wasn't leaving town. She had groceries. Groceries that needed refrigerated. He would wait for her at her house.

Cut 27

Keep a Knockin' But You Can't Come In

Sloopy had finished shopping.

Should she go home? It was probably safe. Even though she had received a package this morning, whoever had delivered it would be long gone.

She didn't want to go home right away, but she didn't know what else to do. Besides, if she kept the groceries out too long, some of the meat might spoil. She had a paperback Janet Evanovich she was halfway through. There was a park northeast of town. She thought of going out to her favorite place, a couple of benches that faced a little wooded area in the park but then thought better of it. It was just too damn hot.

Instead she would go home and draw a bath, spike it with some mint bath salts, and spend a couple hours turning into a prune, while she soaked away some tension and got lost in the world of Plum.

At home, she thought she recognized a van at the end of the block, but after putting away the groceries, she looked out several windows and didn't see anything to arouse suspicion.

She went outside and walked around the house. Nothing out of the ordinary. The van at the end of the block was no longer there.

She went upstairs and started the bath. It was a Jacuzzi built for two, so she rarely used it, instead using the regular tub in the guest bedroom or the shower. A big boom box in the guest bedroom had a three CD changer on top. She filled it with Leonard

Cohen CDs then slipped out of her clothes and took a look at herself in the mirror. Not an ounce more than she weighed in high school. Not too much sag. She still had it.

She wasn't in the tub more that five minutes when the doorbell rang.

Wouldn't you know it?

Maybe she would just let whoever it was think she wasn't home and he or she would go away.

The doorbell rang again. Then, knock, knock, knock. Then, the doorbell again. Would the person ever go away? Probably not.

She got out of the tub and put on a terry cloth robe. Should she get dressed? She kind of felt like she was in a porn movie answering the door naked except for the robe. The person at the door would be the plumber and she would say she needed her pipes cleaned.

Not good.

So she pulled on jeans and a sweatshirt and went downstairs. Maybe whoever was at the door was gone now and she could return to her tub and book.

No such luck.

She looked out the peephole and saw the face of the man standing on the porch. She backed up and shivered. Why wasn't Louie here when she needed him? Should she call the police? Should she run to the car and just leave? She decided to call the police. Hopefully they would get here before the man did something drastic.

The doorbell rang again.

She didn't have a gun, but there was a big butcher knife that could do serious damage if she got close enough to the man. As she was walking to the kitchen, she dialed 911. The operator answered as she was rummaging through the drawer where she kept the knives.

"How may I help you?"

"Could you send a police unit over to 308 Edgeway Drive?

There's a man outside my house, at the front door, and I think he wants to hurt me."

Sloopy found the knife just as she heard a big thump on the back door that led to the kitchen.

"He's no longer at the front door, he's at the back door and he's just about to break in. Please hurry, there's not much time."

Cut 28
Needles and Pins

The Man with the Lightbulb Head had been watching Susan Petrie's house with needles in his butt for an hour when she came home. He had checked out the place when he first got there from downtown Tivoli and found the package he had delivered to her still unopened. It was still on the table in the kitchen.

He went back to the van. He couldn't just park on the street for any length of time and not expect to arouse suspicion from the neighbors. So he parked another block away. He had magnetic signs on the side of the van to make it look like a package delivery service.

He checked the rearview mirror. With the baseball cap, large sunglasses and collar of his golf shirt turned up, he looked passable, almost human.

He decided to walk. Not only could he keep an eye on Susan's house, he could check out the surrounding area for alternate getaway routes, hiding places and nosy neighbors.

He circled the block twice and walked up and down the alley behind her house and discovered some interesting things. First, it seemed there were hardly any neighbors around today. Secondly, it seemed that people pretty much kept to themselves in this neighborhood.

He found a couple hiding places protected by shrubs, trees or fences that provided good cover if he needed or wanted to spy on her house from someplace other than his van.

He also found a way to slip into her backyard without being seen from the street or by her neighbors.

He went back to his van and got a clipboard in case he was spotted again wandering around the neighborhood. He made one more tour of the neighborhood—you can't be too careful—and ducked under the neighbor's shrubs and hid in a tiny clearing in a copse of balsam pines.

It was a well-hidden area but he couldn't crouch forever and no matter how carefully he sat down, pine needles would eventually work their way into his buttocks and upper thighs. The heat was a hurting thing, causing even more irritation from the needles and the baseball hat on his head.

After an hour of watching the house he decided to make his move. Whether she opened the box or not, he would get her.

That's when the police car pulled up to her house.

He figured it was time to scoot. But just as he was coming out from underneath the hedges into the alley, another cop car pulled in.

"Stop, right there," the cop said.

No use running. It was so undignified.

He turned around and saw there were two cops, one with his gun drawn.

"Mister City Policeman sitting, pretty little policemen in a row," said The Man with the Lightbulb Head.

"What's your name?" Joe Sizelove asked.

"I am the Eggman, coo-coo-ca-joob," The Man with the Lightbulb Head said. "I see by your nametag you name is Sizelove. So what is it?"

"What is what?"

"Your size, love?"

At that Joe Sizelove had The Man with the Lightbulb Head assume the position to be patted down.

Cut 29
So What!

"Now Tony, what in the hell do you think you're doing?" Police Chief Elliott Blake asked.

"I came to apologize."

"Apologize for what?" Susan's cell phone buzzed. She walked into the living-room to answer it.

As she was talking, Elliott got a call on his walkie-talkie.

Because she was talking on her cell, she couldn't quite understand what was being said in the other room. When she hung up with Louie, she walked back in and both men were looking at her.

The police chief hooked his thumbs on his gun belt and pushed down. It made a crackling noise. "Who was that?"

"Nobody."

He looked at her with the cop stare and a half smile on his face.

"A relative who wants to come and visit." Why did she say that? She didn't owe him an explanation. She made a mental note to not volunteer any more information.

"Are you sure it was a relative and not some boyfriend or another?"

"I'm sure. It's really none of your affair. Could we continue, please?"

"No Susan, it ain't my affair." He stressed the word affair, but she didn't react. "Well, there seems to be quite a ruckus in the neighborhood today. My boys just found another person, another man, sneaking around the hedges in your neighbor's backyard."

"What was he doing there?"

"I don't know. He was nuts or queer or something. Hell, there ain't no crime in being nuts. Or homo. Least not anymore. And it ain't the man we're looking for, 'cuz he's right here. So I told 'em to cut him loose. Which brings us to you." The cop turned back to Tony.

"As I said, I came to apologize," Tony said.

"You have a funny way of apologizing, scaring the lady half out of her wits."

"I didn't intend to scare her. When she wouldn't answer the front door, I went to the kitchen door."

"Well if she didn't answer the front door, why'd you think she'd want to answer the back door?"

"I don't know, I wasn't thinking, I guess."

"Have you been drinking?"

"No, I haven't. Not today. No. Not at all."

"If I was to give you a breathalyzer, would you pass it?"

"Sure, I think so. I mean, yes, of course."

Elliott stared long and hard at Tony Ferman.

"Boy, you're as jumpy as an ice cube on a hot skillet. Are you sure you ain't hiding anything?"

"Nope, everything I told you is solid."

"Okay, since you're this woman's former husband's brother—man ain't that a mouthful—you're practically relations, so I guess that gives you some points. But I still wonder what you're doing here."

"As I said twice now, apologizing." Tony looked at Sloopy and raised his eyebrows.

"For what? Being a dumbass who rings her doorbell all the time?"

"That's between me and her."

"Now son, the minute I arrived, it suddenly became something between you and me and her. It became what I like to call a three-way."

Sloopy hated the snarky smile Elliott had when he said that.

"Now, I can haul you in right now for let's see, trespassing, disturbing the peace, stalking, and lewd behavior."

"I didn't do anything lewd."

"Don't interrupt. Plus resisting arrest. Which would put you in a world of, let us say trouble, believe you me. Because to make that charge stick, I'd have to make it look authentic and to make it look authentic, I'd have to bang you around a little bit."

"Now, Elliott, that's enough," Sloopy said.

"Why, now Susan, don't get all high and mighty. You called me, remember?"

"I made a mistake." She looked over at Tony and gave him a slight nod. "Didn't I, Tony?"

"Yes."

"So what was he here apologizing for?" The cop gave Tony a long stare and then turned to Sloopy.

Sloopy hesitated.

"I, uh, came over…"

"A week late. He was supposed to bring me some paperwork I needed for an accounting thing, and I had to postpone a meeting because he was late. I blew up at him. It was silly I guess." Sloopy shrugged.

"Paperwork."

"Yeah, some divorce things his brother gave him to give me."

Elliott smiled. "It's not that I don't believe you, but I don't."

"Thank you for dropping by, Elliott. I'm sorry I involved the police in this. Sometimes I'm just a bit skittish with what's happened and all."

The cop looked around the foyer and then at Tony. He strolled into the kitchen and scanned the family room. He stopped when his eyes came upon the package, but he didn't say anything.

"Okay, I'll leave now."

Sloopy wanted to ask if he knew anything more about the packages she had given him, but since he didn't bring it up, she didn't ask. Something told her she shouldn't say anything in front of Tony.

After Elliott left, she turned to her former brother-in-law

and put her hands on her hips. "You can leave now too, Tony."

"But, Susan, I did want to apologize for the other day."

"Please leave."

"I didn't intend to hurt you, it's just when I saw you with Louie, I, well I always wanted you and Tim to get back together."

"You were drunk and you hurt my arm."

"I didn't mean to."

"Look, Tim and I are over. So it's none of your business if I see anyone else."

"I know, I'm sorry."

"Please leave and please stay out of my life."

"I truly am sorry."

"Prove it to me by leaving me alone."

Tim opened his mouth to say something else and then closed it again. He walked out the front door and quietly shut it.

Sloopy walked up the stairs. Her bath was ice cold.

Tony Ferman had blown it. He felt awful walking to his car.

Susan was afraid of him. And he hadn't helped himself today.

Today, he hadn't been drunk, but he had been drunk, rip-roaring drunk, when he went to see Susan the other day. He had scared her. He had hurt her by gripping her arm too tight. He had done everything wrong.

He knew of his brother's problems with the booze. He knew of the blackouts, the hookers, the sadism. He hoped and prayed Susan would be the help his brother needed. Tony and his mother loved Susan. She was smart, kind, and beautiful, both inside and out.

Yeah, Tony Ferman had blown it.

He knew that now. He knew that he had ruined any chance of Susan and his brother getting back together, not that there was much of a chance anyhow. He was never told the official reason, but he was sure Susan had discovered Tim's odd appetites. He was sure she couldn't stomach the person his brother could become.

He should never have gone to her house on Thursday. It was

just that when he saw her with that Louie Louie clown, something snapped inside.

He should never have come to her house today. He just wanted a chance to explain himself. Fat lotta good that did. Tony sat in his car and stared out the window. Was there anything he could do to salvage the situation? Probably not. It was beyond repair.

Tony Ferman had blown it.

He had gotten into his car without checking the back.

He turned the key on his ignition, but before he was able to put the car in gear, The Man with the Lighbulb head rose up from the back seat.

Tony Ferman blew it.

He should have ducked his head and pulled the door handle at the very moment he saw the weird-looking man in his rear-view mirror. He might have had a chance.

"Who are..." But before Tony was able to finish the sentence The Man with the Lightbulb Head struck with a ball-peen hammer, sending bits of Tony's skull into his brain.

Tony opened and closed his mouth twice, blinked once and then a long string of drool ran from the right corner of his mouth to his lap as his eyes rolled around crazily. Then stopped.

The Man with the Lightbulb Head let go of the hammer. It remained embedded in Tony's head. He pushed Tony's left shoulder and the dead man slowly fell to his side.

The Man with the Lightbulb Head took out a handkerchief and wiped the gray stuff off his face. Susan Petrie would be next, as soon as she opened that package.

Cut 30
Fight Fire

"Exile on Main Street" by the Rolling Stones blasted through Louie's iPod. It was the third time through what was, in the days of vinyl, a double album. Louie could listen to it three more times and not grow tired of it. It was garage rock long after garage rock supposedly died. To Louie, you just couldn't beat that grungy, sloppily-recorded rock 'n roll. Half past four and Tim still hadn't shown up for work. Louie's neck was sore. Legs were sore. Back felt like it had been kicked.

It was highly unlikely Ferman would show up this late for work, so Louie took out the ear buds, started the car and drove toward Zionsville once again.

Ferman wasn't home. Once again, Louie resisted the urge to disable the alarm and break into the place.

He decided to find a cheap motel and take up the stakeout again the next day. Just as Louie was pulling out of the driveway, his cell phone rang. According to the digital readout it was Carson.

Louie flipped open the cell.

"Commissioner Gordon here." Carson's voice had an eerie, tinny quality to it.

"What's up, Comish?"

"Big news in Gotham City."

"Have to give it to me over the phone, bro."

There was that special silence that means the person hasn't hung up.

"Go to a pay phone."

"Is that really necessary?"

"Dude, a pay phone."

"Okay."

Finding a pay phone in the cell phone millennium was not easy. Louie went to filling stations, convenience stores, fast food joints, until finally he found one in the lobby of an office building near Keystone at the Crossing, an upscale shopping mall on the outskirts of Indianapolis.

Louie dialed Carson's cell phone. Carson answered on the second ring and gave out another telephone number to dial.

"Danger Will Robison," Carson said when he answered the phone.

"Hey, Carson."

"Another one bites the dust."

"What do you mean?"

"I mean another person reported getting animal parts and now he's dead."

"Who was it?"

"Stuart Brown."

"Who is?"

"A guy that lives in Cincinnati who just happened to work for, are you ready? Stuart/Brown Branded Entertainment which, as you remember was a sister company to Wild Imagination Advertising and also the parent company to Flicker Advertising."

"Which is where Mimi worked before she died."

"Yes indeedy, kemo-sabe."

"Well, that is interesting."

"His house burned down."

"What did you say?"

"His three-quarter of a million dollar home is now a big pile of charcoal."

"But, you told me he was murdered."

"He was and then his house burned down."

"That's a new twist."

"Yes it is. The cops almost didn't figure out he was murdered. The killer was pretty clever."

"How's that?"

"Well, he probably caused a gas leak by cutting a pipe or blowing out a pilot light or something and then ka-blooey."

"So all the evidence would be destroyed. Like the body."

"Right."

"So what did our killer do wrong?"

"Well, even though he was clever, he was no demolition expert."

"So?"

"Stuart had a sheet of one-inch plywood between his bedsprings and mattress. Probably had back problems. Whoever blew up Stuart's house, cut ol' Stuey up into chunks on top of the bed. When the house exploded, instead of the bed and Stu disintegrating, the plywood acted as some sort of blast shield so chunks of Stu meat, well done mind you, rained down on the street outside. They could tell that Stuart had been cut up before he was blown up."

"Wow."

"Wow is right. And you and I and the police are the only ones who know it. For now they're still treating it as death by smoke inhalation and not releasing the details to the press."

"Anything else?"

"Isn't that enough?"

"Of course. Thank you."

"However, our man Carson may have something else you'll find interesting."

"What's that?"

"Mimi and Stuart were doing the horizontal bop."

"Before or after she and Tim?"

"Before."

"Curiouser and curioser."

"That's probably why Stuie moved to Cincy and started his

own shop. Timmy boy wanted him out of the way."

"Carson, you've done good."

"Thank you O Louie of the tiny brain."

"You're quite welcome. How's your head doing?"

"Not tingling anymore."

"Good to hear. Oh, tell me about the animal parts the guy received."

"Oh yeah. Just that he received eyeballs and ball balls, ears and paws and all sorts of stuff for about four months before he was killed. Again, Cincinnati Police didn't know about Mimi and vice versa. So there was no connection drawn."

"Were they always animal?"

"Animal, what?"

"Stay with me, Carson. Animal parts."

"Yea, cows, pigs, raccoons and dogs. Stuff like that."

"Any humans?"

"Huh?"

"Any human parts?"

"Not that I know of. But I don't think he reported everything."

"What do you mean?"

"Well, the last month or so, he made no reports to the police about receiving any packages."

"Do you think the packages stopped?"

"I think he just stopped telling the police about them."

"Why do you say that?"

"Just a feeling. I think the cops were starting to view it as an elaborate prank of some sort and Stuart got tired of calling them. Or, maybe Stuart thought it was a prank too. Who knows? I could be wrong."

"It makes sense to me. You're probably right. Is there any pattern to this?"

"What do you mean?"

"Did it go from cow to pig to whatever before the murder? Or, from head to toe? Or, I don't know, any pattern to when or how the packages arrived? Something that would give us an indication when the mad butcher was going to strike."

"I don't know. Let me see if something emerges as I run some comparison programs. Keep in mind I haven't tapped into Stuart's email. I'm sure I'll find out more stuff when I do."

"I bet you do. But Carson, you have to hurry. I feel I'm running out of time."

"Why do you say that?"

"Because we now are fairly certain that whoever receives the packages ends up dead."

"I hear you."

"Now I've got a really tough decision. I'm convinced Tim Ferman is doing these things. Do I stay here until he comes back and try and stop him? Take the offensive, so to speak. Or, do I go back to Tivoli and protect Sloopy? Just sort of wait around and see if I can stop whatever's about to happen."

"You've always been a rather offensive sonovabitch."

"I love you too, Carson."

"You've decided already."

"Yes I have. However, if I've made the wrong decision, the only woman I've ever loved may die."

After Louie disconnected from Carson, he called Sloopy. "Hey, how are you doing?"

"I'd be better if you were here."

"What's going on?"

"Oh, the chief of police and a man who has been stalking me are here with me right now and we're having a little discussion."

"What?"

"I'll tell you about it later."

"Tell me now."

"I can't."

"Have you received any more packages?"

"We'll talk later."

"Sloopy, what's going on?"

"Nothing. It's getting handled."

"But..."

"We'll talk later. When you get here."

"Well that's what I was calling about, I want to follow up on something and I may not be there until tomorrow."

"Well, okay then, I'll see you tomorrow."

"But if you need me, I can come home, I mean to your home. If I leave now, I'll be there in an hour and a half."

"No, tomorrow is fine."

"Are you sure?"

"I really can't talk now."

And the line went dead. Louie tried to call back and got Sloopy's voice mail. He left a massage asking her to call back right away.

An hour later Louie had checked into a Drury Inn and began staking out Ferman's home.

Louie was getting anxious. He tried to call Sloopy several more times and couldn't get through. He was just about ready to give up and race home to her when a car pulled into Tim Ferman's driveway. It was a black Lexus.

From Louie's vantage point it looked like there was just a single driver, a male.

Louie started his car and peeled out, covering the three hundred yards to Ferman's drive in seconds. Louie fishtailed around the turn to his lane. Because Ferman was taking it slow and easy Louie was nudging Ferman's rear bumper before the Lexus made it to the garage.

Ferman stopped the car and was out of the driver's side before Louie could even put his in park.

He was wearing an expensive suit that, Louie noted, was surprisingly wrinkled.

As Ferman approached the car, Louie rolled down the window. That was the bait. Ferman took it and came over to the driver's side screaming at the top of his lungs.

"What the hell do you think..."

But Ferman never finished the sentence. Before he could get

all the words out, Louie doored the irate ad man. Tim doubled over and fell on his ass.

Just to make sure he had his attention, Louie bent over and slapped Ferman's ears, right-left, right-left. Not enough to burst eardrums, but enough to sting and give a very unpleasant buzz.

Louie grabbed the lapels of Ferman's suit, pulled him up and then kneed him in the stomach.

"We have to talk, asshole."

Cut 31

Goin' Outta My Head

"Louie, what do you want?" Tim Ferman had to turn his neck at an uncomfortable angle to talk.

"Let's go inside."

"I don't know what you think you're doing."

"Inside." Louie gave Ferman a shove.

They walked to the side door. Louie's left hand was holding the back of Ferman's suit collar, Louie's right hand was bending Ferman's right arm up behind his back. They walked through what Louie used to call a mudroom, into Ferman's kitchen. Louie let go of Ferman's suit jacket and gave him another push. Ferman had to put both hands on a wooden chopping block island to catch his balance. The chopping block was barely big enough to dress a steer.

"Look, Sloopy and I are over. You can have her. I know you've always wanted her." Ferman still had his back still to the Indiana detective.

"Turn around, very slowly," Louie said.

Ferman turned and the two men were face to face. There were some brown stains that looked like blood splatters on the front of Ferman's white shirt.

Louie looked around. With a couple of hoops the kitchen could have accommodated a full-court basketball game and still had room for spectators. The room was filled with black granite and brass fixtures against hand-painted white tiles. Everything else was shiny white enamel. The refrigerator-freezer was big enough to hold two bodies and a couple jars of pickles. It had, of course, brass handles and a black slate front you could write on in chalk. Next to the chopping block, another island with a knife set on it. Louie grabbed a meat cleaver.

Ferman put his hands up in a calming gesture. "Let's go into the study, have a drink and talk this over calmly."

"Lead the way."

Louie followed Ferman through a living room done in shades of cream, then through a big entertainment room into a study with French doors and wall-to-wall bookcases. Unlike many rich people Louie knew, the library didn't have many knick-knacks and paddywacks, but was actually filled floor-to-ceiling with books.

This was a room done in light oak and forest green. Four comfortable looking club chairs sat in front of the desk with a low, round coffee table in the center. Ferman took one of the chairs. Louie sat directly across from him.

"What have you been up to, Tim?"

"When?"

"Oh let's start with yesterday."

"I honestly don't know."

"I don't like that story, Tim. You can do better than that. Make up something and sell it to me. That's what you're good at. You're a bona fide advertising hero."

"I'm telling the truth."

Louie studied the ad man's face. Ferman didn't have any of the tells Louie recognized from liars. When he was a cop, Louie had interrogated many people, most of them liars, and had developed a pretty good instinct whether someone was lying or not. Ferman wasn't, or was the best liar Louie had ever met.

Louie didn't have the stomach for torture. Never had. Also, a long time ago he had met an old FBI agent who had tortured many people back before it became national policy. The G-man revealed something interesting.

Torture doesn't work.

Once you've beaten a man to the point of giving up stuff, he'll tell you anything he thinks you want to hear, just to get you to stop. So the information you've gathered may or may not be true. Most of the time it isn't.

Something in Louie wanted to beat the hell out of Tim. But Louie didn't think it was the right emotion. It would satisfy something mean inside. Something deep. Something that should stay inside and never be let out. It wouldn't produce anything useful. So, Louie discarded the idea.

"You want to smack me around, don't you?"

How did he know?

"Yes," Louie said.

"I can't say I don't blame you. But, I'm telling you the truth."

"I hope you are. Explain to me why you don't know what you did yesterday."

Ferman shrugged his shoulders. "I just don't."

"Why?"

"Because I have blackouts. I drink and then I don't remember what happens. It's all gone. Poof. My dad had them too. The blackouts. It's why Sloopy and I broke up."

That jibed with what Louie knew.

"So you drank and blacked out yesterday."

"Yes."

"How did you get that blood on your shirt?"

"I don't know. I started drinking here in the library and then I woke up in Cincinnati."

"That's where you killed Stuart Brown."

Ferman flinched as if he had been slapped in the face.

"Stuart's dead?"

Louie could tell Ferman didn't know.

"Yes."

"Oh God no." The ad man buried his head in his hands. He lifted his head "This has got to stop."

"What?"

"The killing."

"I agree. What do you know about it?"

"Nothing. I don't know anything."

"Then why did you say it had to stop?"

"Because it does. It's awful. People I know are getting killed. I'm sure it has something to do with me somehow."

"I thought the very same thing."

"But what? What's going on?" He clenched his fists and pounded on the desk to punctuate each word.

"You really don't know."

"I don't."

He was telling the truth.

Louie still wanted to rip him apart.

"I need a drink." Ferman looked down at his desk.

"That's always the start of your troubles, isn't it?"

"Yeah, I guess you're right."

"So what happens when you black out?"

"What do you mean?"

"You know what I mean."

"I drink. I black out. I wake up somewhere else. And the only thing I remember is that second drink. It's always the second drink. That glorious second drink. I may drink a half a bottle, but I remember that second drink. It's the one that starts slow and civilized and then..." Ferman stopped talking and stared out the window for what seemed like minutes. "I begin with a sip and end with a guzzle. If only I could stop after that second drink, that sweet, sweet second drink. I'm not an alcoholic, you know. I am not. Really. At a party or a dinner I can have a glass of wine, a martini." Ferman stopped again.

"But," Louie prompted.

"But, sometimes, I have to be alone and drink. It's not an addiction thing. It's. You know, I've never really put it in words. It's a need. Because I never feel the way I do with a woman like I do when I'm... The second drink is magic. It's power. It makes me a man."

"I'm not sure I follow."

"We Ferman men have a *crazy* gene. Some of us do anyhow.

My brother doesn't seem to have it. I've often wondered if we were the children of Cain or are infected with the demons of Lillith. You see, we aren't homo or anything, but women really don't do it for us. Not in the regular way."

"You're impotent."

"Far from it. It's just the only satisfaction we get comes from a bottle and a woman, a paid woman, or two women. One night I had seven women in succession."

"How do you know?"

"I hired someone to follow me. To report on what I did. A private investigator like yourself. He followed me and took pictures and notes." Ferman laughed a mirthless laugh. "Boy, did that cost me."

"What do you mean?"

"He's been blackmailing me for years. The sonovabitch."

"Does that have anything to do with the bloodspots—those are bloodspots, aren't they?—on your shirt?"

"Probably. I mean, I don't know for sure, but my guess would be yes."

"Why?"

"I could really use a drink now."

"Not now. In a minute. Explain the blood."

"The blood comes from women."

"Which women?"

"Women. Always women. Different women. Only women bleed, as the song goes." Ferman sighed heavily. He shook his head violently, like he was trying to dislodge something.

"As I said women and booze are two parts of the equation. But there's something else. Something else I need. Something to unleash the demons, to get the fires burning. To make me a man."

"What's that?"

"Violence. Hurt. My only true satisfaction as a man comes when I'm slapping a woman around. It's something I can't control. Maybe that's why I only use hookers. I'm still enough of a human to not want to hurt someone I love. But I can't really make love to anyone I love."

"You're sick."

"Don't I know it!"

"Have you tried getting professional help?"

"I've spent tens of thousands of dollars with psychiatrists and therapists of every stripe. They all want to go back to my childhood. To find out if my daddy beat me or Mommy breast fed me too long, or not enough. None of that happened. I had a great childhood. It's something deeper. My dad tried to explain it to me. It's a demon in my blood. A crack in my DNA strand. I don't know. Believe me I've paid for my affliction in so many ways."

"What do you mean?"

"Well just the money alone. The shrinks. The blackmail. And every time I go on one of my little midnight jaunts, I try to make sure the woman or women are taken care of. I give them money, So much money. I pay for dental work and hospital bills. I give them money to keep quiet.

"And my personal life is a mess. I know I can't ever be with a woman in the normal way. I found that out with Susan. I also know the madness stops with me. I have made sure I will never have children. It all stops with me. Can I have that drink now?"

"Sure. But only one. I could use one too."

"I have an excellent scotch in my desk drawer."

"Pour us a couple."

That was when Tim Ferman unleashed the darkness.

Ferman got up and walked toward the desk. He sat at the big leather chair behind the desk and opened the lower left hand drawer. He pulled out a brand new bottle of 30-year-old Talisker and two cut crystal lowball glasses.

"Ice? Soda?"

"Not with 30-year-old single malt."

"Good man."

He poured about three fingers in each glass and sat back in his chair. Louie picked up a glass and sat back down. Took a drink. It was golden honey, peat, spices and a mellow warming fire. It was the best whiskey Louie had ever tasted. When he looked up, Louie realized it could be the last. Ferman was pointing the Colt .45 at his forehead.

Oops.

Louie felt more stupid than a box of rocks, and that was an insult to rocks. In every old detective movie he had ever seen, when a bad guy goes to his desk, there's usually a gun in the top drawer. As Amanda had said, well duh. He was about to be killed by a cliché. A worn-out cliché. Which didn't make it, unfortunately, any less deadly. A drop of sweat ran down the side of his face, from scalp to chin.

"You know, I know you have a thing against guns. They say guns don't kill people, people kill people. I never quite understood that one. Lotsa things kill people. Including people. So, are you anti-gun or what?"

"Not really, I just don't think cops should carry them. I wanted to arm the Tivoli police with tasers. Be able to put a man down without killing him. The town didn't agree," Louie said.

"But you're not carrying."

"No."

"Well, you see the advantage I have by having a gun?" Ferman waved the gun around in an erratic pattern. "Your principles may cost you your life."

"What happens now?" Louie asked.

"Well, why don't we drink and talk and then end this thing."

"Tell me about the animals."

"I had nothing to do with the animals. I don't know anything about animals. I don't even have a dog. I hate animals."

"I thought you mentioned you knew about it. In fact, I'm sure you did."

"Oh you mean the animal parts that came in the mail and FedEx and sometimes just appeared on the doorstep? You must learn to be specific."

"You knew what I was talking about."

"I don't know a thing."

Louie started to stand up. He wanted to slap that smirk off Ferman's face.

"Now, now, remember I've got the gun. Let's not be hasty."

Louie sat back down and took a sip of scotch.

"I really don't know a thing about the animal guts and whatnot. Although I think I'm involved somehow. I amend that. I know I'm involved somehow," Ferman said.

"What do you mean?"

"I got a letter a while back that said: 'Roses are red, violets are blue, you screwed me, now I'll screw you.' I didn't think much of it at the time."

"Why not?"

"Every once in awhile a person in a position of power gets a nasty note from a disgruntled employee or something. It's happened before to some of my friends."

"Can I see the note?"

"Nope."

"Why not?"

"I threw it away. It was from a laser printer you could find at any business, Kinkos or library in the world. I'm sure there were no clues on it."

"Why do you think it had something to do with the animal parts, then?"

"Because after Mimi died, I got another one that said: 'now you've seen the first screw turn, a few more and it's your time to burn' and then the night before last I got one that said, 'two down and one to go, and then it's you, enjoy the show.' I didn't even know what it was about, but I guess it was about poor Stuart."

"Can I have those other two notes?"

"Knock yourself out. They're in a hollowed out book on the shelf over there called "The Last Good Kiss." You can get it on your way out."

"Is our talk over?"

"I'm afraid it is."

Louie stood up and walked over to the bookcase against the

east wall. He had to turn his back on Ferman and felt the muscles between the shoulder blades tighten up. Louie stopped before pulling out the book. He wanted to ask Ferman if he knew Sloopy was getting the notes. Louie wanted to ask Ferman if he had any idea who was sending the notes, the animal parts and killing people. But Louie didn't. Before Louie could speak, Ferman raised the .45 and blew off his own head.

Oh crap.

Now what? Louie thought about calling the police, but quickly nixed that idea because he wanted to get back to Sloopy. Louie tried to think if he had left fingerprints anywhere. Probably on the chair and the lowball glass.

Louie went to the kitchen, soaped, rinsed and dried the glass. He took the moist dishtowel and wiped down everything he might have touched.

Back in the library Louie stood looking at what had once been Tim Ferman. Almost all of Ferman's head was completely blown off. There were bits of hair and brain matter all around the floor and on the desk. Ferman slumped to his left on his chair near a dark puddle of blood with bits of what Louie assumed were white teeth floating on top.

The bullet had gone into the ceiling; there was a blood splatter against the wall. Louie wondered if he should go through Tim's desk, but decided against it so as to not disturb the body. He doubted he would find anything. And, frankly, Louie was a little spooked. He wanted to leave as quickly as possible. The house was far enough away from its neighbors and the road, so Louie was sure nobody would have heard the shot.

Louie got the notes hidden in the hollowed out book, wiped the book down and got the hell out of there.

On the way back to Tivoli Louie received a call from Sloopy. She told him about Tony Ferman and how he had bruised her arm by squeezing too hard. She told Louie how Tony had been over that day to apologize and all that had happened later.

"Be careful because he might come back today or tonight."

"Why?"

"Something terrible has happened."

"What? What is it Louie?"

Louie didn't reply.

"What is it?"

"I'll tell you when I get there."

Louie was quiet for a moment. Should he tell her to leave the house? He would be there in a little under an hour.

Sloopy broke the silence. "Another package showed up on my porch today."

"What's in it?"

"I haven't opened it."

"Did you show it to Elliott?"

"No. There's something about him I don't trust anymore. I decided to wait for you."

"Good thinking. Listen Sloopy, other people have been receiving those packages and bad things have happened."

"What kind of bad things?"

"Really bad things. Look, I want you to pack a bag right now and go to Our Prom Place."

Our Prom Place was a little motel that should've gone out of business or turned into something seedy when the new highway was built. However, it was owned by an older biker couple who kept it neat as a pin and cleaner than a hospital.

It was actually called the Rest E-Z Motel. Sloopy and Louie went there after their senior prom. Somehow, Sloopy's father heard about it and was sitting in the room when they got there at 2 a.m. Sloopy's dad took her home and told Louie to stay in the room.

The old man came back at around four and they had a long, long talk. It wasn't one of the more pleasant moments in Louie's life. But Louie was straight with him about everything, including how far Sloopy and Louie had gone, Louie's plans for the future, and his plans for Sloopy.

"I like you Louie, but I swear to Christ, if you do anything to hurt my little girl, I will kill you, if it's the last thing I do," was the father's parting shot.

Sloopy didn't know what Louie meant. Surely, she remembered.

"You know, Our Prom Place," Louie repeated.

"Oh yeah. Now I got it. I will go there, but first tell me what's going on."

"Honestly, I don't know for sure. But everyone who's received the packages has ended up dead."

"Do you think Tim is doing this?"

"No, I don't. Look, I don't want to upset you too much now, but I don't want to keep anything from you. I wish you would've told me about Tony Ferman earlier, so, in fairness. I can't keep this thing about Tim from you."

"What thing?"

"I'd rather tell you when I get there."

"Has he been murdered too?"

"No. I'll tell you if you insist, but it's better to do it when I'm with you."

"Okay, Louie. I trust you."

"Good, I will feel much better if I know you're safe. Please go there tonight."

"I will. How long should I pack for?"

"One night, maybe two. When I get there we'll decide what to do. If you need anything else, we'll just buy it. I don't want you spending too much time packing, the more I think about it, the more I want you to get out of your house. And take the package with you."

"Okay. Louie, you know something? I think I'm falling back in love with you."

"I've never fallen out of love with you." But Louie was talking to dead air because Sloopy had already hung up.

Cut 32
Na Na Hey Hey Kiss Him Goodbye

The Man with the Lightbulb Head was tired of sitting in a car with a corpse. He decided to do something about it. He didn't have much of a plan, but still had to wait until dark to put the half-plan in order.

The strange-looking man got out of the Tony Ferman's car, then walked around the block to make sure he wasn't drawing any undue attention. He walked down the alley behind Susan's house, the alley where he almost got busted by the police. He walked from end to end to make sure everything was cool.

It was.

The Man with the Lightbulb Head used the bushes as cover and snuck into Susan's backyard. He went to each of her windows to see what was going on inside, to see if she had opened the package yet. He didn't see her or the package but that didn't mean anything because she had moved it after the cops came.

He would give her until nightfall to open the package, and then burst in and drag the bitch kicking and screaming to his playpen. There he would force her to open the package. Then the fun would begin.

It began getting dark. The Man with the Lightbulb Head was nervous about having Tony Ferman dead and rotting in front of Susan Petrie's place since the cops had told Tony to leave Susan alone.

The keys were still in the ignition, so The Man with the Lightbulb Head started Tony's car and drove it to a gravel pit east of town.

He drove around the pit two times to make sure it was deserted. The pit was surrounded on three sides by wooded areas and the fourth by a chain link fence. It was about a half a mile back from a country road, which made it impossible to see the pit from the road.

He drove to side of the pit furthest from the road and backed up as far as he could without running into the woods. He ripped off a piece of Tony's shirt not covered in blood and wiped down everything he thought he had touched. Then he used a branch of a tree that he had broken off to push the accelerator to the floor, popped the car into first and slammed the door as the car sped toward the edge of the pit.

It was about a twenty feet drop from the side of the pit to the water below. The car went over the side and then nosedived to the water. The Man with the Lightbulb Head watched the car hit and send up a wall of pit water. When the splash had calmed, he could see the trunk end of the car sticking out.

Damn. Wasn't deep enough. He dreaded the thought of having to find his way down the side of the gravel pit and the try to push the car over until is wasn't sticking out of the water.

He watched for several minutes. Slowly, the car started rolling over on its back. It stopped twice and he planned to climb down and give it a push, but finally it rolled all the way over with just part of the left rear tire sticking out of the water.

That would do. No one would see it from the road, and he just needed it to remain hidden one night. Maybe part of the next day.

It was a two-mile trek back to town, so The Man with the Lightbulb Head started walking around the pit to the front gate he had jimmied open with a tire tool.

This was getting to be way too much work. The Man with the Lightbulb Head was tired and frustrated.

Susan would pay.

Forty-seven minutes later, The Man with the Lightbulb Head was in the garage with crowbar in hand. If Susan came into the garage, he would crease her skull with the crowbar. It would deviate from his plans, but he was really aggravated and his feet hurt. It had been a long walk back from the gravel pit.

Susan opened the back door, stepped outside and made a tour of the yard.

Stupid bitch. What did she hope to accomplish?

She stopped at the area by the kitchen window he had just left. What was she doing? She ran the flashlight beam around. He gripped the crowbar tighter. Okay, enough was enough. He was just about ready to step out into her backyard and bash her skull in when she turned away and walked back inside.

She didn't realize how close she had come to a terminal migraine.

After he was satisfied she wasn't coming back outside, the Man with the Lightbulb Head went to work on her car. Yes, indeedy, he had some big surprises in store for her.

Inside the house, Sloopy tried to call Louie again. Again, no answer. Where was he? What was he doing?

She went to the refrigerator, grabbed a bottled water and sat on the couch. She tried Louie again. Left a message. Another two minutes passed. Louie had told her to go the motel. She had started to pack. Might as well finish up and get to the motel. She wished she could talk to Louie first. But maybe he wasn't near a cell tower. There were a lot of dark areas around Tivoli.

She finished her water and went to the kitchen to throw the bottle away. As she was walking toward the wastebasket that was under the kitchen sink, she thought she saw something move in the window behind the sink. She stopped. Her heart was kick-drumming in her chest. She crept to the sink and looked out the window. It was the soft gray blue of twilight. It took a moment for her eyes to adjust. She thought she caught another movement to the left.

Her eyes locked in on the left side of the yard. She scanned it inch by inch. Nothing. Her eyes swept the property. Nothing out-of-place that she could detect.

She opened the cabinet doors below the sink and deposited the empty water bottle. She looked around the yard again. She decided to grab a couple of waters from the fridge to take to the motel. But first, she wanted to check out the backyard. She went to the pantry to get a flashlight.

She went back to the sink and looked out the window one more time. Still, she couldn't see anything.

She stepped out the back door from the kitchen and flicked on the flashlight. She made a tour of the backyard but didn't see anyone or anything that was suspicious.

She shone the flashlight on the ground in front of the kitchen window. Did the shrubbery looked disturbed? Were those footprints in the mulch? Get hold of yourself, girl, it was nothing.

She walked back inside.

Sloopy put three bottles of water in her tote bag along with a couple of magazines and a bottle of red wine. She looked around the bedroom. Was there anything she had forgotten?

Nope.

She flipped open he cell phone and tried Louie again. Still, no answer.

She didn't leave a message.

Louie had wanted to get to the motel as soon as possible. She had probably taken longer than he wanted, but everything seemed okay. Maybe he was there waiting on her.

Sloopy went downstairs with the suitcase and tote bag. She thought for a second and then went upstairs and got the .38 revolver from the bedside table. She walked back downstairs and put it in her purse, thought better of it and put it in the suitcase and zipped it shut.

She was ready.

She double locked the front door then went around and locked all the windows. She locked the door to the basement. Sloopy again placed her hand over her mouth in thought. She went back upstairs to make sure all the windows were locked. They were.

She wasn't sure why she was worried so much about locking

up. She wasn't going to be here. Back downstairs, she made another tour of the house. Everything was locked tight. She found the extra garage door opener in a kitchen drawer and dropped it into the tote bag.

She went through the kitchen into the garage and locked the door. She grabbed the car keys off a little key holder by the door and pushed the button on the fob to open the trunk of her car. She put the tote and the suitcase in the trunk and slammed it shut.

She heard a sound. She stood motionless for a few minutes. It must have been a mouse. Or, something outside. Or, the neighbors.

She didn't realize she was holding her breath.

She pushed the button on the fob to unlock the car doors. She heard the beep of the doors unlocking. The headlights flashed. She pulled on the door handle. Nothing happened. Another tug. Nothing happened. She gripped her purse tighter. It was dark in the garage even with the light on. Did the car door look funny?

She hit the button on the fob again, heard the locks unlock and tugged at the door handle. Still nothing.

She walked in front of the car to the passenger side. The door wouldn't open. What was going on?

She walked back to the trunk and hit the button on the fob to release the lid. She wanted to get her gun.

As the lid came up she felt the cold steel of a surgeon's blade against her neck. "Oh, I don't think you'll be needing anything inside there."

The man pressed up against her back. The arm that didn't have her in a chokehold slammed the trunk.

"Miss Suzy, if you, excuzy, please. We're gonna go back inside and get a package and then off we go to a special, secret place where we're going to have some fun, fun, fun 'til this daddy chops your T-bone away. Goody, goody, off we go now." The Man with the Lightbulb Head giggled.

Cut 33
Tell Me

Carson called to say he had figured out a pattern.

Of course it took a while to get to the meat of the conversation. When Louie answered the phone Carson said, "Good evening, Mr. Phelps." And then talked a little about this mysterious rash he had.

Finally, he said he'd figured out that the last package each of the victims received was a human part with a note attached.

"By last package, I mean after that, they're murdered."

Louie asked what the notes said. Carson read them. Louie had read the notes from Tim's library earlier.

That's when Louie figured out who the murderer was. Or at least thought he had.

Louie called Sheldon and asked if the pathologist knew anything about the toe given to him. He expected to hear it was Stuart Brown's but was surprised to hear that it was from a teenager.

"Are you sure?"

"No, I'm not sure. But, without running more tests, I would say I'm ninety-nine percent sure."

"Would you mind running the tests? To be absolutely sure?"

"Look, I'm breaking some rules here. What have you gotten yourself mixed up in? I mean a human toe, for Christ's sakes. I should report this."

"Sheldon, I wouldn't ask if it weren't important. Please?"

"I don't like it, but I will. You owe me big time."

"I'll buy you a case of scotch."
"Call me tomorrow night."
"I will. And Sheldon, thanks."
"Be sure to call."
"You've got it."
Louie never made that call.

Cut 34
You Gotta Run

Louie crossed into the city limits of Tivoli and the cruiser was on his tail. It followed all the way to his apartment. When Louie got out of his car, Elliott got out of the cruiser.

"Louie, we've got to talk."

"Haven't got time right now."

"That pretty little piece will wait a few minutes longer while we chew the fat."

"I don't know what you're talking about."

Louie was leaning against his car. The police chief was standing behind the driver's door of the cruiser. Elliott shut the door of the police car and walked toward Louie and stopped about a foot in front.

"Well sure you do. You've been hound dogging after that fancy ass since high school. You know it and I know it. Can't say that I blame you."

"Why don't you drop it."

"Or what? You gonna stamp your feet and run to Suzie Q and have her wipe your nose?"

Louie walked past the cop bumping shoulders on the way. Childish move. Louie walked up the stairs to his apartment, let himself in and closed the door. He was heading toward the bedroom to get his bag when he heard pounding at the door.

"Now Louis, that wasn't very polite."

"Go away, Elliott."

"I'm telling you we have a few things to talk over."

"Later."

"No, now, asshole."

And with that, the door exploded inward.

"What are you doing, Elliott?"

Elliott had his gun drawn. "Give me a reason. Just one good reason. Put your hands behind your head. Lace the fingers. Now!"

Louie did as he was told.

"Now down on your knees."

"Oh come on."

The policeman cocked his revolver. "I mean it."

Louie got down on his knees.

Elliott walked over and jammed the gun barrel in Louie's ear, drawing a trickle of blood. "Not so tough, are you, asswipe?"

"What do you think you're doing?"

"Touch your nose to the floor."

"Gimme a break."

"Nose to the floor. I'm losing my patience."

Louie started to bend over slowly, but Elliott gave his head a push. Louie turned his neck just in time to avoid a nosebleed.

"That's better. Now let's see what we have here." Elliott kicked Louie's legs apart and started slapping his back and sides. The police chief put his foot on Louie's neck and straightened up. "Well, my, my, it appears to be a gun."

"Hold on a minute, I wasn't carrying a gun. I never carry a gun. You know that."

Elliott waved a revolver in front of Louie's face and then slapped it on the kitchen counter. "Shut up." He kicked Louie in the ribs. "Stay down."

Louie couldn't see what was happening but he could hear Elliott rummaging around the apartment.

"Do you have a search warrant?"

Elliott didn't answer. In a few minutes he came back into the kitchen. "Okay, stand up."

Slowly Louie made it to his knees, then stood up, putting his hands back on his head, looking straight at cop the whole time.

"Turn around."

"What are you doing?"

"Arresting you, asshole. Put both hands, palms down on the kitchen table."

"On what charges?"

Elliott didn't answer. He just yanked Louie's right hand behind his back, then the left, and slapped on the bracelets.

"I want to call my lawyer."

"Walk."

So, Louie walked. Out the back door of the kitchen and down the stairs leading to the alley behind his apartment. Louie looked around, hoping to see if anyone was witnessing the scene, but didn't see a soul. Just before he got to the police car, a stick of dynamite exploded in his head and everything went black.

Cut 35
I Fought the Law and the Law Won

Louie woke up in a four by six foot cell. There were three cells total in the basement of the police station. Louie was in the one furthest from the door. A single forty-watt bulb illuminated the space. It was surrounded by a metal cage lined with screen wire.

Three concrete walls were painted gray. The fourth was made of bars.

There was a stainless steel sink, cold water only and a stainless steel toilet, no seat or lid, one roll of toilet paper on the floor. Louie laid on a cot with a two-inch foam mattress on top of a steel slab. The legs were bolted to the floor. The only other furniture was a steel chair with legs bolted to the floor.

On top of the steel chair was a food tray like the kind you see in most school cafeterias, but this was made of aluminum. Resting on the tray was a single serving box of cornflakes. No milk. No sugar. No eating utensils.

Louie sat up. His head felt as if it had been hit with a medicine ball. Something hot and acidy rose in his stomach, but he kept it down. Louie felt the back of his head and there was a bandage.

His mouth was hot and dry. He thought about walking over to the sink and getting a mouthful of water. But even the thought of moving caused his head to throb painfully. And the thought of swallowing anything made him nauseous.

His watch was gone. The forty-watt bulb would be on 24/7. No natural light came in from anywhere, so Louie had no idea whether it was day or night or how long he'd been there.

"Hey, anyone else down here?"

Louie heard nothing except the echo of his own voice.

The basement was soundproofed, so there was no use in screaming. No use whacking the tray against the bars. No use doing much of anything except think.

Louie stretched out on the mattress. This was the position that hurt the least. He was worried about Sloopy.

The single bulb in the cell blurred. Louie rubbed his eyes. A small dot of black appeared on the ceiling. It grew bigger and bigger until it engulfed his entire world.

He drifted away.

Cut 36

Love's Gone Bad

Dr. Brian, the dentist, was frustrated. He had driven all the way to the police station to see Elliott Blake and Elliott Blake wasn't there. Joe Sizelove was there. Dr. Brian didn't want to talk to Joe Sizelove.

Joe was a little bit like that other guy. What was his name? Louie, that was it. Louie. Louie just wouldn't play ball, didn't understand how things went down in this town. Look what happened to Louie. Didn't get that police chief job.

Dr. Brian wasn't sure of Joe Sizelove. Joe could be a stickler for the letter of the law, too. Which was pretty damn inconvenient when you had a kid that stomped all over such niceties.

There were too many damn laws, anyway. How was a young person supposed to have any fun? Why, hell, when he was a kid, he and his buds used to chug Vicks 44, blow up mailboxes with cherry bombs, and beat up the town sissies just to have something to do until football season.

Anyway, his kid was missing. Probably passed out in a cornfield somewhere or smoking pot with his friends at the gravel pit. But he had been gone twenty-four hours now. The doctor wanted the police to look for him, but didn't want it to get all official. That could get sticky.

Elliott would know what to do. And if the dumbass kid had done something a little south of the law, Elliott would fix things. So when Joe Sizelove asked if he could help, Dr. Brian turned around and walked out the same door he came in.

He would teach the kid a thing or two when he got home. Since Dr. Brian didn't believe in corporal punishment of any sort, he wasn't sure what to do to make an impression on his knucklehead son, but whatever it was would be unforgettable.

Maybe he would ground him. Was that too juvenile? Would that even affect Lee? He had his own suite of rooms upstairs. They were filled with the latest toys, the latest PlayStation, Rock Band, Wii, flat screen TV and who knows what else. The kid had a mini fridge stocked with energy drinks and beer.

Nope, grounding wasn't the answer. Lee didn't mind hanging out in his room. How about taking the car away? Yeah, that was the answer. He would take away Lee's car for two days and his credit cards for a whole week. Lee would learn that his old man could really put the hammer down when he wanted to.

Cut 37
Inside Outside

Louie kept having nightmares of Tim Ferman blowing his head off. He awoke again on the steel cot staring at the forty-watt bulb in the prison cell. He sat up. The old noggin' didn't hurt as bad, but his mouth was hot and dry and tasted like dirty laundry. He walked over to the sink and hand cupped several mouthfuls of water. They went down with no problem. The water tasted clean and sweet.

Someone had been in the cell.

The tray on top of the table now included a little box of raisins with the single serving of cornflakes. Louie was hungry so he sat on the bunk and ate the raisins one by one.

Louie needed to get to Sloopy. What could he do? When Louie worked for the police, the cells weren't wired, but they might be now. He went to the bars and looked in both directions trying to spot a video camera. There were two in the opposite corners of the hallway that ran parallel to the cells. By their angles, it didn't seem as if they could see into the cell, but only the hallway if somebody escaped. Maybe they had a microphone attached.

"I have a right to an attorney," Louie screamed at the top of my lungs.

"You don't have no rights down here, *ese*," a voice with a pronounced Latin-American lilt to it answered.

"Who are you?"

"My name is Hector."

"Hi, Hector, I'm Louie."

"Louis?" He pronounced it lew-eese.

"Close enough. What are you here for, Hector?"

"I work at Dal Thomas Farm. No papers."

"Are you from Mexico?"

"*Si*, yes."

"How long have you been here?"

"Two *horas*."

"What day is it?"

"Tuesday"

"Morning or afternoon?"

"The afternoon."

Louie had been in jail a little more than 48 hours.

"Hector, when you get out of here, will you make a phone call for me?"

Louie told Hector the telephone number of Mike Adams, the attorney Louie sometimes did work for.

"Tell Mike I'm in jail and to come here and get me out. He'll know what to do. Are you sure you have the number?"

Hector repeated the number.

"Promise me you'll do it?"

"*Si*, yes *senor*, I do it."

"Thanks Hector. I will pay you something when I get out."

"No need, *senor. I don'* like Senor Elliott. He is a bad man."

"Yes, he is Hector."

There was nothing to do now but wait. Louie wanted to smash his fist against the wall, but that wouldn't help. Louie vowed when he got out of jail Elliott would pay. But first came Sloopy.

Stan Martin was a turkey farmer's son. He was a tall, skinny kid with dishwater blond hair that always looked a little greasy. His dad owned a farm west of town. Because the price of feed kept going up and the big supermarkets sold turkeys as loss leaders during the season, poor Gene Martin, Stan's dad, fell on some hard times.

Stan had a lazy right eye that turned in alarmingly. He wore glasses with Coke-bottle thick lenses that didn't help his appearance much and magnified his weird eye.

The kids at school teased him and called him "Clarence the Cross-Eyed Lion." They called him "Goony Eyes" and "Wacky Wall Eyes" even though a wall-eye was different than a cross eye.

Elliott and Louie were a couple of jocks in school. They weren't friends, but were both on the football team. Elliott was big for his age and because of his size, was somewhat of a bully. As everyone knows who attended high school in the United States, there's quite a class system. It was an intricate structure based on who your parents were, who your parents knew, whether or not you had a car, and whether or not you were a jock or cheerleader.

Louie didn't pay much attention to the system, because there were a lot of jocks he didn't like and a couple nerds, like Carson, he did. Poor Stan just fell through the cracks, no one liked him.

One time after Phys-ed, Elliott was giving Stan a particularly hard time. Louie came around a corner and heard Elliott say to Stan, "Don't look at me like that."

Of course all the guys laughed. Stan just ignored Elliott and kept on getting dressed.

"Did you hear me, goony eyes? I said don't look at me like that." Elliott grabbed Stan by the shoulder. Stan shrugged the hand off and that made Ellott even angrier. He gave Stan a shove to the ground and started kicking him in the ribs.

Dad had always told Louie to "never kick a man when he's down."

After about the second kick, Louie stepped between them and gave Elliott a little shove backwards. "Touch him again, and you'll have me to deal with."

"Aw Louie, this is none of your damn business."

"I mean it, Elliott."

Elliott started to say something and then stopped. He tried to stare Louie down for a minute, turned and then walked away.

Elliott never got over that. Whenever he was drunk and he was near Louie, he said one day he'd repay Louie.

Louie figured that day had come.

Elliott Blake was having a hard time keeping things from coming unraveled. First, there was the idiot at the ZipMart. No matter how hard he tried, he couldn't convince the numbnuts that the guy in the photo was the person who tried to rob the store.

"We got evidence that says he is." Elliott held up a photo of Louie.

"Doesn't matter, that ain't the guy."

"Look closely. Are you sure?"

"I can look closely, I can look across the room, I can hold the photo sideways or upside down and this guy," he pointed to the photo, "ain't the guy. He's too old. His hair is too short."

"Maybe he grew out his hair."

"It ain't him."

"Are you sure?"

"Positive."

Elliott gave up at that point. He'd lean on the ZipMart idiot a little later. Threaten to bust him for selling liquor to kids in high school. He'd call in a favor from some kid he'd let off to use as a witness. Maybe he could talk the owner into at least not being so sure. That would work with all the other stuff he had in place. But damn, things were sure getting complicated.

Back at the station, Joe Sizelove informed Elliott that Doc Brian had been around. What the hell did Daddy Dentist want?

Elliott went to his office and called the dentist.

"Have you seen my son?" the doctor asked as soon as he clicked on.

Damn cell phones. People knew right away who was calling.

"No, doc, I haven't."

"Well, he's been gone for a while. Not sure how long. But I haven't seen him in at least twenty-four hours."

"I'll keep my eyes peeled for him."

"Just bring his ass home," the dentist said and clicked off.

What an arrogant piece of crap. Talked to Elliott as if he were the hired help or something.

There was a knock on the door. Now what?

It was Joe Sizelove. That guy drove Elliott crazy.

"What is it, Joe?"

"There's something you ought to see."

"Can it wait?"

"I don't think so."

Joe and Elliott walked to the interrogation room. It wasn't used very much. Behind the mirror was a tinier room, no bigger than a hallway, where you could observe what was going on without being seen. In the viewing room were several old-fashioned VHS tape machines. Two of them were connected to cameras in the basement cells. Joe fiddled around with some switches and got the cells up on the two monitors. He switched on the amp so they could hear sound from downstairs.

"What is it, Joe? I don't see nothing."

"What are the two guys doing down there?"

"What two guys?"

"Louie and Hector Rios."

"Well, I believe Hector is here because he's what we in law enforcement call an illegal."

"What about Louie?"

"He robbed the ZipMart."

"Bullshit."

"Be careful, Joe."

"Lee Brian robbed it. You know it and I know it."

"The evidence tells me something different."

"What evidence?"

"Are you calling me a liar, Joe?"

"I'm just saying."

"What? What are you saying?"

"Well, neither of 'em is logged in and neither of 'em has been charged with anything."

"You're right, Joe. Bring Hector to me."

"But what about Louie?"

"I said, bring Hector to me."

Joe walked away mumbling under his breath.

Elliott felt like firing him. What a pain in the ass. Nothing today was easy.

The cameras recorded in real time. There was a single microphone in the ceiling. Both tapes picked up the same audio. As Joe was getting the prisoner, Elliott decided to rewind one of the tapes just to see if something might have been said by either prisoner that could be of interest. He wasn't sure why he did it, but he was glad he did.

As the tape rewound there was burp on the monitor, a jump of the tiny VU meter. Elliott stopped the tape and pushed fast forward and came to the sound and seesawed back and forth until he was cued to the section and was able to hit play. Of course there was nothing to be seen because there was nobody in the hallway, but he did hear the conversation in which Louie asked Hector to call his lawyer. Hmmm, we'll have to do something about this, Elliott thought.

He looked at the monitor to see what was going on in the basement. He saw Joe walk to Hector's cell and unlock the door.

This might be interesting. He turned the sound up.

Yes, it was very interesting.

Cut 38

Why Pick on Me

Louie woke to the sound of someone in the hall. "Hello."

No answer.

"Anyone there?"

Louie got to his feet and walked to the bars. He couldn't see anyone to the right, but to the left he saw the shadow of someone in front of Hector's cell.

"Hector?"

"*Si?*"

"What's going on?"

"I think they're letting me out."

"Remember what I said, Hector."

"Yes, I remember."

"Who's letting you out? Is that you, Elliott?"

"It's me, Joe. Joe Sizelove."

"Hey Joe, how're'ya doin'?"

"I'm good, Louie. And you?"

"I've been better, Joe. I sure would like to know what I'm doin' here."

"There's evidence you robbed a convenience store."

"What evidence? What store? The ZipMart?"

"I can't say, Louie."

"But Joe, Joe, listen to me. I haven't been charged with anything. I've been here two days and haven't been booked. I haven't been allowed to call my lawyer. What's that all about, Joe?"

"I don't know anything about that."

Hector's cell door squeaked closed.

"Joe, see if you can't do anything to help me out here, will you, bud?"

"I'll put a word in with Elliott. Now that's enough out of you."

A handcuffed Hector started to shuffle down the hall with Joe at his side.

"Joe, Joe, one more thing, could you check up on Sloopy… uh, Susan, Susan Petrie for me?"

Sizelove stopped and turned around.

"What's wrong with Susan?"

"Well, I hope, nothing."

Louie told Sizelove about the packages Sloopy had been receiving.

"I haven't heard nothing about them."

That one slammed Louie in the gut.

"Maybe Elliott is investigating himself. Keeping it under the radar or something." Deep inside, Louie knew it wasn't true.

Joe did too.

"Maybe," Joe said.

"Joe, you gotta help me get out of here. C'mon, you know I'm a standup guy. It's not for me, it's for Susan."

"I'll check things out."

"You gotta hurry. You gotta hurry, Joe. And remember what I said, Hector. Please remember."

Hector didn't answer.

"Hector?"

The door at the end of the hall closed.

What was going on? What robbery? What had happened to all those packages Sloopy gave to Elliott?

A deep-throated scream of frustration burbled from Louie's lips.

He punched the concrete wall. It hurt. It felt good. He punched the wall again and again. His knuckles were bloody. Stop, Louie, he said to himself.

He kept punching.

Elliott turned down the sound. He had heard the entire conversation between Joe and Louie. Shit, more complications. Oh well, better to be forewarned.

He heard Louie's anguished scream. Oh, that was rich. Maybe he'd break the sonovabitch. Yeah. That would be perfect. Leave the mighty Louie Louie a slobbering shell.

Okay, it was still gonna take a lot of work, but things were definitely moving in the right direction.

Cut 39
It's-A-Happening

Louie sat in the cell, throbbing hands cradled between his knees. He rinsed them off under the faucet in the sink. There was nothing to dry them with.

"Hey, can someone bring me a towel?"

The forty-watt bulb didn't answer.

He dried his hands on the sheet.

The knuckles were scraped raw and swollen. He looked at them for a minute then sat on the cot.

Something bad was going down.

Well, that was obvious.

But something really bad was about to happen. He knew it. He felt it. And, couldn't do a damn thing about it.

Hector was in Elliott's office. Joe Sizelove stood next to him.

"Joe, why don't you leave ol' Hector here for a few minutes. We've got a little jawing to do."

"I don't think so."

"And why would that be?"

"I need to know what's going on, Elliott."

"What do you mean?"

"Well, for one thing, I'm supposed to be Assistant Chief of Police."

"I think the best way you could assist me right now, would be to let Hector and me have a few minutes of private conversation."

"Why?"

"Because I said so, and you are the assistant to me. That means you're an ant that assists me. Assist. Ant. And you know what I do with ants? I step on their ass. So take your ant ass out of here before I promote someone who puts more assist than ass in assist-ant. Okay little Joe?"

In the quiet office Elliott heard Joe's teeth grind. He snorted out his nose and said, "I'll be back in an hour."

"Well that sounds just fine. And it would be of great assistance to me if you'd get me some carryout coffee from somewhere's or another."

"When I get back, I'd like to talk to you a little bit about Louie."

"Whatever you say ass-instant."

Joe walked out of the office and shut the door with an intentional slam.

"Hector, it's too bad you tried to escape custody."

"Senor Elliott, *I don'* tried no escape."

"Sure you did." Elliott brought up the gun he was holding. Elliott pulled the trigger and Hector fell to the floor.

Elliott walked over to the Mexican jerking on the ground. He got some nylon cuffs and bound the ankles and wrists of the semi-conscious body. He then put a wadded up piece of paper in the Mexican's mouth and wrapped duct tape around his head three times.

❧

Louie heard the door open at the end of the hallway. There were footsteps.

It was Joe Sizelove.

"Hey Joe, have you come to let me out?"

"Sorry, Louie."

"Why are you here, then?"

"I brought you something to eat."

Louie walked to the bars. Joe had a ham sandwich, the kind you get out of vending machines and in convenience stores, the kind wrapped in plastic. It was on a tray. Louie took it.

"Thanks."

"No prob."

"What can I do to get out of here?"

"I'll talk to Elliott as soon as I can. He's gone now."

"I appreciate it."

Joe stood there looking at Louie.

"What are you doing, Joe?"

"I'm waiting until you finish your sandwich to take the tray back."

Joe leaned with his back to the bars. This was too good to be true. Louie came up from behind and got Joe in a light headlock and scratched around his holster until he had the gun. "Okay now open up."

"You're making a big mistake."

"You'll be making a bigger one if you don't do as I say."

Louie loosened the hold and Joe got his keys. The cop shrugged and opened the door.

"Elliott will be back anytime and he's going to be pissed."

"Give me your keys, Joe."

"Okay, it's your funeral."

"Now, get undressed."

As Joe unbuttoned his shirt, Louie realized what had happened. Sizelove had purposely given Louie an opening to grab the gun and make an escape.

"Thanks, Joe."

Joe handed over his clothes. "For what?"

"I think you know."

"I have no idea what you're talking about."

Twenty minutes later Louie was in one of the three Tivoli city police cars. Joe Sizelove was handcuffed to the cot in Louie's former cell with the door locked. Louie had disabled the radios in the station and yanked enough wires out of one of the other cars that it wouldn't start for a good long time.

The escaped man sped down a country road on the way to the motel. He wore the uniform of a police officer, a federal offense. But that was the least of his problems. Louie had broken enough laws to be put away until he was a very old man.

Sloopy wasn't at her house, so Louie had to make sure she was safe and try and catch the killer and then figure out a way to get out of the country.

He was in deep shit. And it was about to get much deeper.

Time was Louie's enemy. He could feel time. He could smell time. Time was a physical presence. It clutched at him. It was trying to set a trap. Time would be what brought Louie down.

He was at the Rest E-Z Motel. Sloopy wasn't at the Rest E-Z Motel. Bad. Very bad.

According to the desk clerk, there were only four units occupied. None of them by a single woman.

Each minute tightened around him like a noose. If there wasn't an APB out for him yet, there would be one any minute.

After parking the cop car in the back of the motel, Louie walked to his room, unlocked the door and slipped inside. He immediately went to the bathroom sink and washed his face. He looked at the water-spotted mirror. It was a stranger's face staring back. It was a face that was much older than Louie remembered. But it seemed like a face that had a few more good years left.

Life was over as he knew it. Before time got hold of and destroyed him, he had to save Sloopy. That had to be the first priority. He didn't have the foggiest notion where to begin.

Louie grabbed a chair from the built-in desk and set it in front of the window. He opened the drapes just enough to look outside while effectively masking the inside.

There was nothing going on. Louie pulled out his cell phone and started to make a call, then remembered cell phones had some sort of locater device in them. He turned the phone off. He wondered if phones could be tracked even when they were off. He reasoned that the technology would be too sophisticated for Tivoli. He reasoned it might take them a while to get hold of that technology even if they were so inclined. He just hoped the cops were as reasonable.

He walked over to the desk and tried to pull the motel phone over to the window. The cord wouldn't stretch far enough.

So, he gave up watching for Sloopy from the window. Logic told him she wouldn't be coming here. Louie started making phone calls.

First call, Carson.

"*Gort. Klaatu barada nikto,*" Carson said when answering the phone.

"Carson, sorry man, I haven't got time, you gotta listen to me, dude."

There was a long silence. Louie could tell Carson was still on the phone by the slight electric hum that signals a line is open. "C'mon, talk to me, man, I'm really in a bad way and I need a little help."

Silence.

"Carson?"

"What is your problem, Earth man?"

Louie told Carson everything. When Louie finished telling about the incarceration and escape, Carson whistled.

"You in heap big trouble *kemo sabe*."

"I know. I want you to call the lawyer I work for. His name is Michael Adams and he practices in Carmel. Tell him about the arrest, that I swear I didn't do it, and tell him how I escaped and to please do whatever he can to start building a defense for me."

"Why don't you call him?"

"He'll insist I turn myself in and I just haven't got time to argue. Tell him, I'll give up as soon as I make sure Sloopy is okay."

"Dude, you gotta ditch the cop car and uniform like ASAP if not sooner."

"I can't."

"Why not?"

"My car is impounded. I need wheels."

"Take mine."

Carson had a Ford 150.

"Nocando."

"Why not?"

"You'll be an accessory to whatever I finally get charged with."

"I'll handle it."

"I'm not gonna do it."

"Listen, I'll tell 'em that, you know, I keep the keys in my visor and so you took it without my permission."

"I'll think about it."

"Just do it."

Louie didn't want to. He wanted to keep Carson out of the whole mess.

"Listen, Carson, if anyone asks you about this call, tell them you were trying to talk me into giving up."

"They'll never find out."

"They have ways."

"Dude, this phone doesn't exist."

"Sure it does, we're talking on it."

"You're not hearing me. It does not exist. It never existed."

"Oh. I understand, I guess."

Cut 40

The Spider and the Fly

Sloopy snapped awake. She couldn't move. What was going on?

She realized she was duct taped to a chair—wrists, ankles, stomach and head. She didn't know how long she had been unconscious. She remembered going into her house with the weird-looking man and retrieving the package. At knifepoint she walked to a white van with a side door. The man with the weird-looking head opened the door. She was about to step in when everything turned black.

He must have chloroformed her because she woke up with a chemical taste in her mouth. A taste like rubber. No, latex. Like the inside of a latex glove without the talcum.

There was a cold dampness in the room. The last she remembered, it was extremely hot outside. The light was the pale green of fluorescent tubes. She must be in a basement somewhere. Where? Still in Tivoli?

The Man with the Lightbulb Head sat at a workbench with his back to her. He didn't know she was awake yet. She decided to keep it that way for as long as possible. She kept her eyes open just enough to see.

She tested her wrists, her ankles, tensing her stomach muscles. He had done a good job in the binding, she had little wiggle room, yet it wasn't so tight that her circulation was cut off.

She could move her right wrist a little and started to move it back and forth millimeter at a time. Her wristwatch helped cut the tape ever so slightly.

Although there was tape over her mouth, she moved her lips and her tongue to moisten it and loosen it. It would be a long process, but eventually something would have to give. She didn't know how long she had. Hopefully, it was long enough.

As she exerted herself, vomit rose in her stomach. She mustn't throw up with the tape on her mouth or she could drown in her own vomit. She stopped straining and breathed very steadily through her nose. Finally, her stomach calmed.

Was there anyone that knew she was missing? Louie would figure it out when she didn't show up at the motel. Would he have any way of tracing her? Would he get the police involved? Would they...could they trace her? She had heard somewhere there was a little homing device in telephones. Would that work? Could they pinpoint her location? She didn't take any luggage when she went to the van, but her phone was in her purse. Was her purse here somewhere?

She didn't see it, but that didn't mean it wasn't there. She couldn't see very well in the pale florescent light. Her purse could be in one of the shadows by the workbench or in one of the corners. It could be behind her. It could be still in the van, if the van were nearby.

The panic adrenaline sloshing through her body was causing her mind to redline. She mustn't lose control. She had to remain focused. She had to do the one thing she could do, and that was to loosen the tape that bound her to the chair.

She strained again.

The Man with the Lightbulb Head turned from the workbench against the wall. He looked straight into her eyes and smiled.

He walked over to Sloopy.

"Now let's not pretend we're asleep anymore, shall we?"

Sloopy opened her eyes.

"That's better. How was your little nappy-poo?"

Sloopy tried to speak but the tape prevented much more than a gurgle.

"What's the matter? A little bit tongue-tied? No? Maybe I should tie something to it."

The woman in the chair tried to jerk free. Her neck looked like it was made of cables covered with flesh-colored rubber.

"Now, now, I was just kidding. You're such a pretty thing; no need to get your looks all messed up. That's my job. Now just calm down my little pretty."

Blood vessels had burst in her right eye and the blue pupil was surrounded by red webbing.

The Man with the Lightbulb Head turned and walked back to the workbench. When he turned to face her, he had the package he had sent earlier with a box cutter sitting on top. He walked to Sloopy and placed the package and box cutter on her lap.

"You know what we're going to do now, Suzie Q?"

Sloopy just stared at him. A nauseating smell rose from the box. It was like rotten meat only sweeter.

"We are going to see what's inside. And then we're going to see what's behind curtain number two. But that'll be a little later. For now let's see what's in the box. What do you suppose it could be?"

He picked up the box and shook it. The movement increased the intensity of the odor. Sloopy was afraid she might throw up. Her stomach heaved but she was able to keep it down.

"Wow, I thought you were a ghost, there for a second. Don't rush things dearie, it'll happen soon enough."

He put the smelly package back on Sloopy's lap.

"You know, I really think you should have stored this in the refrigerator. I'm afraid the contents have seen better days. Of course that was probably true before I delivered the package."

He walked back to the bench and put on a surgeon's face mask.

"I put a few drops of camphor oil on the cloth to help defray some of the smell. I'll bet you would like one of these too, wouldn't you? I have an extra one. But I'm not going to give it to you. No-no. I'm sorry, but as the recipient of this little present,

I think you should experience it in all its odiferous glory. Don't you, Suzie Q?"

He rubbed his hands together rapidly. "So what do you suppose is in the mystery package? Let's find out, shall we?"

He took the box cutters and cut the tape on the middle seam where the two top flaps came together. "Oh the suspense is just killing me...yet for you it's doing quite the opposite. The time we take opening the package just postpones things for you. Do you suppose that's what they mean by irony?"

Each side of the flap was taped to the main body of the box. He sliced down each side. He pulled the two flaps up.

Sloopy was hit in the face with the most repulsive smell she had never imagined. It was thick, physical. It filled her nostrils and her head. Her stomach revolted. She was choking on her own vomit.

"Oh, my, my, I believe we must continue this a little later. I don't want any sick to get on my sick little present here."

The Man with the Lightbulb Head moved the package back to the bench. He returned with a plastic pail. He ripped the tape off Sloopy's mouth and put the bucket under her chin to let the vomit splash into it. Because Sloopy's neck was taped tightly to the chair, she didn't have much freedom of movement, so some of the vomit dribbled down the front of her sweater.

She heaved again and again, until she was heaving without anything coming up. Finally the stomach convulsions subsided.

"You are quite a messy thing, aren't you Miss Suzie?"

He took the bucket to a spot behind her and ran some water. There must be some sort of utility sink back there. She heard him rinsing out the pail and then he returned with a wet towel.

He wiped the vomit off her face and re-taped her mouth, wrapping the duct tape completely around her head.

"Thank you for not screaming, not that anyone could hear you, but I find the noise rather annoying. And you don't want to annoy me, trust me."

He walked behind her and returned with a clean towel.

"It seems you splattered a little on your sweater. Here, let me get that."

He wiped off a spot just above her collarbone. And then he wiped at her breasts.

"Oh these are such perky things. Are they real? Oh, heck, I don't care. I could just do this all day long."

He wiped her breasts for several minutes with the towel and then started rubbing them with his bare hands. "Oh if only your husband could see me now. I would call this tits for tat, wouldn't you?"

Sloopy strained against the tape to keep the man from mauling her, but his hands wouldn't be distracted. Finally he stopped.

"Now that was fun, wasn't it?"

She channeled the hate she felt through her eyes, but he seemed unaffected. When...if, she got free, she would kill him.

Cut 41
Complication

After Louie hung up on Carson, he called Indianapolis. First, Tim Ferman's Agency. He wanted to talk to Amanda. The agency was closed, as expected, but it didn't have one of those phone directories you could punch in the first name and get the person's full name. It had a voice mail for the entire agency, so he left his name and cell phone and asked Amanda to call. It seemed that everything pointed to Paul Dabrowski being involved somehow in the animal parts packages. He was the only person Louie could think that might be angry enough to want revenge. The revenge was unreasonable. It was beyond nuts. But, if it weren't Dabrowski, then who? Louie didn't have a clue.

Then, Louie called Tim Ferman's house. On the second ring a deep male voice said "Yeah."

Okay, someone was there, more than likely the cops. If not, they would be there soon.

Outside the window, no new cars. No one milling around the parking lot.

Louie took off Joe Sizelove's shirt, he had a T-shirt on underneath. He got a plastic trashcan liner from the receptacle in the bathroom and put the cop's shirt in it. He took another look out the window and stepped out into the unmerciful heat.

On the way to the car, Louie buried the shirt in a dumpster. He was going to find Paul. The address Amanda gave was a little country town south of Indianapolis, just east of Anderson, called Andora. Louie started the cop car and pulled out of the parking lot. Should he risk taking the police cruiser to Andora? He would stick out like a biker at an Amy Grant concert. Yet, he didn't want to get Carson in trouble. However, Carson was willing to take the risk. If the computer whiz kept cool under questioning, they couldn't pin anything on him.

Louie turned toward Carson's house.

There was a cornfield about a mile from there. Louie drove the cruiser to the field and drove several hundred yards into the stalks of corn, put the car in park and didn't shut off the engine. There was about a quarter tank of gas left. As Louie got out, he locked the doors. With Joe Sizelove's gun, he shot out two tires. With two flats and if the car burned all the gas before anyone got to it, no one would be able to drive it for a while.

Louie hiked to Carson's house. It was a little two-story job with a detached garage. All the lights were on. The garage was unlocked. Louie slipped in and found the keys where Carson said they would be. Louie opened the garage door as quietly as possible, started the truck and took off. As he was pulling out, Louie saw Carson on the front porch waving.

It took a little more than an hour to get to Andora. Louie couldn't find the road to Paul Dabrowski's house. So, he took a chance and stopped at a filling station. He filled the truck up and went inside to pay. A lone teenager manned the cash register. The teenage cashier was decked out in a typical goth uniform, baggy black jeans, black T-shirt with a blood-red skull on it and a black watch cap with the letters FLCL. Three tiny hoop earrings in one ear and a cross earring in the other, a stud in the lower lip and another small hoop pierced the right nostril.

Louie asked if the goth knew Paul Dabrowski. The teenager sighed heavily and told Louie no. Louie recited the address. The teenager didn't recognize it, but after much questioning, said the road was a gravel road west of town with only a few houses on it, so there shouldn't be much trouble finding it. The goth mumbled directions to the road.

Louie realized he hadn't eaten since the ham sandwich earlier.

So, he bought some beef jerky and an energy drink.

As Louie drove toward the road, he tried to devise a plan. He couldn't think of any except to go to the house and knock on the door and see what happened. It was the no-plan plan. Louie found the road and maneuvered slowly, looking at mailboxes.

The road was only five miles long. The houses were few and far between. All the mailboxes were on the left. Although the numbers were in order, they weren't sequential. Louie couldn't quite figure out the pattern. One house might be 5910 and the next 5915 and the one across the road 5912.

Dabrowski's address was 5977. There was a mailbox for 5970 and then, about a half a mile up, a box for 5982. Louie drove back and forth three times. He stopped. He pulled Caron's pickup off the road and got out. He walked from the 5970 mailbox to the 5982. On the mailbox side of the road, there was nothing in-between. Just corn. He crossed the road and started back. As Louie walked, a truck pulled up from behind. It slowed beside Louie and the passenger window rolled down.

"Need some help, friend?"

The man inside the truck had one of those pulled-taffy bodies that never seem to fill out, like a teenage boy after a particularly robust growth spurt. Long arms. Long legs. He had a long, craggy face permanently copper colored from too many days of too much sun. His hair was bleached-cotton white and cut by a barber who was probably proud of getting people in and out of the chair in less than ten minutes and wouldn't know how to respond if offered a tip.

He was wearing a worn but neatly-pressed short-sleeved madras shirt and tan slacks. A fashion statement Louie could appreciate.

Louie started to wave the truck on but stopped.

"I'm looking for 5977."

"Up that lane over there."

About ten yards up ahead was what looked like an access road for farm equipment between two cornfields.

Louie thanked the long tall stranger and walked up to the lane. He had to walk a couple of hundred yards between the cornfields and came to a big clearing and a rise in land too small to be called a hill. It was all overgrown and weedy. He didn't see a house or a barn or anything. Just an unkempt plot of weeds and brambles.

However as Louie got closer to the crest he saw the foundation of what had once been a house. The poured concrete was stained the color of an undertaker's suit and there were remnants of the structure in chunks of charred wood and sooty broken glass.

Louie walked around the rubble of the burned-down house and saw another lane that led to the woods in back, but there wasn't much point in following it.

As Louie got to the road, he noticed the red pickup truck parked next to Carson's white one. He walked up to the driver's side window.

"Why didn't you tell me?"

"You didn't ask," the tall stranger replied.

"So what are you doing here?"

"Thought I'd stick around. Figured you might have some questions."

"You have a lot of time on your hands, don't you?"

Exhaustion and worry enticed Louie to say something that strict upbringing and small-town ethics would have censored. He didn't know why that wise-ass remark came to mind. He didn't know if that would offend the tall man or not. Instead the old guy broke out in a throaty laugh shellacked with years of nicotine and bourbon. The laugh became a cough that quickly subsided. The stranger wiped the corners of his eyes with a handkerchief pulled from his back pocket.

"Aren't you Mr. Sassy-Pants." The tall man smiled and then broke into another coughing spell.

"I apologize."

"No, I deserved it. That is your truck, isn't it?"

"Sort of."

"Well why don't you sort of pull it into my driveway up there. We'll go to town and get ourselves a donut and a cup of coffee."

"I don't know if I have time."

"What else you gonna do? Go on, you oughtta get the truck off this road. You don't want some drunk hillbilly sideswipin' it and scraping off all the paint, do you now?"

After Louie parked Carson's truck, and as the pair rode into town, the tall stranger said, "I used to own 800 acres of good farm land. My grandfather bought it up during the depression. Daddy gave it to me. Thought I'd pass it on someday to my son or daughter. Had an accident when I was harvesting one year and anyway, the doc said I'm shooting blanks. So I sold it a few years ago. Made a pretty penny. Now's all I own is the half-acre my house sits on.

"Ruby, my wife, and I used to like to travel. But now that she's passed, well, there's really not a lot of fun in discovering new things and trying new restaurants. The fun's in the sharing. But listen to me, an old coot just chewin' your ear off. You look like a man who's got some concerns."

"Well, I'm trying to find someone."

"Even a dumb old fart like me can figure that one out."

"I'm looking for Paul Dabrowski."

"You were just on his farm, or what's left of it. I think he sold most of the acreage himself."

"What happened to the house?"

"Gas leak. Some folks say, Paul may have been trying to commit suicide, tried to gas himself to death. But there was a spark and then, well you saw the result."

"Why do folks think that?"

"Think what?"

"That Paul tried to kill himself."

"Apparently, he said some things while the doctors were working on him. We're here."

They pulled into a gravel parking lot of a place called Golden

Crèam Donuts. The old farmer told Louie his name was Wes. Wes ordered a coffee and two Long Johns, Louie got a coffee and a glazed.

"So Paul lived through the blast."

They sat at a tiny booth with red vinyl seats. Everything in the place looked old, but remarkably clean.

"It was more of a flash fire, really. Not enough gas escaped to blow up the house like you see in the movies. Firemen pulled young Paul out of the house but weren't able to save the structure."

"Where is he now?"

"I don't know. I seen him once a while back in town. Poor boy didn't look too good. They had to put grafts of skin all over his head and face and his neck was all shriveled. It was hard to look at him. Ain't seen him since. No clue what happened to him."

"Do you think he tried to kill himself?"

"Don't rightly know. He was a little bit strange. His whole family had some peculiar ways about them. I don't think he liked coming back here. He was a hotshot advertising guy at one time and got fired or something. Kinda dinged his pride a little, I reckon."

Louie was at a loss. With every minute, he felt Sloopy was in more and more danger. Louie's gut told him Paul Dabrowski was somehow involved. But Louie had no proof. And no idea what to do.

Cut 42
Mindrocker

"Before we were so rudely interrupted, I believe we were about to see what was in the box." The Man with the Lightbulb Head held up the still-unopened package.

He brought the container and set it on Sloopy's lap. He still had on the surgery mask. The smell was still awful. However, there was nothing left in Sloopy's stomach. Although she gagged a couple of times, she didn't vomit.

He opened the two flaps on the package. The contents were wrapped in tissue paper like that in which fine department stores wrap a new blouse or shirt. Some fluid had seeped out and there was a brownish-red stain. On top of the carefully-folded tissue was an envelope with the handwritten note that said, "Open me first."

"Well, my pretty, it looks like the wicked witch of the north sent you a little note. I wonder what it says? Let's open it, shall we?"

He picked up the envelope and slit the top with a scalpel. "How very interesting. I think I shall read it aloud. Yes, that's just what I'll do. It says, 'Someone stole my brain, so I decided to steal one back, baby, the brain must fall, just like that.' Well, it doesn't quite rhyme. What's that called? A false rhyme? Assonance? Yes, I think, that's it. Assonance. Do you understand what it means? Do you understand the note? Well, I do, because I wrote it. Now that doesn't mean much to your husband. He couldn't care less. But I care. Pride of authorship is very important. Anyway, I'll explain it to you as we go along, but for now, I'm just dying to see what's inside the package. Aren't you? I'm sure you are. Let's look, what do you say?"

The Man with the Lightbulb Head wadded up the note and the envelope and threw it in a plastic trash basket next to Sloopy's chair.

He unwrapped the tissue and there was a jumbo clear plastic bag with a moldy gray-brown wet mass.

"Well, what do you know? It's a brain."

The Man with the Lightbulb Head held the baggie with the brain in front of Sloopy's face until he could see her eyes water. The stench was awful. He dropped the brain and picked up a straight razor. He slashed the air gleefully. "I've come to a conclusion, my little pretty."

Of course Sloopy couldn't answer.

"You are such a remarkably beautiful woman, I think what I'm going to do first is destroy your looks. Transform you from awfully pretty to pretty awful. What do you think of that? Not much, I imagine, but you know there is some poetic justice in that, don't you think? Of course, you probably wouldn't understand why I'm doing it it. I believe you and your hubby were divorced at the time. But because of him, I look like this. All these little skin grafts and the little holes for a nose. How come my skin grafts look so rubbery you might ask. Hmmm. I guess I don't know. It's my own skin. Came off my very own ass. I had a pretty supple ass if I remember correctly. And look at this neck! Eek, double eek and ick. No elasticity at all in the skin. I can't stand to even look at myself in the mirror. God knows how others must feel.

"I heard some little kid say my head looked like a light bulb. It's true, you know. The little circular scar kinda looks like the GE symbol, don't you think? My skin is so white. White like a lightbulb. And doesn't my neck look like the base of a bulb? All brown and twisty.

"Your husband is such a charmer, he talked me into leaving my good job in Chicago to work with him. It was my way to make a name for myself. We could be the next Fallon, or Crispin, or one of those shops that no one outside the industry ever heard of. One of those places that does great work and everyone in the biz reveres. And yes, I would be partner one day and blah-de-blah blah blah."

Sloopy strained against the tape. She was making sounds, trying to speak. The Man with the Lightbulb Head only heard muffled mumbles. He put the blade against Sloopy's right eye.

"If I ruined your eye, that would ruin your looks in two ways. The way you look, your physical appearance, and the way you look, the organ you use to look at things. That's kind of funny, isn't it?

"Of course, if I poke out your eyes right at first, you won't be able to see the reconstructive surgery I'm doing on the rest of your face and body. Now that would be a shame, wouldn't it? Maybe I should cut off your breasts, see if they're real. Felt pretty real to me. But with the advances they've made in plastic surgery.

"Naw, I'll save the melons for desert. I'm gonna work on your face first. Maybe your nose. Or, better yet, your ears."

Cut 43

Out of My Hands

Louie decided to call Carson. “Excuse me a moment, Wes.”

“I got nothing but time,” the old farmer said.

“Great Caeser’s Ghost, is that you Kent?” Carson said when he answered.

“Hey Carson, what’s up?”

“Well, I’d tell you about my problems, which involve some weird things happening to my eyelashes, but I figure yours are much worse. What do you want first, the bad news or the badder than hell news?”

“What did you find out from Adams?”

“Well, that’s the bad news. It seems the only evidence the cops have against you is a stocking cap with some hair samples and saliva that belong to you. This cap was supposedly found on the floor of the ZipMart right after the robbery.”

“So that’s what they pulled over my head,” Louie said.

“Who?”

“The guys in the van.”

“What guys…”

“Never mind. What’s the badder news?”

“Oh, grand theft auto, assaulting a police officer, impersonating a police officer, destruction of public property, breaking out of jail.”

“Nickel and dime stuff.”

“Dude, you’re going to be spending some serious time in the Graybar Hotel.”

"I'm tired of paying for my own meals."

"If I was you, I'd hit the road, Jack and don't come back no more, no more, no more."

"I'm going to keep looking for Sloopy until the cops catch me."

"What happens if you find her before the cops catch you?"

"I'm hitting the road. Could you tell Adams that the stocking cap is a plant, and also that I think a man named Dabrowski kidnapped Susan."

"Dabrowski."

"Yep. And Carson, I probably won't see you again unless you visit me in the slammer. So, thanks for everything."

Louie hung up with the very real feeling that many things in life he cherished were about to come to an end.

Elliott Blake hadn't wanted to kill Hector, but there was really no choice. Things were spiraling out of control way too fast. That runt, Joe Sizelove, was nosing around in stuff he shouldn't. Louie was in a police cruiser someplace, having broken out of jail, and his lawyer was raising all sorts of hell. And Doc Brian was causing a commotion about his dumbass kid.

It was times like these that Elliott got a real stiffness between the shoulder blades and a headache that just wouldn't quit.

Well first things first. Take care of Hector. Then go back to town and tell Louie's lawyer it was all a big mistake about the ZipMart robbery and to let bygones be bygones. He'd forget all about the jailbreak and stolen police vehicle, if Louie would just return it.

Shit, all he wanted to do was get asshole Louie away from Susan Petrie. But hell, no trim was worth this aggravation. Besides there was a tight little high school fox that he'd caught with some grass. She'd probably be willing to provide a little extra-curricular fun if he were to forget all about the bust.

Well time to drag Hector out of the trunk, have him dig a little hole and then cap him in the back of the head. Problem solved. Elliott opened the trunk.

"Hector, wake up. Need you to do me a little favor and then you're free to go. Hector? C'mon Hector, you're not dead or anything are you? It was just a taser, man, so you can't be damaged too bad."

The body in the trunk didn't move. Elliott thought maybe had set the charge too high or something. Would anything go right today?

"Hector, I mean it, move!"

If this wasn't a shit sandwich with pickles on top, he didn't know what was. He grabbed the body by the belt and tugged it out of the trunk. After the body hit the ground, Elliott felt for a pulse. Still alive. He kicked Hector in the ribs.

"Wake up, you silly beaner."

The body didn't move.

There was a shovel under the spare tire. Elliott turned back to the trunk and unscrewed the base of the jack that held the tire down, wrestled the tire out of the trunk and got the shovel.

As he was straightening up, he heard rustling in the distance. Hector was seventy or eighty yards away running toward a cornfield.

"Hector, now you stop. You hear me, Hector?"

Shit.

Elliott unsnapped his holster and pulled his Glock. Damn if the little beaner wasn't zig-zagging. Elliott squeezed off a shot. Hector kept running. If Elliott kept firing, he might draw too much attention, even though the nearest house was about a quarter mile down the road.

It was too damn hot to run.

Elliott got in the police cruiser and started driving in the direction Hector was running. Damn, that little Chihuahua was fast.

Thumpity, thump, thump, the undercarriage was slapping the ground and bouncing around like a speared fish. The cop car wasn't really made for off-road driving. Elliott felt like his teeth were going to shake loose.

He had to slam on the brakes; there was a big drainage ditch up ahead.

He got out of the car and ran toward the ditch and stopped. He couldn't see Hector. He listened. He heard some noise to his right. A shadow moving in the center of the ditch. He aimed his pistol in the direction of the shadow. There was no movement.

The last thing he wanted to do was climb down into the ditch and get his pants all dirty. He waited. A twig cracked to his left. He wheeled around. It must've been a rabbit.

"Hector where are you? Come on back, my man, we'll talk things over. However, if I have to chase you..."

Well crap. He would have to slog around in the muck at the bottom of the drainage ditch and get all sweaty chasing Hector.

This day was totally in the crapper. He just hoped someone flushed before dropping another turd on him.

Cut 44
Psychotic Reaction

Sloopy faded in and out. The Man with the Lightbulb Head had been carving on her for the better part of an hour. The pain was bad, but the loss of blood was draining her will to live.

Obviously, he could have killed her quick, but he preferred to spend much of the time railing against her husband while making terrible puns and rhymes.

They were taking a break at the moment. He had been at his workbench for a half an hour. She heard knives being sharpened, the clatter of tools and instruments being handled, and what sounded like newspapers being crinkled or folded.

Her right wrist was raw from trying to loosen it, and blood was seeping out of the abrasion. She had loosened the tape around her mouth so she could breathe easier, but it still wasn't loose enough to really be able to scream.

She gave another jerk on her right arm. The duct tape tore a little. This was the first positive sign since she woke up here, wherever here might be. She looked over at the table. The weirdo still had his back to her. She worked her right arm some more. The tape split about an inch. If she could get another tear, she might be able to pull her right arm out from the mass of tape that was encircling it. But she had to be careful not to make too much noise or breathe too hard or the man would come back.

A stool scraped. He was standing up.

Had he heard her? Was he coming back?

No, wait, he was walking toward the back. A door opened, then closed. He was gone.

Hopefully she had a few minutes to free herself before he came back.

Sloopy pulled and twisted and yanked and flexed and finally got her right hand free. She was weak from the effort and loss of blood.

She freed her other arm and used both of them to free her head and mouth.

She took in big lungs full of air. It tasted rich, almost perfumed, even though the dank dark space must've smelled moldy. She slowed her breathing to listen for the man. And heard nothing. Her luck was holding.

Hurry.

She unraveled the tape that bound each of her feet to the front two legs of the chair. She started with the right leg. She pulled and pulled and still there was more tape. This was taking forever. She could say one thing for the bald nutcase with the knife, he didn't scrimp on duct tape. He must've wound the stuff around her ankles and shins at least fifty times.

God how she wished she had a knife, or a box cutter, or anything.

Now, the left leg. The man was sure to come back any time. Her hands were slick with blood, so she kept losing her grip on the tape. But she peeled it off, layer by layer. Sweat or blood or something kept getting into her eyes.

Finally she was free.

She stood up and took a step. And fell flat on her face. Her legs were numb from either the tight tape or loss of blood. This couldn't be happening. She pounded her calf muscles trying the get some blood in them, some feeling, anything. She got up to her knees and used the chair to get to her feet.

Fine, she would use the chair as a walker until she could get her feet working right. She pushed the chair ahead as far as she could and then took three steps. She repeated this maneuver four times until her feet got some feeling. They burned terribly, but at least they were working again.

She stepped away from the chair but held on to it with one arm for a few wobbly seconds. She tried another step. And another. Each step burned a little less. Each step gave her a little more strength. She was almost walking normally. She hobbled toward the workbench because the only door she could see was next to it. There were also tools and knives she could grab.

When she got to the workbench she thought about picking up a hammer, oh how she would love to bash in her tormenter's skull, but she didn't know if she had the strength. She decided upon a surgical knife.

If he got close, she would make sure she did some damage to repay him for the damage he had already done to her.

For a fleeting moment, she wondered if Louie would still be attracted to her with all the carving Lightbulb Head had done. Stop it! How silly. She had to concentrate on getting out of here, alive.

She gripped the knife tightly and walked to the door. At the door she stopped and pressed an ear against it. She heard noise of some sort, but it wasn't human. It didn't seem to be the sound of anyone bustling about. It sounded mechanical and distant. Like an air conditioner or water softener. Well, it was now or never.

She turned the knob. The the door squawked like an alley cat in heat as she pushed it open.

Sloopy looked into another room. It was shadowy and windowless like the one before. She took another step until she was even with the doorjamb. Nothing much in the room except a very old bathtub and shower combination and a big utility sink. Another door at the far end must lead to the outside or a stairway to somewhere.

Sloopy held the knife out in front of her with her right hand and took a step inside. Before she was inside, something bumped her wrist. The knife hit the floor and clanged several times before the pain started.

"Now, don't run off, the fun is just starting," The Man with the Lightbulb Head was standing against the wall just inside the door holding an old fashioned meat cleaver.

Blood dripped from the blade.

The man bent over and picked up something from the floor.

"Dear, I'm afraid if you're not careful, you'll ruin your outfit."

He offered something to her. "Here, let me give you a hand."

Sloopy looked down to see what The Man with the Lightbulb Head was holding out to her.

It was her severed right hand still clutching the surgeon's knife.

Cut 45

Put the Clock Back on the Wall

Louie drove Carson's pickup back to meet with Wes. Amanda hadn't returned his call and he still couldn't reach her with any of the numbers he had.

Wes and Louie had talked about Paul Dabrowski, but the old farmer didn't offer any insights into where Paul might be found. Louie was coming up empty everywhere.

"So tell me more about Paul's family. You said they were a little odd?"

"Well first thing you gotta understand, a lot people who live on farms have their own ideas about things. Living away from other folks, you don't get quite as homogenized as people from towns, even small ones."

"I understand. I know a few farmers myself."

"So were the Dabrowkis weird compared to any other farmers? Not so much. However, they did have their own slant on the world."

"Could you give me some examples?"

"Well, sir, let's just say when a lot of folks saw daylight, the Dabrowskis saw only saw shadows. You know, they were all worried about Y2K. Believed 9/11 was a plot by our own government. Uh...still think fluoride is some sort of conspiracy. Hell when Tom, Paul's dad, would come over, I put on an extra pot of coffee, because I knew I was going to hear about everything from how the Catholics ruined the Bible by taking out books they didn't like to how the big car companies were in cahoots with big oil to kill the electric car."

"What happened to them?"

"Most of 'em went bankrupt. Had to have the crooks in congress bail 'em out."

"No, I mean, Paul's family."

"Oh. They're in Sun City, I believe it's called, outside Phoenix. One of them retirement communities, you know."

"Do you happen to have their telephone number?"

Louie started driving to Indianapolis. He still couldn't get hold of Amanda, but was on the phone with Paul Dabroski's mother. Her tone of voice had the tang of a suspicious woman.

"Who did you say you were again?"

Louie told her.

"And what is it you want with Pauly?"

Louie said Paul was an old friend from way back and Louie was trying to look him up.

"Where did you and Pauly meet?"

"Northwestern."

"What year?"

Louie told her.

"Well, I don't know where he is."

"Don't you keep in touch?"

"We keep in touch, I just don't know where he is."

"I really would like to find him."

"Call him."

"Do you have a number where I can reach him?"

"If you're such gosh-darn good friends, you should have his number," she said.

"I told you, I haven't seen him since college."

But Louie was talking to dead air. She had hung up.

Louie was about to call her back when a big "what if" kind of thought pinged around his brain. He slammed on the brakes and skidded to the shoulder of the road. He looked at the steering wheel for several seconds

He banged a yoo-ee.

Louie had a feeling in his gut. There was a very slim chance he was right. But it made sense. Perhaps it was wishful thinking. The logic didn't have much meat on it, but instincts told him that he had gotten his teeth into something substantial.

Back on Dabrowski's farm, in the wreckage of the burned-down house, Louie kicked around through the rubble.

Wes drove up in his truck. The old farmer rolled down the driver's side window. "You're back."

"I am."

"What are you looking for?"

Louie continued to kick around the ashes and coal. "You mentioned that the Dabrowskis were conspiracy freaks. The kind of people who might have built bomb shelters. Or, maybe some sort of shelter for Y2K."

"Yep, they were the sort of folks that would do something like that."

"Did they?"

"I don't reckon I know. If'n they did, they kept it to themselves. I heard tell of them buying supplies to last them a year in case some emergency or other struck. But they did that way before Y2K. I hear they was always buying up silver dollars, too."

"Did they have a shelter of some sort?"

"Again, I wouldn't know it if'n they did. But it sure wouldn't surprise me if they made an old root cellar or storm cellar into a shelter of some sort."

Wes pitched in as they moved aside charred wood and rubble looking for an opening to a basement or cellar.

"You know, for a fella that's just lookin' for another fella, you sure are going to a lot of trouble."

Louie decided to tell Wes what was going on, leaving out the parts about getting arrested and stealing a cop car.

"So you think it's Paul that's been chopping up animals and

sending them to people."

"Not necessarily. But he's involved somehow."

"Now you're afraid he's gonna chop up your old girlfriend."

"I'm worried about her. I want to make sure she isn't hurt."

Actually, Wes verbalized exactly what Louie was thinking.

"It sounds pretty damn crazy to me, but I'll keep helpin' you out, just to set your mind at ease when you find out you're wrong. Paul may be a bit off-key, but he certainly isn't gonna kill the choir."

Louie wasn't sure knew what that meant, but nodded sagely.

The pair kicked and cussed and moved carbon around for a couple more minutes when Wes said, "It looks like I've found something."

"What?"

"Well, if I'm not mistaken, it looks like the door to a cellar."

Indeed it was.

Louie ran back to Carson's truck and got the revolver and a flashlight. He hadn't fired a gun in a long time. He hoped he still could remember all the stuff he learned when learning to be a cop.

On the outside of the house, buried under a pile of charred rubble, were slanted twin steel basement doors. Since there was no sign of a basement in the foundation itself, Louie figured this led to some sort of cellar that wasn't under the house.

By the time Louie got back to the scene, Wes had them pretty well cleaned off.

There was only one handle. Both Louie and Wes tugged on it. They couldn't pull it open.

Wes rummaged around and found a metal pipe about four feet long. Louie worked the pipe into the opening in the middle and used a couple cinder blocks as leverage. They worked on the door together. The third time they pushed down, the door slowly bent open with a loud, low-throated moan.

Well, if anyone were down there, he knew someone was coming. Louie pushed the door all the way open. It hadn't been locked, but the heat from the fire had caused the two doors to warp and fuse together.

Louie pulled out the gun and told Wes to wait.

"If I don't come back in five minutes or if you hear any shooting, call the police and ambulance right away."

The stairs were concrete so Louie could take them rather rapidly without making much noise.

At the bottom of the stairs, there was nothing.

Nothing.

Barely enough room to turn around.

Louie shined the flashlight around. Some cinderblock walls and a drain. No latches. No openings. No doorways of any kind.

No Sloopy.

Nothing.

Cut 46
Light Bulb Blues

"Eenie meenie miney moe, what's the grand finale of the show?" The Man with the Lightbulb Head said in a sing-song voice. "You know you really are quite the party-pooper. I thought you'd be a little more of a cut up."

The Man with the Lightbulb Head walked around the barely-alive woman in the bathtub.

"I really want your husband to know how you've suffered. I should have video-taped this."

Sloopy felt a tingling in her temples. She tried to keep her eyes locked with his, but couldn't. She bowed her head.

"Well, listen, I've a good mind just to undo that tourniquet and let you bleed out. You're about as much fun as a dead fish. But I'm not going to do it just yet. There's one more thing I want to find out. Are those real?"

He put his hand on her breast.

"Or, are they silly putty, I mean silicone?"

The man walked out of the room and returned with a scalpel.

He walked over to the tub and slapped the slumping woman hard on the face.

"Wake up. Time for our little experiment."

"Dammit, it was just a storm cellar." Louie's head was throbbing.

"Well it's pretty far-fetched to think he would be living in some sort of fallout shelter anyway."

"I guess you're right." Louie hit the door with the injured hand. It started bleeding again. "I just don't know what to do now. I guess nothing. I feel so…I don't know. Well, anyway, thanks for helping me out, pardner. Walk me to my truck?"

"Sure thing. Hey, I gotta tell you, this investigating stuff is alright. You ever need help on anything else…"

Louie and Wes were walking past the burned out house.

"Hey, Wes, what is that?"

"What is what?"

"Over there."

"Oh that's where the old barn used to be."

"No, that thing."

"I think it's an old well that's been capped and boarded over."

The boards were fairly new two by sixes, almost flush with the ground and held down with several big rocks. However, they didn't seem to be bolted or in any other way attached to the round concrete and limestone structure. Wes and Louie were able to remove the rocks and wood planks in less than five minutes. It did appear to be an old well. On the inside of the opening were iron rungs that could be used to descend downward. Louie peered down but saw no reflection of water. He dropped a pebble and heard it hit what sounded like gravel.

"That don't mean nothing," Wes said. "A lot of folks fill in old wells with gravel or bentonite chips before they cap it. To keep dead animals and leaves and whatnot from polluting the water table."

"But they don't usually have a built in ladder to get to the bottom."

"You're right about that."

"I'm going down," Louie said.

"You want me to go back to the truck and get the flashlight first?"

Louie had put the flashlight back in the glove compartment, although he still had the gun.

"Get the flashlight and come back. But I don't have time to wait."

Louie started climbing down the manmade hole in the ground. When he reached the bottom, he was standing on gravel. On the south side of the well was a tunnel big enough to crawl in. Although he couldn't see any light, he heard a man's voice coming from the end of the tunnel.

Cut 47
Hang on Sloopy

Blackness, total blackness. No sight. No sound. No noise. Sweet, sweet nothingness. After all the pain, no pain. Sloopy wanted it to stay that way. Stay that way forever. Forever black. Forever darkness. Surrender to it. Let go. Stop the world, she was stepping off.

A voice penetrated the darkness. Soft. Muffled, very far away. The voice sounded like Louie. Go away, Louie, let me sleep. Let me stay in the darkness. Then, another voice. The Man with the Lightbulb Head. Sloopy tried to push the voice away. To bring back the cocoon of dark. Louie's voice again. Sharper this time.

And then pain. Pulling. Tearing. Yanking her hair. Jerking her head back. Cold, sharp steel against her throat. She mustn't let herself go. She had to fight the pulling.

But it was so much easier to accept the comforting embrace of oblivion.

Louie had a clean headshot. A killshot. He almost squeezed the trigger, but everything he believed in impelled him to try to take the man alive.

"Drop the knife now, or I'll blow your ugly head off."

Louie still had a shot.

The Man with the Lightbulb Head, head bowed, was looking down at the broken and battered Sloopy. The man raised his head slowly and turned in the direction of the voice.

Louie had an even better shot. The only danger was a ricochet in these tight quarters.

"I'm sorry, you haven't introduced yourself."

"Put the knife down now," Louie screamed.

"I don't think so." The ugly man dropped to his knees. He laid the blade against Sloopy's throat.

Louie didn't have much of a shot anymore.

"I'm not sure who you are, but I think my business is finished here."

With one swift stroke, the Man with the Lightbulb Head slit the throat of the only woman Louie had ever loved.

The first shot blew off the lightbulb head. The next one slammed into the ugly man's chest. Louie emptied the revolver as he ran over to Sloopy. Because his eyes were so watery, Louie couldn't tell how many shots had hit the target. Later the cops reported that the Man with the Lighbulb Head took every bullet.

The monster had cut off one hand, shaved her head, etched several cuts into her face and scalp and cut off all of her toes.

Louie prayed that God in His mercy would soon return Sloopy to glory in the next life.

Louie barely heard the sirens through the roaring in his head. He was on his knees by the bathtub with his hands over her bloody neck and her head against his chest.

Louie felt hands on his shoulders pulling him away. He jerked forward and wouldn't let go of the lifeless woman. He was on his knees covering the wound on her neck with one hand and had his face pressed against her cheek. He closed his eyes.

A voice in his ear whispered, "Louie, let me go,"

Louie raised his head and looked up to the ceiling and choked. "I can never let you go."

"No, I mean it darling, let these men take me away and fix me up."

Cut 48
That's Cool, That's Trash

The state police held Louie for twenty-three hours before Mike Adams sprang him. They decided not to press charges against Louie for shooting Paul Dabrowski, although all agreed emptying a pistol into him went beyond self-defense.

After much negotiation, Mike told Louie that the Tivoli cops finally dropped any charges for breaking out of jail, assaulting a police officer, stealing a police car and vandalizing the car.

To save face, Elliott admitted the stocking cap with Louie's hair fibers on it, might have been a mistake. Some evidence had gotten mixed up. In fact, the police chief now claimed to have pretty strong evidence that Louie didn't rob the ZipMart. The local police think it might have been Lee Brian.

No one had seen Lee Brian for days, but the theory was he left town.

In Louie's mind, the rotten cherry on top of the curdled whip cream of this sick sundae, was the Tivoli Police claiming Sloopy never gave them any of the packages with the animal pieces.

Louie figured Elliott thought the packages were coming from Ferman and was too lazy to investigate. The small-town cop probably thought if they could keep the whole thing quiet, he could use it to get to Sloopy. The poor deluded fool never realized she found him repulsive.

Tim Ferman's estate was valued at a little over three and a

half million dollars. Two of the millions were used to put Sloopy back together again.

Her chin had saved her.

When the Man with the Lightbulb Head slashed at her throat, he sliced off the bottom of her chin and only cut the surface of the skin on her throat. There had been an extreme amount of blood, but he hadn't punctured the trachea or the carotid artery.

She had been taken to Memorial County Hospital where they stabilized her, and then flew her immediately by helicopter to St. Vincent's Medical Center in Indianapolis.

G. Everett Gaunt, a world-renowned hand surgeon, was flown down from Chicago and miraculously he and his team were able to reattach her hand. It took three more surgeries to get it functioning again, although the tips of her fingers still felt numb and, even after two years of painful therapy, she was never able to close her hand fully.

The toes were lost.

Plastic surgeons in Beverly Hills and Rio de Janeiro brought back most of her beauty and minimized the surface scarring.

She emerged three years later, after all the surgeries and procedures, after months and months of physical and mental therapies, a beautiful woman.

But the scars ran deep.

With monetary help from his father, Louie was able to be by her side during the surgeries and support her through the therapies. He asked her several times to marry him. She didn't say no. However, she never really answered the question, either.

After one of the last abrasion procedures in Beverly Hills, Louie and Sloopy stayed another three days to relax and enjoy some pampering. The night before they were to fly out, they had dinner at the Ivy in West Los Angeles.

They sat on the patio surrounded by the restaurant's signature white picket fence. The night was soft and blue, fragrant from the roses that adorned the patio. The stars were out. The food was excellent. Or, at least that's what Sloopy said. Even though the food was considered classic American cuisine, some critics called it "comfort food," Louie would have preferred a chunk of mile-high meatloaf and cherry pie from Dixie's Diner in Tivoli. He couldn't wait to get home.

After dinner, the couple shared a piece of apple pie, which Louie thought was delicious, maybe even better than the pies at Dixie's.

But even though it was a perfect ending to a perfect evening, something was wrong. Louie couldn't quite figure out what it was, but Sloopy was different. She had been different for the past three years. But this night, sitting under the bowl of stars among the flowers on a cool night in L.A., she was even more subdued than usual.

He noticed she didn't meet his eyes. Hadn't all evening.

"You're not flying back with me, are you?"

She looked at him for just a second, took a deep breath and looked at her hands. "There are too many memories for me in Tivoli. I have too many nightmares." There were tears in her eyes.

"We can live wherever you want. I don't have to live in Tivoli. You name the place; I'll live there. I'll find work."

She took a sip of coffee. Didn't say anything. Didn't look Louie in the eyes.

"I'll turn in my ticket tomorrow. We can stay out here in la-la land for as long as you want. Then we can go wherever you want."

"Louie, you'd never be happy any other place than Tivoli. I know you."

"Yes, I can. I can be happy anywhere, as long as I'm with you. I—" Louie stopped. He looked at Sloopy a long time and then nodded his head. "That's not it, is it?"

"No. No, it's not. Not really." She took another sip of coffee. Looked Louie right in the eyes. "Remember when this whole thing started? You told me nothing would happen to me. Remember?"

"Yes."

"Well, I trusted you. Deep in my heart I felt you could protect me from all that is mean and ugly in this world."

"I tried."

"But you couldn't. You didn't. I don't blame you. Not really. But, I thought I would be safe with you. I wasn't. I'm not. I just can't forget that."

Louie felt his eyes burning. There was nothing more to say. Not really. Part of him didn't want to speak. Another part won. "If you ever need me, ever need anything at all. I'll be there. If you can ever get past all this, I'll be there. If you call, I'll be there."

Louie stood up and started to walk away.

"Louie?"

He turned around and looked at her.

"Thanks." That was the last word she said before he walked out of the restaurant and out of her life.

Cut 49

Nothing But A Heartache

Louie hadn't been back in Tivoli for more than two or three days at a stretch for three years. He had kept up with things by talking to Carson and hanging out at Dixie's Diner and the Tic-Tock.

First thing, he spent a couple of weeks hidden inside a bottle of bourbon and then decided to climb out and get on with life.

But life was different. He still got assignments from Mike Adams. He still ate lunch at Dixie's Diner and spent time at the Tic-Tock Bar. He played softball and flag football with his buddies. But something was sour. The charm of the town was gone. There seemed to be an undercurrent of defeat. Was it him or the town?

He tried to pull himself out of the funk. Spent an entire day listening to the blue-eyed soul that always cheered him up. Mitch Ryder and the Detroit Wheels. The Young Rascals. The Escorts. The Righteous Brothers. Bill Deal and the Rhondels.

He went to the Muhammd Ali Museum in Louisville. Hung out at the Checkerboard Lounge in Chicago. Took a day trip to the Stax Museum in Memphis.

But nothing worked.

Tivoli was a town full of soiled memories and spoiled dreams. There was something oppressive about it. The "howdy neighbor, good to see yas" seemed a little forced. The smiles weren't as quick. Everyone was carrying a weight they didn't want. Everyone was carrying around a hurt they couldn't quite heal. Everyone was doing time. Waiting for something.

But what?

Doctor Nicholas Brian missed his son. The boy disappeared three years ago. Didn't take any clothes. Didn't take a car. Just disappeared. Off the face of the earth.

Sure Lee Brian was a knucklehead. Sure the boy smoked too much dope and was always getting in trouble with the police. But he'd grow out of all that. His heart was good. Dr. Brian loved his son. He wanted the boy back.

One day Dr. Brian sat across from Louie at Dixie's Diner. He asked Louie to find Lee.

"You are perhaps my last chance. My only hope. It's been three years now. The police seem to think Lee ran away. I know they're not trying very hard to find him."

"How do you know?"

"Elliott Blake thinks he's so clever. But I'm not an idiot. He's not looking. I know he's lying. He's a jerk."

Louie took a bite of his mile-high meatloaf. Didn't say anything. The dentist hadn't touched his chili.

"Will you find him? Please. Will you find my boy?"

"I can't promise anything. But I'll give it my best shot."

"That's all I'm asking. I'll pay you. Money's no object."

"For me neither."

"What's do you mean?"

"I don't know. I'll look for your boy. You don't have to pay me anything."

"I'll pay your expenses and five hundred dollars a day."

"Expenses will be fine."

"I don't expect you do it for free."

"Okay, whatever you want."

"When can you start?

Louie took another bite of the meatloaf. "Now. Right now. I have one condition, though."

"What's that?"

"If I find your son and he's fine and in no danger but doesn't want to come home, I leave him alone. I won't bring him back. I won't tell you where he is."

The dentist threw his shoulders back. "Now you just hold on a minute."

"That's the deal, take it or leave it."

"But."

"No ifs, ands or buts. No negotiations. You've got thirty seconds to decide."

The father scratched the back of his head. He started to speak and then closed his mouth. Finally, he said, "Deal."

They shook hands.

Louie was determined to find Lee Brian. Or, find out what happened to Lee Brian.

Two months later Louie had to tell Doc Brian he didn't know anything about Lee. No idea what had happened to the boy. No clues. A lot of dead ends. He just seemed to disappear off the face of the earth. Louie didn't think spending any more time would help. The case was too cold. Louie said he was sorry and didn't want any money. The doc insisted and wrote Louie a sizable check.

Louie felt guilty about taking Doc Brian's money. He hadn't told the dentist the truth.

He knew exactly what happened to Lee.

He interviewed the owner of the ZipMart. He talked to the girls who were at the ZipMart the night Lee disappeared. He talked to Lee's high school friends and began seeing a picture of the teen's relationship to the chief of police. Louie listened to the rumors as told by Junkyard Slim and the Belladonna boys. He talked to Joe Sizelove who didn't really say anything, but it was what wasn't said that helped Louie put sort things out.

And then, one night, the chief of police showed up at Louie's apartment.

Louie answered the door. "What do you want?"

"Are you going to invite me in?"

"I don't see why I should."

"Oh now, Louie, don't be like that."

"What are you after, Elliott?"

"Well, I just thought I'd drop by and chat. We've been kinda on the outs since I mistakenly arrested you a while back. I feel real bad about that and figure we ought to find some way to put it behind us. We need to talk."

"I don't have anything to say to you."

"Well, that's odd. I hear you been talking a lot about me around town. Seems you been asking a lot of questions about me. Maybe it's time you talk to me instead of about me. Get it straight from the horse's mouth, so to speak. What do you think, pardner? How about a little man to man? I would be happy to answer any question you might have."

Louie looked at the policeman standing in the doorway. "Sure come on in." Louie stepped aside.

"You know, a beer would taste awful good right now Got any to spare?" Elliott walked around the Louie's massive great room. "Whew. Four of these old record machines. That's quite impressive."

"It's my hobby, I guess."

"Weird hobby. Now, personally, I wouldn't want this old junk messing up my house. But you and I have always had different views about things."

Louie handed the cop a bottled beer. "I guess I agree. For one thing, I'm not quite as loose with the law as you."

Elliott laughed. "That's rich. Loose with the law. I like that. Mr. Louie, I happen to be the law. So it looks like me and the law are pretty tight."

Louie took a sip of beer. "What'd you do with the boy, Elliott?"

"Well now there's another area where you and I don't see eye-to-eye. Can you imagine if I'd a spent the last three years looking for him? What a waste of time and money. You see, I'm pretty convinced the boy ran away. He's quite a wild one. Got a hair up his ass and decided to go somewhere to smoke dope all the livelong day. All night, too, more than likely. All the evidence seems to point in that direction. "

"What evidence?"

"Well, now Louie, you gotta understand I don't answer to

you. Used to. But no more. The city council thought you were too big a pussy to be a police chief. So now you're nothing. And I'm the king dog. I don't gotta tell you nothing. See where I'm coming from?"

Louie nodded. "I understand you."

"And as the chief of police, I've come to the conclusion that spending more of the town's limited resources chasing down a runaway kid just ain't in anyone's best interest. He'll come home when he's good and ready. Or not."

"Or, not."

"Are you trying to say something here, Louie? Are you trying to insinuate something? Because if'n you are. Why don't you just stand up like a man and say it?"

"You killed Lee Brian. You know it and I know it."

"Well, you got bigger balls than I ever imagined. Yes indeed you do. But, once again, I think you're just a bunch of wind. You ain't got no proof. So, I think you better keep that pussy mouth of yours shut. Because if you don't bad things might happen."

"Are you threatening me?"

"Well if I was, just what in the hell are you going to do about it? I'm the one with the gun and the badge; all you got is that pussy mouth of yours making wild accusations. But, hell no, I ain't a-threatening you. No sir. I'm just talking. Just jawin' with my old pal Louie. Like I said, I think it's pretty foolish to waste the town's resources chasin' down Doc Brian's runaway kid. But I might come to the conclusion it might be worth the money to get your lesbian friend off the streets."

"What do you mean?"

"Well, Dixie, the dyke. Dixie's Diner. You had to know she's a rug muncher."

"She's never done anything wrong."

"Well you see, I bet if I look hard enough, I can find a couple of underage teenage girls who would testify that Dixie did some improper things with them. Yes sir, I bet if I put my mind to it, I could find evidence of that."

"You wouldn't dare."

"And those boys who smoke belladonna. I bet I could find some drugs and paraphernalia on their persons or in their cars. You know, life could get awfully mean for folks around here."

"You're a prick."

"You know Louie, I'm gonna forget you said that. But don't you ever talk that way to me again." Elliott pulled the gun out of his holster, a Glock 9, and jammed the barrel in Louie's crotch. "If you ever disrespect me again, I'll blow those big balls of yours right off." The cop put the gun back. "And If I decide you're spending too much time stirrin' up trouble over Doc Brian's boy, I just might decide to use the town's resources investigating, let's just say, other crimes. Do we have an understanding?"

Louie nodded slowly.

"Well, I'm glad we could have this little chat. Thanks for the beer." Elliott wiped his mouth and set the bottle down. He started for the door.

"Elliott."

The cop turned and looked at Louie.

"You know, you never did deny killing the Brian boy."

The policeman grinned. "I guess you're right. I didn't, did I?"

Louie wanted to bring down the policeman so bad it hurt. Elliott Blake was what was wrong with Tivoli. A little town was built on its people, bound by decency and character. But the acid of corruption eats into the connections between people. If left unchecked it can rot away at the foundation of what makes a town good. And the weight of one man, one bully, can bring the whole thing down.

The town would never be right unless Elliott was gone.

For sure, Elliott had crossed the line with Lee Bryant. It should not go unpunished or the whole town would suffer.

Louie just didn't have any proof. And he didn't know where the body was buried.

That night Louie dialed a telephone number in Chicago. "Hello Dad. Is that job still open in your firm? I think I'm ready to stop playing around here in Tivoli and get serious about a career."

Cut 50

Run, Run, Run

His life was all stored away in sixteen book boxes and three wardrobe boxes. Most of the book boxes filled with actual books and 45 rpm vinyl records. A few DVDs. Some odds and ends. Plus, four juke boxes wrapped in bubble wrap, carpet padding and miles of duct tape. Louie looked at his last day in Tivoli.

The moving truck would pick up his stuff in the next day or so. To take advantage of the best rate, Louie's move was to piggyback on another from Indianapolis. The rich folks from Indy got the movers first, at the time they wanted. Louie's was whenever the movers were done packing up the Indianapolis home.

Louie went to the bank and cashed Doc Brian's check. Got a thousand in cash and the rest in savings bonds.

He walked over to Dixie's Diner. Had a piece of coconut cream pie.

Dixie and her sister Dot were at that asexual age and weight. Pudgy but not really fat. Feminine in facial features only. Louie wondered if what Elliott said about Dixie were true. And decided as long as Dixie weren't dipping into the underage crowd, it didn't matter to him.

"We're going to miss you, Louie." Dixie actually had tears in her eyes.

"I'll come back and visit from time to time."

"Thanks for saying so, but somehow, I don't believe you. People who leave never come back."

"You'll see too much of me, Dixie. You'll get tired of my dropping in."

"I wish you weren't leaving. This town needs you, Louie."

"What do you mean?"

"You provide a balance."

"Balance."

"To the meaness. This town could get pretty mean without you. We need people like you to balance things out."

Louie thought he knew what she meant. But there was nothing he could do. He was powerless. Against the meaness. He didn't have any proof. And he didn't know where the body was. He didn't know where the bodies were.

He collected his change and walked out.

Louie got in his car. One last stop before leaving town. Probably for good.

"What happened, Diane?" Louie walked into the house. The cute little house on Church Street. He had an envelope with $20,000 in U.S. Savings Bonds for Diane's son. For college or starting a business or buying a car or whatever the boy decided to do with he when he reached 18.

Diane Baker had a bruise on her cheek. Slightly yellow-green now with still a hint of purple and red. But substantial.

"Nothing. I ran into a door. Clumsy me."

"You didn't run into a door."

"It's all right. Nothing to worry about." She smiled. "So, you're leaving town. Come to say goodbye?"

"To give you this."

"Louie, how many times have I told you, I don't want your money."

"It's not my money. They're savings bonds. For your son."

She took the envelope. Started to say something and then turned, walked to the small dining room and put it in a drawer in the maple hutch. When she came back she smiled. "So, I guess this is it. The goodbye part."

"Tell me what happened to your eye."

"Quit asking me. It's not important."

"It is. Just tell me."

"Some guy got a little frisky." There were tears coming down her cheeks.

"Which guy?"

"Elliott."

"Elliott." Louie turned away.

"I got it under control," Diane said.

"Did he, you know, do anything?"

"No. Not like that. But..."

"But what. Tell me Diane."

"He threatened me. Said he could make my life miserable if I didn't...if I didn't..." She buried her face in Louie's chest. The sobs were made her whole body jerk.

Several minutes later, she pulled away and hiccupped softly. "Now look what I've done, I've gotten tears and snot all over your shirt. I'm sorry."

"Don't worry about it. You take care of yourself."

Cut 51
Let it All Hang Out

It was one of those cool summer afternoons that lured you outside and seduced you into staying as long as possible. On the tiny balcony of Louie's apartment, he could smell cinnamon from the bakery across the street. He watched the kids playing baseball in the vacant lot next to the Baptist Church.

However, Louie didn't stay outside on the balcony, he went inside the Tic-Tock Bar waiting for nightfall. The faint nicotine odor, the aroma of old grease and spilled beer, and a faint sour milk smell never left the place.

The air was too chilly from the cranked-up air conditioner and oily from the rush hour burgers-and-fries service.

There were only two people in the bar besides the Louie and the bartender.

No one commented about the oddly-shaped satchel Louie put by the coat rack as he walked in. No one commented about the thick leather jacket he wore on a day when most people were in shirtsleeves, a light sweater at most. One person commented they hadn't seen Louie in a while. Louie said nothing.

At about six there was another small rush for burgers and tenderloin sandwiches. Louie decided to have a double burger patty on toasted rye with double cheese, fries extra-crisp and a bock beer. When the burger came he ate half of it and lost interest.

By eight, the crowd thinned out. Left was another solitary drinker, a Mexican-looking fellow. Two tables in front by the windows looked out on Harrison Street, the main street.

Neither the Mexican nor the bartender said a word when Louie took his beer, walked over to one of the two tables, picking up the satchel on the way, and sat next to a window.

Around 8:15 or so, Joe Sizelove walked in, nodded and sat at the barstool closest to Louie. That meant the softball games were over.

Some of the other cops who played softball would be at the station having a couple of beers.

Doc Brian came in a little later. He looked at Louie a second and said hi and then took a seat three stools away from Joe.

At 9:30 Louie picked up the satchel and walked outside. He put the satchel on the sidewalk and leaned against the plate glass window of a men's clothing store.

It was Thursday night; there wasn't much traffic.

A car turned onto Harrison from the cross street that ran in front of the police station. As the car rounded the corner, Louie stepped out into the middle of the street and pulled out a double-barreled shotgun from the satchel.

The car moved slowly toward Louie. He pulled back both hammers on the shotgun. A loud double click echoed down the street. The car stopped about half a football field's length away.

Elliott got out. Louie started walking toward him.

"I thought you didn't believe in guns," Elliott said.

"Sometimes a man changes his thinking."

"Now Louie, I've stopped the car, so there's no need for that gun. Let's talk about whatever it is that's got you all fired up."

"It's Sloopy. It's the town. It's..."

Louie took aim and fired.

And then began walking back in the direction of the bar.

"Now, dammit, Louie, that's my own personal vehicle you done shot. Look at that. I'm gonna have to get a new radiator now."

Louie kept walking.

"Louie, you listen to me, I'm thinking you better pay for that or you and me's gonna have some trouble."

Louie stopped in front of the bar. Elliott had followed, but kept a good twenty-five yards back. Louie put the shotgun down and turned around. Elliott started walking backwards slowly.

Louie took off his jacket. He slid the holster belt around so his new revolver was on the right hip and not in back.

"Now what are you doing, Louie?"

Louie unsnapped the leather strap that fit over the hammer.

"Now this is just plain crazy."

"I'll let you go for your piece first," Louie said.

"What's going on here? Why in hell do you wanna do this?"

"Because of you, Sloopy is gone. She will never be whole again. Because of you, this town is sick. You're an infection."

"Now that's just crazy talk. You ain't got no proof."

Louie didn't say anything.

"Let's just sit down and have a couple of beers and hash this thing out. I had nothing to do with Sloopy. Nothing."

Louie pulled out the revolver and shot Elliott in the thigh. The police chief fell on his face and started pushing himself up. Joe Sizelove came out of the bar and was pointing his pistol at Louie.

"Put the gun down, Louie."

"Not gonna do it, Joe."

"Put it down, Louie. Now. Put it down nice and slow."

Louie started to lower his gun. Elliott, in a crouch, raised his. Louie fired off another round and caught Elliott in the center of his chest. Ellott was knocked over backwards and didn't move.

By this time Doc Brian and the Mexican had come out from the bar. Nobody rushed to Elliott. Joe had his gun trained on Louie. Louie slid his gun back in the holster and started walking toward his apartment.

Joe lowered his gun and looked at Louie.

"Come get me if you want to, Joe. I have a few letters to write first."

Joe looked at the Louie a few seconds. "Do what you gotta do."

Louie shrugged and walked on. He stopped when he got to Elliott. Sightless eyes told the story.

"He's dead," Louie said.

"Yeah, I was afraid of that."

"I'm still gonna write those letters Joe. Can you let me do that?"

Joe Sizedlove shrugged. He turned to Dr. Brian. They locked eyes for a few seconds. He turned to the Mexican and whispered something in his ear. The Mexican nodded.

"I'm gonna need you to stick around Louie."

"I'll come to the station in a couple of hours. You trust me, don't you?"

"I trust you, but you know as well as I do, the fresher the witness, the better the testimony."

"You got your witnesses, Joe. I'm a suspect and I'll sign any confession you want."

"Well, let's just make sure we got our details right."

"I think I saw the same thing you did," Doc Brian said to Joe.

"He was shot in the line of duty." Joe pointed to Elliott's body.

"Yeah, it's a damn shame he got shot before he could even fire his gun," Doc Brian said.

"I wonder if we'll ever catch those two guys who tried to rob the tavern?"

"I wonder."

"Louie, you think long and hard, because right now, I'm having a little trouble remembering what they look like."

Louie contined toward his apartment and his beloved jukeboxes. There was something broken inside of him, something he would never be able to fix. There was something broken in the town Louie loved. But maybe it could be fixed. Not to perfection, but so it worked a little bit better. Maybe the town could be a little bit more what it should be.

Of course it would never be the same. Nothing ever is.

ABOUT AUTHOR RANDY ROHN

Randy Rohn's short story, "The Man Who Fell in Love with the Stump of a Tree," was picked as one of the BEST AMERICAN MYSTERY STORIES of 2009.

New York Times bestselling author Jeffery Deaver said this about Randy's writing: "The dialogue is witty and the characters wry and appealing." Randy has had many mystery and thriller short stories published in L & L Dreamspell anthologies. This is his first full-length novel.

Randy lives with his family in Indiana.

CPSIA information can be obtained at www.ICGtesting.com
Printed in the USA
239288LV00001B/5/P